EXTINCTION ISLAND

JANICE BOEKHOFF

Lost Canyon Press
P.O. Box 624
Bettendorf, IA 52722

Trade Paperback ISBN 978-1-948003-06-3

E-book ISBN 978-1-948003-05-6

Cover by Kim Mesman (mesmandesignco.com)

For Todd

You are always there to make it worth while to leave my fictional worlds. Thank you for making my real life wonderful.

In a world where genetic manipulation is the newest superpower, dinosaurs are brought back from extinction and released on the American population. After several gruesome fatalities, the military hunts down each specimen and transfers it to a sanctuary—the newly formed island of Costa Rica. Contained by an expanded Panama Canal to the south and the freshly dug Nicaraguan canal to the north, the dinosaurs flourish in the tropical climate.

However, the cost required to purchase the land, evacuate the residents to nearby countries, and construct the sanctuary leaves the United States saddled with enormous debt. This cost, coupled with an overworked prison system—a result of a decline in the moral fabric of the country—leads to the signing of a new death penalty bill, dubbed by the media as *Jurassic Judgment*.

After four months of accelerated appeals, death row inmates are given a choice: immediate execution ... or exile to Extinction Island.

A LOW MOAN escaped from Oakley Laveau's lips. Her synapses worked in slow motion. She scraped her dry tongue along the roof of her mouth. Her limbs dragged on her like dead weight. The effects of the alcohol penetrated every crevice of her brain.

With a massive mental push, she forced her eyes open as if they were on rusty hinges. A dark curtain draped in front of her eyes—her own sable-colored hair. *Stupid.* She brushed a hand over her face to clear her vision.

She lay face-down on a bed with a vaguely familiar yellow zig-zag comforter. Yellow was her best friend's favorite color. With a jolt, Oakley pushed up to her knees. Pale yellow walls, white ornate dresser, and a painting of a gigantic sunflower over the bed. How did she get into Monica's apartment?

She gave herself a quick once over. Jeans and an LSU

T-shirt. The same clothes she'd worn yesterday. So, why couldn't she remember the rest of last night?

She flipped over to lay on her back. At the bar, Monica had apologized for her part in the betrayal. Had Oakley forgiven her? No, she hadn't. Instead, she finished the vodka and club soda and grabbed something from her drink. What was it? She dug through her mind for the tidbit. A gold coin had been in the bottom of her glass, given to her by a man. She plucked it out and then ... nothing.

Nausea swelled in her stomach. She'd never experienced a black out before. It couldn't have come from just one drink. Had she stayed for more? Maybe Monica had taken her home because she couldn't drive?

Her cottony mouth begged for water. She scooted off the bed and walked in bare feet to the main living area of the small apartment. "Monica?"

No answer. A small measure of relief. She needed time to sort out her feelings before facing Monica again. As her brain finally kicked into gear, she remembered Monica's name listed on the schedule for today. She must have already gone into work.

Oakley made her way to the kitchen and sucked down a large glass of water. She put the glass on the counter next to a shiny set of keys—Monica's keys. Had she left them so Oakley could lock up? But the car key fob was still attached. Did Monica have another set of keys? If not, how would she have gotten to work?

Maybe in my car. Oakley patted her jeans pocket. Nope, she had her keys.

Unless Monica was still here.

"Monica?"

On her way back to the bedroom, she tripped over a black sandal. Her sandal. At least she knew where one of them had ended up.

Aside from the small rumpling of the comforter where Oakley had lain, the rest of the sheets were undisturbed. Perhaps Monica was in the bathroom. She tapped on the closed door. "Monica, are you here?"

When she received no response, she put her ear to the wood. No sound of movement or running water.

She tried the knob and pushed the door open. "Monica?" This time it was almost a whisper.

As the door swung open, she saw a foot resting on the edge of the tub. She quickly turned her back to give Monica privacy. "I'm sorry. I didn't realize you were taking a bath."

The next minute dragged on, punctuated every few seconds by her awareness of what she *didn't* hear. No exclamation of surprise. No splash as Monica tried to cover up. No harsh words about the door being closed. Nothing except the tiny drip, drip of water.

She cleared her throat. "Are you okay?"

No answer.

She pressed a hand to her throat as she slowly turned back around. Her gaze found the foot, then traveled farther along the tub. Monica's legs and body were submerged in about a foot of water. She stepped closer to peer fully into the tub. Monica's submerged face rested unmoving beneath the water, her mouth frozen in a small exclamation of surprise. She searched for air bubbles, movement, anything to indicate life, but Monica lay absolutely still, her half-shuttered eyes staring at the ceiling.

Sorrow, mingled with confusion, created a sloshing mixture of burning acid in her stomach. If only she could remember something after the conversation at the bar. What happened last night? How had Monica died?

CHAPTER ONE

FOUR MONTHS LATER ...

THE STINGING, salty wind blew Oakley's hair into her eyes, the individual dark strands sticking to the moisture on her cheeks. Every second that ticked away brought her closer to the island of her nightmares.

She swept her hair up with one hand and focused on her dad, memorizing his features—dull brown hair with one gray shock on the right side, placid green eyes, and wrinkles like twin commas creased around his mouth—but his image kept blurring with her tears.

Behind her, the horn on the prison ship let out a protracted bleat. She didn't have much time left. As a felon, convicted and sentenced to death for murder, her future had died with her three fast appeals.

Dad reached out to cup her cheek, and she let her hair

go wild again. Her tears rolled over his thumb. She turned her eyes down to where the droplets splattered on the white planks of the dock, creating a wet stain.

"You have to stay strong." Dad's deep voice broke on the last word.

She searched his face, turned as hard as stone. He said what she'd expected him to say. The only advice he'd ever given her. As a kid, she'd used the mantra to make him proud in school and while playing soccer. Then, when she was a teenager, staying strong had meant winning at all cost, and she'd used it to battle against the few rules he'd given her.

Now, when her life and career should just be beginning, the words fell flat with meaninglessness. No matter how strong she became physically or emotionally, it wouldn't be enough for where she was going.

"Did something happen to your eye?" Dad lifted her chin. "It's bloodshot."

"It hurts." Without thinking, she rubbed her left arm that also ached at the spot where they had inserted her tracker. Every prisoner had to get one. "The nurse said my eye was an unusual reaction to the anesthesia."

At the time, Oakley hadn't pressed the issue with the nurse because a frantic guard had burst into the recovery room in a panic. Apparently, someone at the hospital had lost track of Oakley during the implantation procedure. Of course, they mustn't let a dangerous criminal get a chance to escape. What could she have done while cuffed to a hospital bed anyway?

At the insistent sound of the horn, Dad grabbed her and wrapped her in a desperate hug. She stood frozen like that. Her bandaged arm hurt under the pressure, but she wouldn't ask him to stop. She might never feel his arms around her again.

From behind, Officer Lewis cleared his throat. "We need to leave to avoid an offshore storm."

Dad pulled back and gripped her hands. His fingers skimmed across the stubs of her pinkie and ring fingers on her left hand, taken by a gator just before Monica's murder. First her fingers, then her best friend, and now her freedom. What else would she lose? She had only her life left to give.

Reaching up toward her ear, Dad barely touched one of the silver fleur-de-lis earrings that had been her mother's. The guards let her keep a single personal item, and she chose the one with the least amount of memories attached. Anything else would have been too painful.

"Oak, you're a fighter like your mother. Don't give up. I'll be working to get you back."

Typical. He'd waited to bring up her mother until Oakley had to go, so he didn't have to address any of her unanswered questions. But even if he released some of those mysteries from the past, it wouldn't do her any good now. Just staying alive would be her most pressing battle.

Pushing her small shoulders up, she turned to follow Officer Lewis to the boat. The gray transport ship wasn't much bigger than the boats from the Lazy Lizard—the swamp tour where she used to work—but it seemed more menacing.

Don't look back. She held her posture square. If she could just make it up the gangway.

Halfway up, she couldn't stand it. She turned her head until she saw him. Dad stood with a hand over his mouth and an arm clutching his stomach. A sob wrenched out of her at the anguish on his face.

Officer Lewis halted to give her a minute. "Best get it all out now. No room for emotion where you're going."

With the back of her hand, she wiped away the remnants of her tears. Time to be strong. Despite her missing memories and regardless of what the jury said, Oakley wouldn't believe she'd killed her best friend. Her only hope lay in Dad finding evidence to free her. With a deep breath, she stepped through the metal door in the hull, feeling surprisingly hollow. Despair had drilled a cavern into her heart and the hole was growing by the minute.

THE NEXT TWO days at sea shredded Oakley's nerves. Her stomach twisted and turned with the waves that shoved the prison transport ship around like a toy bobbing in a bathtub, but her anxiety wasn't solely because of the sea. The needles stabbing at her gut had more to do with the other passengers aboard.

Four in total—two police officers with long rifles

strapped to their chests, the ship's captain locked securely in the bow, and Daric Perkins, the recently convicted serial killer from California. Daric's fierce gaze followed her everywhere on deck.

"I don't belong here," she said to Officer Lewis, hoping he would agree.

He raised his thin and strangely manicured eyebrows in a disinterested gesture. Probably every convict had given him the same story, and that was all she was now. A convict sentenced to live on an island where she would be hunted by reptiles much more lethal than the alligators she had come to love.

She turned to her right and locked eyes with Daric. His ferocious stare marred his innocent blond, blue-eyed surfer appearance. She hadn't strayed more than two steps from an officer since yesterday, when Daric attacked her in the lower level bathroom. Every time she closed her eyes, she saw his black tennis shoes, splayed at a cocky angle, just before he climbed on top of her. She fought him off with a dirty toilet wand to the face, then she ran like crazy. For a man like him with a body count of ten, capital punishment made sense. He'd slaughtered women as prey. Now he would be the prey.

But for her? She couldn't even remember her crime, only the strange man who'd been at the bar before it happened. During the trial, the prosecutor said she made Jim Durham up—an imaginary scapegoat to avoid the impact of what she'd done—but he was wrong. If only she could have found Jim afterward.

Since she'd boarded the boat, all hope of escaping her fate drowned in the open ocean surrounding them. There were so many things she'd miss. Her dad, of course, was the one constant in her life. Her ten-year-old half brother, Eric, kept her roaring with laughter at his antics, but he hadn't been allowed to come to the boat to say goodbye. Felice, Oakley's stepmother, had once again protected him from what she referred to as Oakley's bad example. Saturday afternoon soccer games with her friends in the cool Louisiana winters were over. Her friends would move on with their lives and forget about her.

Even her career as a reptile expert was finished. Ogden "Raptor" Greene—her boss at the Lazy Lizard— might miss her unusual confidence with the gators, but he'd find someone to replace her.

She let out a shaky sigh. The reptiles on Extinction Island would welcome her—as a source of food. Would they be anything like the marshmallow-eating alligators she'd studied and cared for the last two years?

Officer Lewis bellowed from the head of the stairs, his commanding voice rising above the wind. "Both inmates, report below for a briefing on the island."

Daric gestured for her to go ahead. She didn't like turning her back to him, so she quickly navigated the rubber-lined stairs and entered the first door available. As she stepped over the threshold, she gasped and covered her mouth with her hand. Raptor stood with his hands raised to the low ceiling, adjusting some projection equipment.

She ran to him and stretched up to throw her arms around his thick neck. "You have no idea how good it is to see you."

His muscular arms encircled her tightly. The same dreadful mix of comfort and sadness enveloped her. After a moment, he patted her gently on the back and pulled away. He must have been on board all along, but he hadn't come to see her. His dark gaze assessed her, sweeping across her reddened eye and over her two missing fingers.

She held them up, trying not to cringe at the memory of the gaping jaws of the fifteen-foot-long alligator they called Blackie. The gator died within seconds of taking her fingers, then sank into the swamp. She wanted to ask Raptor if he'd ever found its body, but she couldn't seem to force the question out. "They've healed fine."

He gave a pinched smile. "It's good to see you. I just wish it wasn't like this."

"You've been on board?"

He pressed his lips together before answering. "I'm not allowed contact with the inmates except for the briefing."

Obviously, he'd come here in his official capacity as the reptile expert for Extinction Island. His professional demeanor reminded her of the day he'd promoted her to assistant manager of the Lazy Lizard—a week before Monica's death. A bittersweet pang of loss squeezed her heart. Monica had perished, then when Oakley was accused of her murder, Raptor lost both of his full-time employees.

Officer Lewis took up a post near the door and tossed her a frustrated glance. "Sit down," he barked.

"Yes, Sir." She avoided his gaze as she took a seat in one of the few chairs in the room.

Daric sat next to her, his arm brushing hers as he lowered his body to the seat. Officer Lewis once told her that Daric had killed four girlfriends and six women who were unknown to him. He'd used a brace on his leg to make them think he was harmless. Sort of like a blond Ted Bundy. She hadn't seen the press coverage since she'd been occupied with her own trial at the time, but she hadn't needed to. From the moment they met, his surfer-boy good looks hadn't fooled her. She knew a predator when she saw one.

She scooted her chair away from him, the wooden legs screeching against the floor. He raised both eyebrows and smirked.

"Let's get started," Raptor said. "The government allows me twenty minutes to brief you. The U.S. Death Penalty Detention Center in Costa Rica is a dangerous place because of two factors—the convicts and the dinosaurs. The good news is, it's a big island and has only about a thousand surviving convicted inmates."

A thousand? The number made her stomach jump through her throat.

"How many people have died so far?" Daric blurted out.

"In the five years since inmates have been trans-ported to the island, we've seen a fifty percent casualty rate within forty-eight hours." Raptor turned sad eyes toward her. "And of those who survive, the statistics show another fifty percent casualty rate within two years."

Daric shifted in her direction, whispering loudly. "Hear that, Snow? If one of us has to die, it's probably going to be you."

She crossed her legs, making sure to kick him in the process. He grunted, but winked at her. No way would she ask him why he'd decided to call her Snow. Better to keep the communication with him to a minimum.

But then, Raptor asked for her. "Snow?"

Daric tipped his smile to one side. "You don't think she looks like Snow White? She's even got those eyes like blue ice." He cocked his head in her direction. "I get shivers just looking at her."

If only she gave him shivers of fear rather than lust. She scooted her chair farther from him.

Raptor folded his thick arms and fixed a glare on Daric. "The dinosaurs will be your most dangerous and most numerous adversaries." He switched his focus to Oakley. "To beat them, you have to use the one thing they don't have, your creative brain."

Oakley raised her hand. "Aren't some of them smart?"

"Yes. Small Theropods, especially the raptors, can be extremely smart, and we're just starting to understand how they communicate." He took a deep breath. "As you've probably heard from the media, some of these dinosaurs were genetically manipulated when they were brought back. Several species will have abilities you wouldn't expect."

"Like what?" She tried unsuccessfully to keep the tremor out of her voice. She hadn't realized genetically modified meant more dangerous.

Raptor stuffed his hands in the front pockets of his jeans. "Enhanced stealth properties like camouflage, manipulation of electrical fields, the ability to poison through skin contact and in aerosol form, and of course, superior vision, especially at night. Don't assume the dinosaurs can't see or sense you. Keeping still might work for a few species. As a whole, it's a terrible strategy. And so is running. It only triggers their prey drive. Trust me, they will out-predator you any day."

Daric threw his hands up. "What are we supposed to do then?"

Raptor gave him a condescending look. "Use your brain, genius. Outthink the animals. You have to assess each threat and respond to it appropriately." He spared her a glance. "In that respect, my money is on Oakley."

"Why?" Daric asked.

"She's a trained herpetologist. I'll let one of the officers define that for you later."

Daric scoffed. He wasn't as stupid as Raptor assumed. The glint in his eyes said he knew what her degree could mean in a place like Extinction Island.

"If all else fails, try climbing a tree."

What? She hadn't climbed a tree since she was ten-years-old.

"Some dinosaurs can climb decently with their back legs, but they have trouble holding on with their front." Raptor switched on the projection equipment, displaying a slide of the island. A dozen yellow highlighted areas were scattered on the map. "Returning to the humans, defined groups exist with some people mixing in between. Think of them like the cliques from your junior high years, except these guys are bigger, stronger, and armed."

"So they're like gangs?" she asked.

"Not really. Gangs are better organized with a code and a purpose, usually to make money or control territory. Most of these groups don't inspire loyalty and their only goal is to survive. However, there is one exception. The Cazador Gang, named because *cazador* means *hunter* in Spanish, behaves like a pack of wolves. They are loyal to the current alpha male who leads them. He gets the best of their food stores, the best sleeping arrangements"—his eyes found Oakley again, pity and fear etched on his tanned face—"which includes first pick of any available females."

Her mouth went dry as his words set in. On the island, her body would be a commodity, a resource, and heaven forbid, a bargaining chip.

From the back of the room, Officer Lewis spoke up. "We're almost there. Inmates, head upstairs. The terrain is rough, therefore each of you will be issued hiking boots when we dock."

She bristled. How kind of the government to make

sure her feet were protected, right before they dropped her off to die.

She stood and gave a parting look to Raptor. His stocky physique and close-cropped brown hair were the same as always, but his dark eyes revealed the despair of losing a loved one. Just ten years older than she, he had always treated her as a little sister, and she loved him like an older brother. He bent down to give her a hug. "I'll check on you in a few days when I can get back to the island."

She barely nodded, staring after him as he left the room. He turned right to head deeper into the ship. A moment later, she turned left to climb the stairs, flanked by Officer Lewis. Her head throbbed, her heart ached, and her throat burned from fighting off unshed tears. In a few moments, she'd be immersed in a jungle that concealed more dangers than she could count. Forget a few days. Would she survive the first few hours after they docked?

As she stepped onto the deck, the ship tilted. She grabbed a metal support pole to keep from falling.

Officer Lewis came around her and shuffled to the side of the ship, barking instructions to his partner. "Get ready to jump to the dock and tie us off."

The other officer scowled at having to do the manual labor, but he climbed on the rail to wait, hanging on by another support pole.

Hot breath filled Oakley's ear. "Soon you won't have anyone to help you." Daric grabbed her elbow and squeezed until she bit back a cry. She wouldn't give him the satisfaction. Instead, she whimpered just loud enough for Officer Lewis to hear.

He put a hand on his rifle. "Back off, inmate."

"What are you going to do, give me the death penalty twice?" Daric asked.

Officer Lewis glared daggers at him. "I can make sure the one you already have is carried out sooner rather than later."

Daric backed away with a smirk playing on his lips.

A loud thump sounded as the other officer jumped from the ship to the landing area. Then, the swaying deck began to stabilize.

"Oakley." Officer Lewis gestured for her to meet him at the railing. When she joined him, he lowered his head and his voice so only she could hear as he swept a hand toward the jungle. "Out there it's kill or be killed. Once we release you, take your supplies and run." He gave a quick glance to her small physique. "You seem like you'd be fast. Find someplace to hide. Don't let Perkins catch you."

He moved away to check on his partner. She continued to stare out at the mass of green foliage waving in the wind. Run and hide where? Full of convicts and dinosaurs, this terrible place would be her home. A thousand men like Daric and an even greater number of walking fossils armed with serrated teeth made this the most dangerous place on the planet.

At the top of a nearby cliff, something stationary amid the blowing leaves caught her attention. A man stood in front of the trees with his body turned toward the boat. A convict? He wore clean khaki pants and a white shirt, not the outfit she'd expect for an inmate. She narrowed her eyes to focus on him. As his features crystallized, she stepped back in shock. The unruly dark hair. The slender, aquiline nose. She'd only seen those prominent features twice. First, on her tour boat the day she'd lost her fingers to the gator, and again on the worst night of her life—Monica's last night alive.

Her heart pounded against her ribs. *Jim Durham.* The man who'd been at the bar that night. Her last memory was of a gold coin he gave her. He'd teasingly dropped it into her drink, then he disappeared, along with her memories. Where had he been during her trial? Why was he here now? As her disbelieving eyes tracked him, he slowly turned and entered the trees. The waving green leaves swallowed him up.

She gripped the railing tighter. Officer Lewis was more right than he knew. She needed to run straight into the jungle. To discover what information Jim Durham had about Monica's murder. If she could survive long enough to find him, perhaps she could prove her innocence and end this ordeal.

An unexpected worm of doubt squirmed its way into her mind. With her amnesia, she'd had a hard time explaining away some of the evidence presented at her trial. Like why her sandal had been found under Monica's body. Or how Monica had been electrocuted alone in the tub with no appliances anywhere. Though she tried to push the doubt away, it lingered in the corners of her mind. What really happened that night?

As the ship slid along the dock, the nearby trees blocked some of the wind. Daric shuffled his feet on the fiberglass floor of the boat behind her. Was he anxious to get to her or nervous for the landing? She glanced over her shoulder. He held her gaze for a brief second before he slowly ran his tongue over his upper lip. She shuddered and turned away.

The uniform sway of the trees captured her gaze again, as if the island was waving her away. But leaving wasn't an option. A growling roar rumbled from deep in the jungle. No matter how this all unfolded, she wouldn't get through it unscathed. Even if she fought off the evil behind her, she still had to confront the evil in front of her ... and possibly the evil inside her.

CHAPTER TWO

METALLIC GRINDING FILLED THE AIR. A riveted door the size of a large man opened in the side of the ship. It lowered slowly, exposing the moss green expanse of trees surrounding them like a menacing wall. Her heart beat wildly, slamming painfully into her rib cage with every thump. They'd arrived too fast. She wasn't ready for this.

The door clanked as the metal hit the concrete landing dock.

One of the officers strode through the door, holding his rifle at his waist.

"The gun is to encourage you to get off." Officer Lewis said. "This is the hardest part of the journey."

The hardest part for *them* maybe. For her, much worse awaited outside that door.

Officer Lewis walked to a storage box, lifted the latch

to open it, and removed two large backpacks. With a side-long glance at his partner, he announced, "Arming the prisoners." He handed one backpack to Oakley, the other to Daric. "Inside, you'll find a week's worth of food, rope, matches, and a short sword for protection. Here are your boots." He held out a pair of brown leather boots to each of them. She took the smaller pair and quickly put them on.

Daric waved them away. "Those things are too clunky." He pointed to his pitch-black tennis shoes. "I can get along just fine in these."

With a shrug, Officer Lewis placed the pair back in the storage box. "We suggest you find shelter immediately as the sun is going down and many predators hunt by night. In the dark, humans are at a disadvantage."

She would have agreed except perhaps darkness would help her slink away from Daric. The boat shifted as a large wave pounded the hull. The storm they'd managed to outrun on the way here had almost caught up with them. The crew would have a tougher time on the return trip.

Officer Lewis put his palm out toward Daric's chest. "She'll go first."

He pressed a square object into her hand, then motioned for her to go. She looked at what he'd given her. A taser. Though she probably wouldn't be able to charge it, at least it would carry one shock. She gave him a grim smile.

The other officer pointed with the rifle toward the

open door. With a gulp through her dry throat, she walked out and down the gangplank.

At the end, she stepped onto the concrete landing platform about the size of a two-car garage. The trees closed in on all sides. The humid air wrapped her in a cocoon. Sweat trickled down her forehead.

Her heart raced out of control. She sucked in a jagged breath, fighting off the panic.

The wall of leaves and vines appeared impenetrable. She flinched at every movement caused by the steady breeze. Above the sound of rustling leaves rose several voices shouting to each other. She backed away from them, her muscles tense. Where should she go?

Wide hands closed over her shoulders. "You're still here, Snow?"

Her stomach lurched. She should have run when she had the chance.

The voices from the trees grew louder.

"We have to get there before the gang," a man shouted as he broke out from the trees to the platform. He wore torn jeans and a navy long-sleeved T-shirt. A bow was slung over one shoulder, and he gripped a sword in his left hand. When he turned slightly, the top of a quiver shifted along his back. His light hair, more strawberry than Daric's platinum blond, blew in waves across his high forehead.

The man's gaze flickered to Daric, assessing the situation. He raised the sword. "Let her go."

She glanced over her shoulder. Daric appeared

conflicted, but he tightened his grip. She scowled and pulled away. She'd take her chances with this guy. He couldn't be worse.

"Come with us." The man's gaze never left hers as he added, "Both of you."

No, she wouldn't go anywhere with Daric. She stepped away from them.

"Cane." For the first time, Oakley noticed a woman—also armed with a sword—who had joined them on the landing. Slender, short, with dark skin and hair, she looked like a native Costa Rican. "No time."

Cane swiveled his head as if he could hear something else above the wind coming from the other direction. Oakley turned to look and the wind blew her mass of hair across her face. She swept it back just as another group of people came through the trees. She counted at least six men. One of them, with skin as dark as onyx and long dreadlocks, brandished a six-foot-long spear.

The spear-holder and another man took off and ran past her, chasing Cane and the woman who had already fled into the trees.

"I can't believe it." The voice came from near her shoulder. A grungy looking young man, probably in his teens, hungrily stared in her direction. "We've got a girl this time."

"That's not yours, Chubs." The deep voice came from the rear. The group parted for a man who looked a few years older than her. He had creamy, tanned skin, chin-length brown hair that shimmered like volcanic glass, and slate-colored eyes. Hawaiian maybe? With sculpted features, strong shoulders, and a trim waist, he was one of the most beautiful men she'd ever seen. His intense gaze sent a warm, yet tense pulse through her, something akin to the pleasure of hot chocolate right before it burns the tongue.

She started to run, but someone yanked her back. Chubs had a grip on her backpack. She shrugged out of it.

Just as she tensed to sprint, the leader of the group darted at an angle and cut her off. He latched on to her arm. "Not so fast. This place is dangerous. In good conscience, I can't leave you alone out here." There was no mistaking the sarcasm in his voice.

She matched his tone. "I doubt you've ever had a conscience."

She jammed her elbow into his stomach. It was rock-solid. She flipped the switch on the taser, but he was too fast. He snatched it from her grip before she could point it in his direction.

When she tried to wrench her arm free, he laughed, spun her around to face away from him, and pinned both arms to her sides in a bear hug. He picked her up and carried her like a stiff board toward the jungle. She kicked backward at him, furious at the disrespectful treatment. He squeezed harder until she had no breath left to fight.

In the few seconds before entering the jungle, she caught a glimpse of Daric. The gang had taken his backpack, and two members were rifling through it. Daric stood with his head hanging down, feigning submission. If only he'd fight, show his true colors, so the gang would kill him.

She lowered her head. Since when had she become the kind of person to wish for someone else to die? Her stomach knotted as the image of Monica's body came unbidden. Somehow in this situation, it would help to think of herself as capable of murder because then she'd be on more equal footing with these guys.

Fifteen minutes into their jungle walk, the leader finally put her down. She sprinted to the right in an escape attempt. With astonishing speed, he wound his hand in the fabric on the back of her T-shirt, jerking her back and holding her tight. Catcalls came from the rest of the group. One look down and she knew why. Her shirt was taut along her chest and had also pulled up at the bottom, exposing a few inches of flesh above her jeans.

The leader raised his free hand. The group fell silent.

All except for Chubs. "Come on, Kaleo. Can't you share this one?"

Kaleo. It sounded like a Hawaiian name. She glanced over her shoulder.

His brown eyes darkened. His only response was to swing her body around and smash her chest to his. With barely a second of warning, she threw her hands out as a barrier between them. She gulped at the solid surface beneath her palms. He could literally crush her if he wanted.

"You know I turned eighteen a week ago." Chubs

wasn't easily deterred. "Take pity. I've never been with a real woman."

From his lack of reaction, this either wasn't new information to Kaleo or wasn't true. Maybe he didn't react to much of anything. Then again, his intense eyes indicated the simmering brew of emotions hovering just below his calm surface.

"I mean, I've never been with a woman like her. She's the prettiest one we've ever gotten," Chubs continued.

"I agree." Kaleo muttered low, probably only so she could hear. His words sent a disturbing shiver through her.

"You've got to let me touch her before she gets all sunburned." Chubs inched closer. His hand went for her earring like a cat drawn to the shifting twinkle.

"Enough!" Kaleo wrapped an arm around her upper back and neck, forcibly burying her head in his chest. The smell of coconut, lemons, and sweat enveloped her. "She belongs to me. No one touches her."

Just great. The controlling, possessive leader had claimed her. Should she be happy she wouldn't be passed around to all of them or worried this man would kill her as soon as he got what he wanted? Instinct told her she would have been better off with the other man, Cane, but he'd left her to this gang. Maybe they were the Cazador gang, the hunters Raptor had talked about.

Kaleo's chest expanded as he drew in a big breath. His chin nuzzled her ear. He was smelling her hair. Just before they landed, Officer Lewis had allowed her a shower. Now she regretted using the peach-scented shampoo.

She yanked her head back, and Kaleo allowed it. Over his shoulder, Chubs flashed her a complicated look, part anger, part desire, followed by disgust when he came side by side with Kaleo and saw her left hand. "She's damaged."

Still securing her with one arm, Kaleo ran his fingers over the stretched skin and empty space where her left ring and pinkie fingers should have been. She flinched, not because it hurt, but because it felt too personal. One of his eyebrows quirked up, though he said nothing.

"It's time to go," the onyx-skinned man said with a nervous edge to his voice. He must have caught up to them so quietly that she hadn't noticed his presence at the back of the group.

"Camocroc?" one of the men whispered.

The man shook his head, his dreadlocks flying, even as his expression increased in intensity. "We have to go now."

Kaleo leaned down again to whisper in her ear, "Taye is our tracker. When he says go, it's smart to listen."

She wriggled her elbows in between her chest and his to create more space between them. "How 'bout we stay right here? All these beefy guys will be the first items on the buffet, and I'll just run along while the dinosaurs are eatin' y'all."

Kaleo gave her the same amused look the northern tourists had given her at the Lazy Lizard when she let her southern accent out in full bloom. Men found it charming. Maybe that would be useful later.

"Taye, do you still have some rope?" Kaleo asked.

The onyx-skinned man nodded, dug around in his shoulder pack, and pulled out a ten-foot length of braided cord.

Kaleo let go of her long enough to loop the rope around her waist. He knotted it, then coiled the rest over his elbow. Her blood pressure ratcheted up a notch, but she had to give him a little credit. The way he held it meant she couldn't go anywhere, and yet, if he happened to be attacked by an animal, the rope would fall, and she could escape. Not that she had any safe place to go. If she could get away, she'd most likely start the search for Jim Durham at the cliff where she'd seen him.

A curtain of darkness fell over the jungle as they continued to walk. Her gaze darted around, trying to identify threats behind dark bushes and shadowed tree trunks. With hesitant steps, she trailed behind Kaleo just far enough to keep the rope taut in case he loosened his hold.

It seemed they had been traveling roughly uphill the entire time. As the sun went down, so did the temperature and humidity. Or perhaps the humidity had decreased due to their higher altitude.

She sucked in a deep breath that tasted like earthy moss and oddly reminded her of home in Louisiana. The foliage tightened around them, minimizing the trail. She ducked through a circular archway of branches, unnerved by the cramped passage. Night predators must already be skulking around. Had they picked up the trail of seven men and one peach-scented woman?

She took peculiar comfort in Kaleo's confident swagger as he led the group. His hips rolled and his shoulders dipped like a stalking predator himself.

"Can we take a break?" she asked.

He spoke over his shoulder, not missing a beat. "Too dangerous. It's not far."

She rubbed her sweaty hands on her jeans. Noises skittered through the trees. The others paid no attention. Maybe they knew something she didn't.

Just as she was about to ask, Kaleo shot a concerned glance at Taye, whose dark features she could barely make out in the low light. Taye held up a hand. In a quick motion, he sliced it through the air twice to the right.

Both of Kaleo's arms encircled her, dragging her into the bushes bordering the trail. She gasped, but he put a firm hand over her mouth to cover the noise.

From the corner of her eye, she saw all six men also taking cover.

Strong, pounding steps ran down the trail straight at them. She held her breath.

A thirty-foot-long *Iguanodon* rushed past, zig-zagging along the trail. As it cleared their hiding place, it changed course and crashed into the underbrush away from them.

Before she had a chance to release her captive breath, another dinosaur raced into view. A ferocious *Velociraptor* with claws extended and nostrils and teeth bared.

At the point where they were concealed, this dinosaur

came to a halt. Bits of earth and leaves sprayed out from beneath its feet. The hairs on the back of her neck and arms stood at attention.

It drew in a great draught of air and huffed. Did it smell them?

Kaleo tightened his hand over her mouth. He needn't have worried. She had no plans to scream. Hadn't even dared to breathe yet. The scaly green beast stood at least a foot taller than her, and had two curved sickle-like claws. It could rip her to shreds in seconds. She was rather partial to keeping her guts on the inside.

A loud crash broke through the air. The *Iguanodon* must have tripped. The raptor's gaze shifted to the noise, then back to their hiding place. After a few seconds of indecision, it pivoted, dug its claws into the dirt, and took off in pursuit of the *Iguanodon*.

When she couldn't hear movement anymore, she let the air leak out of her desperate lungs. Kaleo released his hold on her mouth, and she took in a deep breath.

"That raptor must not have liked peaches," he said with a smile.

She swallowed to wet her dry mouth and just stared at his shadowed face. Any witty or sarcastic comment failed to materialize in her fear-numbed brain. His easy tone gave her insight into the first lesson she had to learn about Extinction Island. If fear paralyzed her again, it could be fatal.

As they crept out onto the trail, a loud, heartbreaking sound met her ears. Part wail and part howl, it signaled the torment the *Iguanodon* suffered. Had the raptor been one of the genetically modified ones? Why would anyone want to make killing machines like dinosaurs even more deadly?

She rubbed at the rows of goosebumps popping up on her arms. Her expertise might not matter on the island as much as Raptor led her to believe. In terms of reptiles, she was definitely out of her league.

CHAPTER THREE

AFTER THE CRAZED raptor had disappeared into the foliage, Oakley no longer strained at the rope tethering her to Kaleo. What might happen once they got her where they were going wasn't nearly as terrifying as a night out here unprotected.

They walked for about ten more minutes until the path dead-ended at a cliff. Kaleo took a hard left, ducking under an archway of vines. She followed him through the remains of a grand gazebo with rotting wooden supports and a carpet of musty leaves covering the floor.

Beyond the gazebo, a large structure rose in several angled peaks. Definitely a hotel, probably a luxury one from before the evacuation. When the United States had purchased this land and ordered the evacuation five years ago, many companies resisted, until they eventually accepted that the arrival of the dinosaurs would mean the death of tourism on Costa Rica. No tourist wanted to be eaten by the wildlife.

Then, an American politician proposed a brilliant way to offset the cost of Extinction Island and, at the same time, clear out the most dangerous criminals from jail. Hence, the choice with no real options: immediate death or trying to survive on this island.

As Oakley took in her surroundings, she also scrutinized the men around her. Were any of them part of the first group of death row inmates or had all of those original men died?

An overgrowth of vines and bushes blocked half of the hotel entrance from view. At one time it probably would have had sliding glass doors, but one side was covered with thick wood. The other door had cracked glass and a crudely carved handle. Kaleo grabbed the handle and yanked the door hard.

It slid sideways to reveal a man with shaggy brown hair and a beard, holding a shotgun. The man's light brown eyes went wide at the sight of her.

"Wyatt, all six back, plus two extras." Kaleo turned to her with raised eyebrows.

He didn't know her name. She could make something up, but what would it prove? Even so, she dug her heels in defiantly and focused on the broken marble tiles of the foyer.

Still looking at her, Kaleo flipped his thumb at Wyatt. "This guy has the shotgun because he's the sniper who killed twenty people last year on Highway 30. You might want to play nice."

She chewed on the inside of her cheek. He had a point. She would have a better chance of getting out of here and finding Jim Durham if she cooperated—to an extent. "I'm Oakley Laveau."

Wyatt shifted the weapon to his shoulder and stepped within inches of her face. His rank breath soured her stomach. "What did you do, Oakley?"

This time she wouldn't answer. Mostly because she didn't know for sure.

"She killed another girl in Louisiana. Monica somebody." Oakley spun around. Chubs had opened her backpack and was holding up a piece of paper.

Kaleo sported a satisfied smile. "They always send you off with a statement of your conviction. I guess they don't want you to forget why you're here." He looked her up and down, his ravenous gaze making her squirm. "Guess I should be careful when I get you in bed tonight."

The rest of the men laughed. She wrapped her arms around her torso.

Wyatt backed away and gestured over her shoulder. "What about the new guy?"

They had passed Daric's backpack to one of the other men whose name she didn't know. He read the statement, while Daric looked perturbed that they hadn't recognized him. But how could they? It wasn't like they could watch the news.

Kaleo whistled long and slow. "Ten women. Impressive. Too bad you couldn't make it an even dozen before getting caught."

For once, Daric blinked with no idea what to say. Oakley suppressed a smile.

"Give our new serial killer a room down the hall from Wyatt," Kaleo said.

"You mean Luis's room?" Chubs's voice wavered.

"Yeah." With a firm hand on her back, Kaleo steered her past Wyatt and toward the hall on the right.

"Who's Luis?" Daric asked.

Before Kaleo and Oakley turned the corner, Chubs responded. "Luis *was* my best friend. Red Grizzly got him. Huge *Utahraptor*. We only found pieces and blood. Lots of blood."

Her feet slowed, then stopped. How could she escape with all the creatures out there? And the close call with the *Velociraptor* still brought a heavy weight to her chest. She might know and understand reptiles, but not those that hunted people for food.

Before she could leave here, she'd have to find out more from Kaleo about how to travel safely. Unless, of course, it became unbearable to live with him. Because if he forced her into anything, she'd have to take her chances with the dinosaurs.

"Let's go," he said.

He'd waited when she stopped, the firm pressure on her back constant, but not insistent. If she ran, she'd only run right into Daric or Wyatt. At least Kaleo didn't have a gun at the moment. She pushed her feet forward and he guided her to double doors at the end of the hall.

She walked past him to enter the room. It looked like a palace, not a prison. The bed had a bright orange comforter and six fluffy white pillows. The hardwood floors still held their shine. A small sitting area to the left consisted of pale green chairs set across from each other. Glass patio doors farther down the left side of the room opened to a wrap-around deck with some sort of small pool or hot tub outside.

She tried to keep her reaction from showing. What would he expect for keeping her in this kind of luxury? She twisted her lips into a frown. "What, no butler or chocolate-covered strawberries?"

He laughed, a deep, almost enticing sound. "Actually, we can find strawberries. Chocolate is much harder. We make it from cacao beans, coconut oil, and honey, but it's not the same. You get used to it, once you've forgotten what chocolate from the mainland tastes like."

The mainland. Chocolate was the least of what she'd miss from home.

He closed the door, causing her to flip around to face him. She was defenseless. There was only one weapon in the room. A sword resting by the hinge-side of the door. Without it, and probably even if she wielded it, Kaleo would have the advantage. He towered over her by a foot and had at least seventy-five pounds on her. Whatever he wanted, he would take.

He raked his eyes over her body. The open raw

hunger flipped her stomach in somersaults. But then, his dark creamy irises met hers with curiosity. He moved to a chair in the sitting area. "Let's talk."

Talk? Was he serious? She let out a long sigh and sat in the chair opposite from him.

He reached over to grab her left hand. She flinched, but allowed it. With one thumb, he gently rubbed circles over the back of her hand, slowly moving toward the area he'd touched earlier. The circles stopped at the stub of her ring finger. He brushed the pad of his thumb over that nub and then the nub of her pinkie finger. "Not a birth defect. The edges are too straight. What happened?"

"I lost a fight with a gator."

She expected him to assume it was a joke and laugh. Instead, he appeared thoughtful. "There are worse things than gators, Oakley." He said her name long and slow. A shiver ran up her spine. "Things they didn't tell you about on the boat."

"Like what?"

He shook his head. "Tomorrow. What were you doing hanging out with gators?"

He asked questions in a curious tone, his expression soft and open as if this was a blind date. Despite his efforts to appear non-threatening, she couldn't dispel the twisting in her gut. This man had complete control of her. "In my former life, I was a herpetologist."

"Drawn to reptiles, huh? Well, at least I don't have to worry I'm not good-looking enough for you."

She gave him a sarcastic snort. He had to know how

gorgeous he was, and she didn't appreciate the false humility.

"Were you going in for a kiss with a gator or what?"

She straightened in the chair. There wasn't any harm in telling him the truth. "I jumped in to save a boy who fell into the water."

He leaned back and crossed his legs, staring at her like she was an unknown specimen. Maybe he didn't believe her.

She, however, would never forget the routine swamp tour that had gone wrong. She'd just spotted Blackie weaving toward the boat when, from the corner of her eye, a small figure leaned over. A dark shape bumped the boy, and then ... splash. Without thinking, she jumped in to get him. Blackie was too fast. A migraine had erupted in her skull, but she managed to hand the boy up to Jim Durham just as the gator closed in. The next few seconds were a blur of screaming and blood. In the end, her fingers were gone and Blackie floated on his side, clearly dead. She still didn't know what killed it.

Kaleo spoke in a smooth and steady voice. "Okay, Captain Hook. I don't think you're lying, but if you're the kind of girl who saves little boys, how did you end up here for murdering some woman?"

Captain Hook? Not a nickname she would have chosen, although she'd always loved pirate adventure stories. She shook her head, mirroring his earlier response. "Tomorrow."

A few seconds ticked away before he stood. "Fair enough."

He strode to the door and flipped the lock. Now what? A dagger of panic sliced through her. Would it matter to him that she'd never been with anyone, or would it make her more desirable?

"I need you to come here." His commanding tone left no room for argument.

She gave him a confused look. There was nothing on that side of the room except the door and the wall. She'd expected him to throw her on the bed.

Like a switch flipped in his head, he stomped over, pulled her by the arms, and dragged her to the wall. She grunted and groaned at the pressure from his hands digging into her upper arms.

"You're mine! You do what I say!" He shoved her into the wall, stealing her breath. Her head narrowly missed hitting the corner of a picture frame. He slammed his open palm just above her head. The picture vibrated, drawing out the impact. She ducked and let out a scream.

With one hand, he yanked her back up by the shoulder. With the other, he cupped her cheek. Leaning down, he whispered in her ear. "I'm not into beating women. Or forcing them. But I've got to protect my position here. I'll make you a deal. I'll sleep on the floor, you can have the bed, and I'll never touch you"—he trailed a finger from her ear lobe down to her clavicle. Despite her fear, or maybe because of it, her body responded with floods of tingles —"unless of course you want me to. But in front of the guys, we have to act like lovers, and you have to be submissive."

He would sleep on the floor? Hard to believe. But perhaps the slamming and screaming were for the benefit of those on the other side of the wall. After all, he hadn't hurt her. Did she somehow hit the jackpot and manage to find the one respectable guy on an island full of criminals? If so, there might be one problem. "How submissive?"

He backed away from her, a glimmer of amusement in his eyes. "Yeah. I get that it doesn't come naturally for you. It's okay for it to look forced."

The unspoken consequences made her shiver for a different reason. If the others thought Kaleo couldn't handle her, then someone would challenge him. She could imagine Daric Perkins would love the opportunity to lead. On the exhale of a deep breath, she nodded, and said, "You've got a deal."

CHAPTER FOUR

OAKLEY AWOKE to the first shafts of dawn tentatively flickering through the glass patio doors. The ghostly remnants of her missing fingers twitched. She rubbed the aching stubs. It was part of her morning ritual as if every day her brain needed to be convinced those fingers were gone.

Kaleo's bed had all of the fluff of a half-dead goose, but she'd probably slept better than he had on the floor. Amazing that he'd kept his end of the bargain.

Last night, while listening to his soft snores, she'd fallen asleep thinking of her teary goodbye with her dad. Dad would beg the authorities for her release, but it probably wouldn't help based on how swift her conviction had been. Besides, he had Eric and Felice to worry about. Felice would have no problem disregarding Oakley's plight, but ten-year-old Eric sobbed when they told him Oakley wouldn't be coming back. No more throwing the baseball with him or burning cookies he would still eat anyway. No catching geckos so he could give them goofy names like Little Godzilla or Slinky. In the dark of night, all of the things she'd never do again had twisted through her soul like a grief tornado.

This morning, though, she refused to indulge in self-pity. She needed to move forward, to decide her next move. She was stuck on this island and ironically, the one person who could have made a difference in her trial ended up here as well. It couldn't be a coincidence. If she stayed with Kaleo, where she momentarily felt safe, she probably wouldn't find Jim Durham, which meant she wouldn't get answers.

Leaning over, she peered at Kaleo, who still snored softly in his sleep. His relaxed expression deepened the set of his eyes and minimized the intensity of his jawline. He looked innocent, almost joyful in dreamland.

She rolled back over and pictured Jim's face as he congratulated her on saving the little boy from her tour boat. He'd dropped the gold coin in her drink, claiming it was a reward for her heroism. After that, her memory was a blank chalkboard.

Although she needed to locate him, she couldn't afford to turn down the deal Kaleo offered. For whatever reason, he was willing to protect her with no strings attached, except a little bit of acting. If she could be patient and let him teach her how to survive, then she could slip away to go after Jim when the time was right.

She shifted in the bed. One of the springs gave a loud

creak. Kaleo sat straight up, his hair sticking out haphazardly, the peaceful expression gone. His frantic eyes found her. "You okay?"

Her safety was the first thing he'd thought of? Her mouth had gone dry, so she nodded.

He relaxed back to the blanket and pointed to the bathroom with a tilt of his head. "In there, you'll find a toothbrush and a pasty compound we use as toothpaste. It even tastes a little like mint, but mostly like silly-putty."

"I'll confess I've never tasted silly-putty. Here goes." She took care of her business in the bathroom, noting that he was right about the consistency and probably the taste of the toothpaste.

When she came back out, Kaleo lay on the bed with his feet crossed at the ankles.

She sat uneasily on the edge, away from him. "How does the toilet work?"

"Good question. We chose this resort for two reasons. It's set into a cliffside, which makes it easier to defend. And it was built as a completely green resort. There's a cistern to capture rainwater and solar panels to run the lights and the electric water purifier. The toilets drain to a septic field at the bottom of the cliff."

"I see. What about food?"

"Some fruits and vegetables grow close by. I also grow berries on the patio. For meat, we hunt every couple of days. And you're in luck, today is one of those days."

Hopefully, he would take her with him, not leave her trapped here like some princess in a tower. She pushed down the sensible part of her that preferred being alone in a tower to being eaten in a jungle. "Were you hunting yesterday when the boat came in?"

"Nope. Every two weeks, we meet the boat. Their schedule only deviates if they run into a tropical storm."

"You're always looking for new members?"

He shook his head. "I've got my hands full with these guys. We meet the boat so we can get more supplies."

She glared at him. "You mean steal them from people."

He stared back, unrepentant. "The definition of stealing gets pretty loose out here. Besides, I usually give the new inmates a chance to join us." As if she'd had a choice. When she didn't respond, he hopped off the bed. "You'll find more clothes in the closet. They're women's clothes, but you'll probably have to roll up the cuffs and sleeves since you're short."

She glanced down at her jeans and jade-colored long-sleeved T-shirt. Maybe a little warm for the area, but the saying on her shirt, "Let's Get Cray Cray," made her think of crawfish and home. "I'm good in these."

"Okay. We leave in ten."

While he took his turn in the bathroom, she rummaged through the dresser looking for a hair tie. She finally found a big scrunchy shoved in the back of the women's underwear drawer. "Wonder how long this has been here."

Nevertheless, she swiped a layer of dust off it, swept her hair up, and secured it with the scrunchy. For a few minutes, she ran her fingers through the ponytail to work out the tangles.

True to his word, ten minutes later, Kaleo escorted her out the front door. Though he carried a bundle of rope, this time he didn't make a move to tie her up. Apparently, their deal had changed the situation in his mind. She could take the opportunity to run and probably beat him in a sprint, but who knew what she'd be running toward.

He pointed at the small courtyard that was walled in by ten-foot-tall shrubs. The gazebo stood as the sole entrance to the area. "You're safe here until you cross over the gazebo, thanks to our electronic pulse system. The sound is an ultrasonic tone most dinosaurs hate."

"Like a dog whistle?"

"Exactly, except it repels them instead of attracting them. It's not foolproof—some of the bigger ones can push through—but it keeps the raptors away." He stopped on the littered floor of the gazebo. His shoes scraped along the weathered wood as he turned around. Leaning forward, he put a hand on each of her shoulders. She felt like a small doll with his large palms stretching from her neck to her shoulder, and his long fingers draping several inches down her back. "Can I trust you to do what I say out here?"

She twisted her lips. If she said no, he would probably tie her up. "Following directions isn't my strong suit."

He pressed down on her shoulders. "This isn't a game, Hook. You could lose a lot more than a few fingers."

She folded her arms, tucking her damaged hand

under her armpit. He didn't have to be that blunt, but telling him so would just sound like a pouting child. "Fine. Let's go."

They passed through the gazebo without seeing anything more than a few startled geckos. She followed close behind him and tried to keep her eyes everywhere. If she let down her guard, a full set of teeth would likely come charging at her.

After an hour of hiking on guard, the adrenaline high overwhelmed her. Her nerves couldn't handle the constant anxiety. She had to relax a little and trust Kaleo to know when they were in danger. He rounded a boulder, took a hard right to avoid a cliff, and continued into the trees. At first, she moved to follow, then she stopped, her mouth agape at the distant view. In the valley below, long, thick necks attached to streamlined heads towered above the tree canopy—sauropods. They might be *Brachiosaurs* or *Apatosaurs*. She couldn't remember the difference between them from her one dinosaur class in college, and Raptor hadn't shown pictures of the sauropods in his brief talk on the boat.

Below the sauropods, a clearing in the trees showcased a herd of some other medium-sized dinosaur, maybe *Hadrosaurus*. Several of them clustered around a grouping of circular nests. The milky white eggs stood out in stark contrast to the dark nest material. It was too far to tell for sure, but likely the eggshells would be leathery to help the eggs stay hydrated as in modern reptiles. If only she could feel them to find out.

"Beautiful, isn't it?" Kaleo's close voice made her jump. He had come back to check on her.

"Amazing."

Who would have thought she could find beauty here? She glanced behind at the jungle crowding her. The fear hadn't completely fled in the presence of her awe, but she was starting to view these creatures as animals. No different from the alligators she'd studied. Except here, balancing the danger with the beauty could prove to be much more challenging.

▭

KALEO FOCUSED on the sounds of the canopy and the movement of the plants around them. As long as the birds chirped and the leaves didn't rustle much, they were safe from the majority of predators, except for a select few. Like the Camocroc. There was no way to know when that creature would show up, and no way to see it when it did.

He ignored the temptation to look back to check if Oakley was still following. Her quiet footsteps reassured him. To be honest, he wanted one more glimpse of her bright blue eyes, her pearl-like skin, and the soft dark waves of her ponytail. Maybe he should let her walk in front so he could watch her curves sway while she walked. *Ugh.* What was wrong with him? He'd never let a woman distract him like this before.

"Do you normally come out here alone?" she asked.

Before answering, he stopped to survey the area. They

were in a little depression near a hill, a safe place for a conversation. He backed her up to the hillside and turned to watch the trees. "Ask your questions. I won't answer the rest of the way to the hunting grounds. Not only will it scare away potential prey, it will make us prey instead." He didn't want to scare her, especially since she was the first woman to agree to come hunting with him—the others had been too freaked out to leave the resort—but she had to learn how to survive out here.

"I normally come out here with Taye or Wyatt, though I prefer Taye."

"Why?"

"Let's just say we have similar philosophies on life and death. Plus, he's a great tracker."

She hesitated a moment before asking her next question. "What did these men do? I mean you told me about Wyatt. What about the rest?"

He pressed his lips together. It was natural for her to want to know, but some levels of evil were better left unnamed. He'd gloss over the details. "Taye was a member of a cult. The leader convinced him to kill another member when they left the cult. He ended up killing an innocent bystander as well. Orion, he's one of the men who walked back with us—the one with dark hair and light skin like you—he's a serial rapist. Never killed any of them, although he raped at least forty women. Don't go near him."

She noticeable swallowed.

He pushed his hands into his jeans pockets to keep

from putting an arm around her. "You haven't met Misty yet. She keeps to her room because she's older and her knees bother her. She killed three husbands in various ways, mostly poison. The guys don't give her any trouble. It's a superstitious thing. Like don't mess with Misty or she'll lay a curse on you." He'd never believed in that stuff, although he was grateful he didn't have to worry about her.

"What about Chubs?"

He blew out a long breath. Chubs wouldn't like his history shared, even though most of the guys knew it. "His real name is Leo Coleman. We call him Chubs because he's the only seventeen-year-old to be shipped here. He still had baby fat on his cheeks when he arrived. Not old enough to vote, but old enough to die. I won't tell you what he did or why. He deserves to decide whether you know."

To her credit, she didn't protest. Probably, she wanted to know about his past most of all. He wasn't ready for that conversation yet.

"How do the native species handle the presence of the dinosaurs?"

He gaped at her. Despite the stress of the kidnapping and near-attack last night, she made an effort to understand her surroundings. He was impressed. Most new inmates didn't handle the transition as calmly.

"What? You said to ask all my questions."

True, and it would seem out of left field, except for her background as a herpetologist, which probably gave her a natural curiosity. "The native wild pigs have been hunted almost to extinction by the raptors. The *Compsognathus*, or compys—those are the small chicken-like dinosaurs—eat the geckos like crazy, but the geckos seem to reproduce fast enough to compensate. The monkeys do fine in the trees. The jaguars eat the compys, but they sometimes get eaten by the raptors. That's about all I've noticed."

She gave him a satisfied smile. "Thanks."

He nodded and began walking again. The bushes in front of them swayed. He tensed and put one hand on the weapon stuck in the back of his jeans.

A soft chirrup floated through the air. He relaxed and lowered his hand as a juniper green *Coelophysis* jumped from under the bush. It balanced on two legs, not quite to his waist, looking like a Great Dane-sized gecko. Though he'd seen them run on all fours when threatened, this one bobbed on two legs, bouncing up and down. It ignored him, staring intently at Oakley. He couldn't blame the poor creature.

"Oh, he's cute." She moved toward it. Another soft chirrup.

"Be careful. The coelos will bite if they think you have food, and their teeth are sharp. This guy looks a little smaller than most, probably a runt."

"He seems friendly."

Kaleo did his best imitation of the sarcastic snort she'd given him last night. "Everything around here seems friendly, until it bites your head off."

She knelt down, putting her face right in the line of fire. The woman wasn't lacking in bravery.

The creature dipped its head in deference and hopped closer. She opened her arms, and it jumped onto her lap, put its rump to her stomach and sat down. Its head rose as high as hers. She stroked the top of its head, then along its spine. Probably felt something like petting a snake with a sparse downy covering.

"Are they always this cuddly?"

He shrugged. "They all run from me."

"Shocking."

Though she didn't look up at him, he smiled at her sarcasm. He could get used to this banter.

She patted the animal's head. "Coelo? Too hard to say all the time. Let's call him something else that starts with a C. How about Cole? Or Cody?"

"I'm not sure Chubs would appreciate Cole since his last name is Coleman."

She snapped her fingers. "Cody it is. Do you like your name, little guy?"

Another soft chirrup.

"How do you know it's a him?"

"It isn't a boy?"

He laughed. "I'd guess so. You're the expert. Lift his leg up."

She squinted at him, her lips pursed in an inviting pout. "I worked on gators."

"I'll bet dinosaurs aren't as different as you'd think."

After a few more minutes of her nuzzling with the

coelo, Kaleo grew impatient. "Come on, leave your new pet. I've got some stuff to show you."

She gently pushed the little pest off her lap. How would she react if she knew he'd killed and eaten many coelos over the years? In this environment, meat was meat.

He led them down a hill and through the small valley. At the bottom, he glanced back to check for predators. Oakley's new pet followed at a leisurely pace several yards behind, partially hidden in the leaf cover. Hopefully, it wouldn't attract any carnivorous attention.

A few yards later, at the site of the marked tree, Kaleo stopped to block her way. "If you're alone, you must watch the trees for symbols." He held a hand out flat to mark her height. "You will have to look up to see them." She frowned at him and he laughed, then quickly turned sober. "If you've got someone with you, the lead person has to watch."

He pointed at the starburst symbol—eight lines spiking in different directions—carved into the trunk at his eye level. "This symbol is for a trap we've constructed. The starburst is the trap and the danger is drawn within it. This one is an arrow pointing right which means spear." He flicked a taut wire set level with his chest and strung between two trees. "Break this connection and a spear launches at a height high enough to kill medium-sized dinosaurs like *Velociraptor* and *Utahraptor*. They are the ones that will hunt you for food. To a *T. rex*, trying to eat you would be a nuisance and this would be a stub of the toe."

"Pardon me if I'm still afraid of a *T. rex*."

"Well, if you stand out in the open and give him a meal, he'll take it, but trust me, he's not your biggest threat."

"Then what is?"

She'd asked a similar question last night and as much as he didn't want to scare her, she deserved an answer. Just maybe not the whole answer. "I've seen dinosaurs out here that can do crazy things. Poison, electric shock, camouflage, it's all out there. Your best defense is to stay alert and stay an arm's distance away from them at all times."

"Are you talking about Camocroc?"

Of course, the herpetologist in her would zero in on something which sounds like a familiar reptile. "It's a *Saurosuchus*, according to the list of dinosaurs posted near the landing site. We call it Camocroc because of its ability to camouflage itself. It's as good as any gecko or chameleon I ever saw growing up on Maui." Truth be told, he'd also had an affinity for reptiles growing up, but this place had spoiled that. "Camocroc is similar to a croc, although it doesn't stay in the water. It killed one of our group at least a hundred yards from the nearest wetlands."

"I'm sorry." Her soft voice and haunted eyes spoke of loss.

He'd have to ask her about that later. For now, back to business. "Other types of traps include a pit full of knives, that symbol is a short rectangular cup with one line inside it. The same symbol turned upside down tells you there's a launching pad powered by springs to throw a dinosaur. A lightning bolt means there's electrical potential in the wire caused by the two ends being dipped in different chemical solutions. Those charges are not powerful, probably just enough to startle a dinosaur, but it could give you the time you need to get away. And then there's the half-arrow pointing up to represent a catapult. Not the kind that throws something. It swings around with a heavy object to smash what's standing there into the forest floor."

She scuffed one boot in the dirt. "Will there be a test on these later?"

He scowled at her. The test could be at the cost of her life. "If you know where the traps are, you can use them to get out of trouble. I have a map you can study back at the compound. Also, I carry this around with me everywhere." He tugged his thick, bundled whip out of the back of his jeans. "It's a little bulky, but it will kill small dinosaurs, like your friend over there." He made a quick move toward the creature. It jumped back behind Oakley's leg.

"And the bigger ones?"

"They will think twice about how tasty you look." He swung the whip, enjoying the zing as it sliced through the air and the smack as it cracked on a tree. "Oh yeah, if you hear that sound while in the jungle, always hit the ground. It either means someone like me is swinging a whip or, much worse, a *Brachiosaurus* is defending its territory. One strike of their tail will take you out."

She crinkled her nose. "Thank you, wise mentor, but I

don't think I'll stumble upon one of those hundred-ton monsters by accident."

He let the whip hit the ground and stared at her. Most people were probably put off by her sarcasm, but he wasn't most people. He actually found it refreshing. She wouldn't give him respect just because he was bigger and stronger. If there came a day when she opened up to him, he would know he'd earned it. "Actually, a *Brachiosaurus* is easy to hear when they're moving or singing. If they're stationary, the jungle can hide their mass."

She tilted her head and shot him a look he couldn't interpret. Something between surprise and anger before her features softened. "Why did you sleep on the floor last night?"

He rubbed at the stubble on his jaw. This woman would keep him on his toes.

"Don't get me wrong. I'm grateful for your hands-off policy, but I don't get it. You're a criminal, used to getting what you want. Plus, you're the leader, you can take what you want. So why not?"

He avoided her gaze for a moment. He'd expected this question, just not so soon. The few women he'd helped had waited longer to ask, probably for fear he would take back his offer. Maybe that was another part of what made Oakley so attractive—her fight outweighed her fear.

He could tell her the whole truth, but his respect for her didn't mean he could trust her. "The problem with getting everything you want is that it all means nothing." He closed the distance between them and placed two fingertips on her chin. He took some satisfaction in the small catch of her breath. "If we discover an attraction, I want it to be real. Not some Stockholm Syndrome, where you think you want what I want because I've terrorized you."

Her gaze flickered away from his to the top of the canopy. She tilted her head again. "What is that?"

He followed her line of sight. A fluffy white pillow drifted across the sky. "What the hell? It's a parachute."

"Who would be stupid enough to come here on purpose?"

Good question. The waters around the massive island were restricted from shipping traffic for twenty miles, and the parachute was too high to be a lost parasailor. The guy had to have jumped from a plane. Not much chance the plane didn't know where he'd jumped. Whoever was attached to the chute had come here on purpose, but why?

CHAPTER FIVE

OAKLEY HAD to push her legs twice as fast as Kaleo's just to keep up with him. Her nerves frayed more with every step because he disregarded everything he'd just told her about moving slowly and quietly through the jungle. He wasn't watching the trees for signs of creatures or keeping a safe distance from creeks. A moment ago, they had splashed through a shallow one, and she saw movement on the other side of the bank. Some animal was hiding there, but she couldn't clearly identify it.

Kaleo continued to bulldoze through the trees and underbrush. She'd given up asking where they were going a while ago, in the spirit of keeping quiet. Their trajectory was taking them toward the landing pad.

She stopped for a second to wipe a line of sweat off her brow. He continued without her. She rushed to catch up. Though part of her longed to escape, another part of her needed the safety he promised.

They broke through the trees on the edge of the concrete pad. Like yesterday, someone else had already arrived. Cane, the man with the strawberry-blond hair and kind eyes, stood next to the same native woman. She appeared older than everyone here, but certainly no older than forty.

Cane nodded at Oakley before returning his gaze back to a spot blocked from her vision by Kaleo's wide shoulders. She stepped around him to see a woman with light-brown hair lying face down on the pavement. The parachute billowed behind her like a flowing cotton dress. She must have hit the pavement hard enough to knock herself unconscious.

Kaleo exchanged a cryptic look with Cane before moving toward the woman. Weird, how he didn't seem intent on capturing Cane now. Perhaps both of them were too focused on the strange woman who had risked her life in that parachute stunt.

The woman stirred and groaned.

"Are you okay?" Kaleo moved closer.

The woman moaned again and rolled onto her back. Her eyes popped open, then shut immediately.

"Do you know where you are?" he asked.

She sat straight up, wincing and holding her head. She peered at Kaleo through pinched eyelids. "Did I make it?"

He put his hands on his hips. "If you were trying to discover a paradise full of teeth and blood, then yeah."

She dropped her hands. The pain cleared from her eyes. "I need to see Daric."

"Daric?" When Cane had spoken to Oakley at the landing spot, the wind had muffled the sound. Now, she heard soothing notes radiating through his almost musical voice, much different from Kaleo's gruff baritone.

"The new guy you saw yesterday," Kaleo answered Cane and turned back to the woman. "How did you know he was here?"

"It's not a secret. Everybody knows the San Diego Slayer was sent to Extinction Island." The woman stood on shaky legs. She was tall, only a few inches shorter than Kaleo. "He invited me to join him. Do you know where he is?"

To join him. Like Daric was staying at his island vacation home and this girl was some starlet he'd invited down for the weekend. What a joke.

Kaleo just stared as if he couldn't decide what to do with her.

"Look, it's not that complicated. I'm Violet Roupp, Daric's girlfriend. I bribed a guard to tell me the location where the boat would drop him off. So where is he?" She put a hand against her mouth. "He's not already ..."

Kaleo held his palms out in a placating gesture. "No, he's fine. He's at our place. I'm just trying to figure out what you're doing here. Daric didn't mention a girlfriend."

Oakley cleared her throat and almost choked. Daric certainly hadn't mentioned anything when he was trying to get in her pants.

Violet glared at her before responding to Kaleo. "If you don't take me to him, he'll make you regret it later."

He crossed his arms over his chest. From the side, Oakley had to admire the bulging muscles. "That's not how it works here. Daric is under the protection of my gang for as long as I say so. I'll take you to him, but give me any problems and both of you will be left to fend for yourselves."

Violet blinked as if seeing him for the first time. With a quick nod, she grabbed her backpack from the ground.

Kaleo quickly scooped it out of her hand. "And this belongs to the group."

She dipped her head, the perfect picture of submission. What was the deal with her? Some sort of serial killer groupie? Or had she known Daric before he'd started his killing spree?

Cane opened his arms wide as if saying there was nothing he could do to help and backed away from Kaleo. As he walked off, he sent several curious glances Oakley's way, but never said a word to her. The dark-skinned woman gave her a sweet smile before she followed him. Those two didn't act like members of a gang. And Kaleo seemed more at ease with them than he did his own gang.

Kaleo led the way from the clearing toward the compound. Violet trailed behind him, leaving Oakley to bring up the rear. Just as they entered the jungle, a soft chirrup met her ears. Violet tensed, but Kaleo merely glanced back with a quirked eyebrow as Cody appeared from the bushes.

She rubbed her new pet's head, smiling as he wriggled into her hand. His smooth skin was coated with a fine downy hair, not nearly as rough as the gators she'd touched at work. When she moved to continue down the trail, Cody bobbed along behind her, more jumping than walking.

As the rear member of the threesome, she could easily slip away, except her new pet would likely follow, and the absence of his bobbing and chirping would be noticed. Plus, she'd only just started to understand the dangers of traveling alone in the jungle. A small smile broke free in the midst of her serious deliberation. Besides, if she left now, she'd miss Daric's reaction to the arrival of his *girlfriend.*

From the way Violet dipped her head whenever Kaleo looked over, it was clear she liked to be submissive to a powerful man. In between demure glances, she glared at Oakley. Definitely, a serial killer groupie, and it turned her stomach. A man convicted of strangling ten women wasn't powerful, he was cowardly and psychotic.

At the gazebo entrance, Violet stepped through tentatively, then stopped when the vine-covered resort opened up in front of them. "This place is massive."

Oakley walked through the archway alone, sidestepping Violet. When she looked back, Cody hadn't followed, probably due to the sound deterrent Kaleo had mentioned. She waved goodbye before striding to the front door.

Inside the resort, men popped out of their rooms like

gophers from their holes, drawn to the shimmery curtain of Violet's long honey-colored hair. They whispered to each other, but no one questioned Kaleo while he searched the resort for Daric. They found him soaking in the large outdoor infinity pool near the edge of the cliff face.

"You've got a visitor," Kaleo barked.

Violet stepped from behind him, and Daric's eyes lit up. A fair rendition of love from someone who could love no one but himself. What seemed like amorous desire in his gaze was only hunger and lust. Violet had better watch her back.

Daric placed his hands on the side of the pool and heaved himself out. Oakley turned away at the sight of him in wet boxers.

Violet raced over and threw herself into his arms. "I've missed you so much."

"I can't believe you came."

Neither could Oakley. She glanced back to see them locked in a deep kiss. Her stomach twisted, sickened that Violet was feeding his passion—that Violet could *feel* any passion for such a monster. Since there weren't many women here, he'd likely keep her around for a while. Eventually, though, his urge to kill would resurface. Men like him didn't change.

A horrible possibility raced through her mind, chased by a spike of adrenaline. What if Kaleo was one of those men? So far, she trusted him because he hadn't forced her to do anything, but she had no idea what he'd done to get here. His patience with her might run out. She glanced at him, searching the tight jaw and sculpted profile as if they would tell her of his trustworthiness. He didn't return her stare. His dark eyes were focused on the two entwined bodies.

He cleared his throat. "I get that this is a happy reunion, but keep it in your pants until you get to your room. It's only fair to the others."

Groans and grumbling followed his announcement. To the others, Violet was just another potential sexual partner that he had taken away from them. Was he letting Daric and Violet be together to keep the peace? If so, it would make Daric happy, but would likely stir up more trouble with the others.

Daric laughed. "Sorry guys. If I were you I'd want to watch. It's the most excitement you'll get"—he locked his gaze on Oakley—"until you decide to loosen up."

She resisted the urge to punch him. Instead, she threw her shoulders back and glared.

Kaleo stepped in front of her, one finger pointing to the hallway. "Get moving."

Daric took Violet's chin to draw her close for a more chaste kiss. "Shall we continue behind closed doors, beautiful?"

She grinned and followed him down the hall, reminding Oakley of her pet *Coelophysis*. With Daric gone, she relaxed, though not by much. The rest of the men stared at her like she was the last candy-coated gumball in the gumball machine.

Kaleo must have sensed it too because he grabbed her around the waist and pulled her close to his side. Her legs were split over his knee and her chest was pressed into his right pectoral muscles. To steady herself, one hand grabbed the strong muscles of his shoulder, the other landed on his rock-solid abs. Her mouth went dry and her whole body tingled. Instinct told her to fight, but curiosity begged her to explore the muscles beneath her palms. Plus, she had no reason to fight. She'd promised to keep up the charade, after all.

Thankfully, he didn't try to kiss her. She really had no clue what her reaction would have been. Instead, he bent low and whispered, "Let's go."

Despite his words, he didn't move. She tried to summon some sort of will to pull away. It was no use. Her senses were overwhelmed by the hum of desire pulsing through her veins. This man was a study in contradiction. Hard and gruff one moment, concerned and tender in the next. She couldn't figure him out, and she ached to know what made him tick. Her gaze focused on his full lips. If he kissed her, would he be gentle or unyielding?

Finally, he took her hand off his abs, spun around, and pulled her back inside the sliding glass door. Once they were walking down the hall, her head started to clear. What was she thinking?

She wasn't thinking, that was the problem. She was feeling—lust, desire, longing—feelings that had no place here in the middle of her nightmare.

Back in the room, Kaleo locked them in and

approached her, a thousand questions in his eyes. She avoided his gaze because she didn't have any answers.

"It's still early," he said. "Let's swim."

Swimming with him sounded like a bad idea. Cool water over hard muscles would only create more temptation.

"It will wash away the long day." His voice lowered, turning husky. "And I don't know about you, but I need to cool down."

He had a point there. Maybe the water would calm them. "Okay."

But when he stripped off his shirt, she just about choked on her own saliva. Ripples of muscles streamed down his chest to those defined abs she'd had her hands on. The top of his shorts circled his trim waist. He opened the patio door and his strong shoulders flexed, sending a flutter through her abdomen. This was a very, very bad idea.

She waited, hoping he would promise her this was completely platonic. But he didn't. If she joined him, she'd be taking her chances.

"There are a few bikinis in the top drawer of the dresser, along with some shorts and T-shirts that might fit you."

The jeans she'd worn all day, and to bed last night, had made her hot and sweaty. Shorts and a dip in the pool sounded heavenly. No way would she go near a bikini.

In the drawer, she found most of the shorts were too big except for a pair of spandex ones. She changed in the bathroom, keeping her sports bra and putting on a long T-shirt over it.

His private pool was big, although half the size of the one on the other side of the resort. Also like the other one, it rested on the edge of the cliff, making it seem as if you could jump from the pool into the deep forest. A smattering of hibiscus plants and overflowing pots of berries surrounded two sides of the pool.

The sun had almost completely fled, leaving only a dusting of pink along the edge of the canopy. It was the most beautiful country she'd ever seen, like the green expanse of swamps in Louisiana, but grander and bolder. Loud screeches and deep rumbles filtered up to them. Unfortunately, this spectacular jungle belonged to the dinosaurs.

Kaleo relaxed against the far side, splashing one hand idly in the aqua water. His eyes moved down her legs. "Sorry about surprising you back there."

She shrugged, her voice not quite matching her casual gesture. "I understand. You were keeping up the pretense."

He splashed water toward her. "Yep, I wouldn't want to touch you otherwise. How gross."

She laughed at the banter and matched his tone. "I know. I had a hard time not throwing up myself."

He took a deep breath and sank farther into the water. "So, tell me, Hook, who's waiting for you on the outside?"

Finally, safe territory. "My dad and my ten-year-old brother, Eric." Then, she realized she'd forgotten to mention Felice. "I have a stepmom too. But she's indifferent to me. Well, to be fair, we're indifferent to each other."

"What happened to your mom?"

She stared at a leaf partially submerged in the water. "She had mental problems. And then she died." There wasn't much more she could tell him anyway. When she reached for memories of her mother, her mind was blocked. Some type of scab guarded the images, like a mental bandage she couldn't seem to rip off.

"I'm sorry."

She tugged her ponytail out and leaned back, dipping her hair in the water. "I don't remember her much because I was young, but I'm pretty sure she didn't want me."

The memories were hazy, but a knot of rejection had lodged deep down in her gut.

He flipped his wet hair out of his eyes. "She really was crazy then."

She smiled at his desire to make things better. "My dad filled the gap."

"No boyfriend?"

It was a complicated question that she decided to answer simply. "No. We broke up."

Kaleo dropped under the water. When he surfaced, he was closer to her. Water dripped from his hair and cascaded down his sleek torso. She meant to turn away, but her eyes followed a single rivulet as it trailed the edge of his tanned jaw, dropped to his pectoral muscle, then coursed down to his toned stomach.

"Did you break up when you were sentenced?"

"No, before." She snapped her gaze up. Time to stop this line of questioning. "We needed a break."

Her eyes had adjusted to the low light, and she caught his smirk. "Meaning he cheated on you."

Apparently, she was easy to read. Her boyfriend, Matt, had cheated on her with Monica. A powerful motive for murder, according to the prosecuting attorney.

He dove underwater again. She bit her lip as water swirled near her legs.

He came up right next to her. He shook the water from his hair, splashing her in the process. He reached out to wipe droplets off her cheek. "I can't understand why anyone would cheat on you. In fact, I can't understand why you're here at all."

She fought the urge to back away while simultaneously ignoring the pull to move closer. Her body locked up with the tension. "Same. Are you going to tell me what you did?"

He gave her a sideways look and scratched his jaw.

"I didn't think so." If only she'd paid more attention to the news, maybe she would remember him being sentenced. National reporters salivated over each inmate sent to Extinction Island, but she'd probably been busy with graduate school at the time. "How about instead, you tell me what the deal is between you and Cane?"

He opened his mouth. His teeth tugged at his luscious lower lip. He appeared to give the idea great consideration. Finally, he shook his head.

"Okay. I'm going to bed." She got out of the pool,

completely aware of how the wet clothes clung to her body.

"One more question?" he asked.

As she looked back, she froze at the sexy image he presented. Water dripped down his chest, his dark hair was tousled over his forehead, his eyes simmered like melted chocolate, and his expression held an open vulnerability. "What?" she whispered.

"Why gators? They're not exactly cute or cuddly."

She almost laughed at the innocuous question. Instead, she gave him an offended scowl on behalf of the animals. "I like their restrained power. They can do real damage to a person, and yet, they only snap for food or defense."

Even Blackie—the gator who took her fingers—had acted solely because of its hunting instinct. Gaining control over such powerful animals gave her a sense of mastery. It was more about technique than brute force. Never approach a gator from the front. Keep leverage on your side by jumping on its back. Pin the head down to prevent the lower jaw from opening. Keep its back legs off the ground to counter the death roll. Every creature could be taken down once its weaknesses were exposed. Including people.

When he didn't ask anything else, she went inside to change in the bathroom. As she slipped on a pair of too-big jogging shorts and a T-shirt she'd found in the closet, she wrestled again with her options. If she told him everything, he might help her find Jim Durham. Then again, why would he care? They barely knew each other. Until she understood him better, divulging more information could be counterproductive, especially since he hadn't shared much of his own story with her. He asked questions, but never gave any answers.

CHAPTER SIX

THE BATHTUB WAS like a white boat sitting on the gray sea of the tile floor. Oakley stared at it, desperately wanting to look inside, yet afraid of what she would find. That was silly. This was her bathtub from the house where she'd grown up, where her mother had bathed her.

Her fascination pulled her toward the tub without her feet having to move. She peered over the side. No one was there, though it was full of water. As she watched, the water sloshed from one end of the tub to the other. With each sway, the color of the water changed. From a rosy hue, to a shade of coral, and finally to red dragon fruit. But it didn't stop there. The water continued to deepen until it looked as dark as blood.

The sloshing grew more violent. The bloody water splashed over the edge, covering her nightgown in dripping red streaks. She swiped at the streaks with her hands, trying to wipe them away, but the more she rubbed, the more of her nightgown turned blood red.

OAKLEY WOKE with her hands wringing her T-shirt. Though she'd always been an early riser, she rarely had dreams anymore, much less a vivid nightmare. The memory of finding Monica's body still invaded the deepest recesses of her mind. One foot hanging out. The rest of her body submerged. Mouth frozen open in a small circle. Bulging eyes staring at the ceiling.

Oakley shook her head to clear the image. As far as dreams went, the bathtub one wasn't new, she'd had it many times in the past, even before Monica's death. Clearly, the stress of this place was taking its toll.

Her heart settled down as the morning sun from the patio door warmed her face. The suite Kaleo lived in was positioned to capture the setting sun, though the persistent mist on the distant hills reflected the rising sun as well. So strange to be in a perfect location in such a terrifying place.

She rolled to the edge of the bed and looked down. Blankets wrapped around Kaleo's legs like cloth from a mummy, and his shirt pulled up at the waist. He stirred restlessly for a minute. When he again relaxed into deeper sleep, his peaceful, tanned good looks made him more perfume model than hardened criminal. She could imagine him in a polished suit, smiling at the camera, leading a woman to his sports car rather than leading a crew of inmates.

Outside the patio doors, the jungle came to life. A distant noise pounded like thunder, probably a large dinosaur walking. Birds twittered closer to the compound. A far-off roar echoed, like a *T. rex* staking its claim. From a distance, the sounds made a symphony, but separately and up close each posed a deadly threat. Was Jim Durham out there facing those threats right now? What if he died before she found him?

Kaleo stirred again, rubbing his eyes before he sat up. He gave her a smile that warmed her insides. "Good morning."

Without thinking, she asked, "How do you wake up in a good mood in a place like this?"

He looked away and shuttered his eyes.

Instantly, she regretted the question.

"It could be worse," he said.

"You're right." Things could have gone much worse for her when she'd arrived. She should be grateful to him, not quizzing him. And yet she couldn't help herself. He'd been nothing except respectful and kind to her, so she chanced asking what was on her mind. "How did you become the leader of the Cazador gang?"

While extremely strong and tall, Kaleo wasn't the strongest or the tallest. Something had caused these hardened criminals to listen to him.

He rolled forward to hug his knees. His hair fell in small waves over his cheekbones. "I became the leader the same way every leader has—by killing the previous leader." He cocked his head. "Except I didn't."

She mimicked his posture, threading her fingers together tight around her knees. "What happened?"

"No one knows this." He raised one eyebrow.

The question was clear. *Can I trust you?* She nodded, truly hoping he would.

A full minute passed before he decided to continue. "I asked Emmett to go hunting with me. I needed to talk to him about Misty." He pointed to the far wall. "My room was next door to this one. Sometimes, her screams still replay in my mind." He ran a hand through his hair, holding it back from his face. "I knew it would be suicide to call him out in front of the guys. While we were hunting, I asked him to ease up on her. Emmett laughed and said she deserved it because she'd killed three men. He was just getting payback for the males of our species. I called him a hypocrite. He'd killed five people in a bank robbery, two were women."

Kaleo went quiet for a moment before he spoke again. When he did, his voice held a steely hardness. "I had to stop Misty's screams. I couldn't listen to them for another day. When he turned his back on me, I took the chance. I jumped him, taking him to the ground. He was bigger and stronger. We wrestled for a while. Eventually, he got on top. He beat on me for only a minute. Turns out, we weren't the only hunters searching for prey that day. Our fight masked the approach of a *Velociraptor*. In less than a second, the animal swept him off me and ripped his guts out."

Her mouth dropped open. She couldn't think of anything to say.

"Thankfully, it wasn't a pack. Just one raptor. I scrambled away, but I knew if I tried to run, it would come for me. And if I stayed there, it would finish eating Emmett and come for me." He blew out a ragged breath. "I did the craziest thing I could think of. I grabbed a rope, tied a loop in one end, and threw the other end over the biggest tree branch I could find. Like a cowboy, I tossed the loop over the raptor's head. After a few tries, the rope circled around its neck. It looked up confused, then went right back to eating Emmett. I grabbed the rope and began climbing, sure that I outweighed the raptor by more than a few pounds. As the rope tightened and pulled the animal up the tree, it slashed out at me."

Kaleo shifted the cuff of his shorts on his left leg. A six-inch-long red scar bisected the muscle.

"Finally, I pulled it up far enough to strangle it." He gave a mirthless laugh. "When I brought the raptor back to the compound, I made it sound like I killed them both with my bare hands. No one wanted to challenge me afterward. A few days later, the rumor started to float around that Misty had cursed all the men who hurt her. Their superstitions allow her to live in peace."

Oakley let the silence stretch. He couldn't stand to see a woman abused and had risked his life to protect Misty. He had some sort of a conscience deep down. She reached out to touch his arm. "No, *you* allowed her to live in peace."

He captured her hand and brought it to his lips. A sweet shiver ran up her arm. "Guess we should get going. Remember the perfect time to hunt?"

She worked her tongue to moisten her mouth. "Mid-morning through mid-afternoon, because you avoid the early rising predators and many animals sleep in the heat of the day."

He jumped to his feet. "Exactly. You were listening to my ramblings before we fell asleep last night. The higher elevations here are part of the cloud forest, so this area doesn't get as hot as the coast, but the nocturnal animals still sleep during the day. When winter comes, the weather changes and shortens the window a little, but not much since we're close to the equator. Either way, it's the same principle. Catch them while they're sleeping and minimize the risk of getting eaten."

Winter was months away. Was he saying he wanted her here long-term? After she found Jim, she hadn't decided where else she would go. Live on her own? Go to another gang? Jim might be bunking with another group. "What other gangs are near here?"

"Several are scattered around. None have as good a setup as we do here. Most of the others are more violent within the gang."

"And Cane's group?" Surely, his wasn't one of the violent ones.

"You know what? We should get going." Before she could push further, he disappeared into the bathroom.

So, he still refused to talk about Cane. That only ramped up her curiosity. Apparently, she'd have to be more subtle about asking. The direct questions had gotten her nowhere.

He came out of the bathroom with a freshly scrubbed face. His dark eyes held her gaze with open intensity, none of the understated warning that normally came from him around the others. Just like last night, she found this version of him, the unguarded Kaleo, nearly irresistible.

"What do you think you know, as a reptile expert, that might help you out there?"

She blinked and shifted into academic gear. "Reptiles are cold-blooded and can't regulate their body temperature, which is not helpful, since everyone now knows dinosaurs have a unique metabolism, a blend of warm-blooded and cold-blooded. Also not particularly relevant is that reptilian skin is cool and dry because they don't have sebaceous, or sweat glands." She tapped a finger on her lip while she thought. "There are specific scents most reptiles don't like, garlic comes to mind. And some of them have a parietal gland on their head, like a third eye, to help them sense changes in light."

"Good to know. Anything else?"

"Nothing that's practical, except"—she grimaced —"most reptiles can't chew their food. They tear off chunks and swallow."

He returned her grimace. "Well said. Let's keep us off the menu. Time for more hunting lessons."

She nodded and slipped into the bathroom to splash water on her face and brush her teeth. Using the hair tie she'd found, she swept her hair into a loose bun.

Ten minutes later, she followed behind Kaleo through the gazebo archway. A high chirping noise set off her alarm bells until she saw the gray-green shape of Cody jumping up and down.

Kaleo playfully lunged at him. Cody jumped back, circled around him, and ran up to her. She swiped her hand along his head and down his back. "Hey, big guy. You coming hunting too?"

Sure enough, Cody bobbed after them. The deeper they moved into the forest, the quieter Cody became.

They walked in silence until they came to the same clearing where they had stopped yesterday. Kaleo turned to her. "Which way would you go to get back home?"

Although she had a hard time thinking of it as home, she pointed to the left.

"Good. Knowing where you are can save your life." He pulled out his whip and angled the handle toward her. "Want to try it?"

"Sure." She grabbed the handle with both hands.

He took on a mischievous grin. "Swing it at your friend over there."

Oakley jabbed his arm with her elbow. "No way."

In slow circles, she spun it over her head. The high-pitched slicing sound cut through the humid air. She smacked it against a nearby tree, savoring the splitting bark and crumpling vines.

A huge thump shook the ground, and she swayed on her feet. Her gaze darted to Kaleo, who had cocked his head to listen.

The same slicing noise ripped through the air, but the whip lay immobile at her feet. Where was the sound coming from?

"Hit the ground!" he yelled.

She dropped to her stomach. Something long and thick swiped close enough to flip her hair out of the bun, leaving it in a ragged ponytail.

A wide, dark-green tree trunk swung through the air as if uprooted by hurricane winds. But it smashed sideways into the other trees and broke them like matchsticks.

It wasn't a tree trunk. It was a tail, the perfect color to blend in and thick enough to crush her in one swipe. They had walked right up to the back end of a big sauropod.

Cody ran off into the underbrush. She stared after him. Maybe they should get out of here too. The tail swung past her head one more time before landing a few feet from where Kaleo lay next to her.

It didn't stay there long.

Slowly, it rose back into the air, shook once, then released a deep rumble. Wait a minute. How could a tail rumble?

"Ah, crap." Kaleo jumped up.

She opened her mouth to tell him to get back down,

that the tail was still up there and could smash him at any second, but the alarmed look on his face stopped her.

"Get up! Run!" he yelled.

She got to her knees, but hesitated. The tail would strike her if she ran the same way it swung.

Her indecision lasted only a second before the smell hit her nostrils and propelled her into action. A noxious, rotten-egg odor scalded the back of her throat like burning acid.

She jumped to her feet. Kaleo grabbed her wrist and took off, half dragging her away. Her heart raced, exacerbating her need for air.

On the other side of the clearing, she tripped over a fallen log and went down hard on her knees and elbows. The deep rumble sounded again.

She glanced back. A wave of cloudy mist pursued them, traveling as fast as a thundercloud.

As she struggled to stand, it engulfed her, choking off her air supply. The smell of moldy, putrefying eggs was bad enough, but the cloud seemed to suck all the air from her lungs. Sharp pains shot throughout her chest.

She tried to cough the substance out. No air could escape from her lungs either. She called out for Kaleo, her words slurring together. "Melp, plez, K ..."

Strong hands scooped beneath her armpits and lifted her off the ground. Kaleo wrapped his arms around her midsection and carried her face-front like he had on their first walk to the compound. Nausea crawled through her stomach. *Please don't let me throw up on both of us.*

As he put some distance between them and the horrible stench, her nausea eased. When he put her down, she collapsed to the ground and rolled over on her back. He sat next to her, concern turning his features darker, more intense. "Are you okay?"

She tried to reach out and ease the frown line between his brows. Her arms wouldn't obey. She took several deep breaths, still air-starved, and nodded. "What was that?"

He pursed his lips. "You might not believe me if I told you."

With her strength returning, she pushed up to one elbow to give him a warning look.

He put both hands up in surrender. "It was a sauropod. You saw its tail. When they feel threatened, they can use their entire back end as a weapon."

No way. He couldn't be serious. "Are you telling me we almost died from a dinosaur fart?"

He laughed, but not because he was kidding. "Yes. It's a big cloud of methane and hydrogen sulfide that eats up all the oxygen in the air, which means we don't get any. I've heard of one person in another gang who died from it."

She let out a strangled cough. "Unbelievable. There are too many ways to die here. I've lost count."

He stretched his palm out toward her slowly as if she were a skittish animal. His hand neared her cheek. At the last second, he aborted the action and let his arm fall to his side. "I won't let you die."

Her heart rate soared again. This response had nothing to do with physical danger, though her body reacted with the same type of fear and anticipation. Just when he began to lean closer, his line of sight shifted over her shoulder. He stiffened, his muscles taut.

She glanced back. A green iguana sat tensely on a branch. The emerald dewlap hanging from its chin quickly puffed out a warning. A predator was nearby. But where?

She shifted back to Kaleo who blinked rapidly, his attention fixed on a particular spot in the trees. Pinching her eyes almost closed, she focused on the same area. A second later, she saw it too. A strange muting of the vines on a tree. A shifting of colors when the wind wasn't blowing. Three dots and a dark slash that seemed to float in the air. She would never have noticed if he hadn't reacted so strongly. Even as she stared, the phenomenon vanished. What was it and why did he fear it?

IN ONE QUICK MOTION, Kaleo squeezed Oakley against his chest and rolled, dragging them both down the slight hill. A huge rush of air followed their path. Dead leaves and dirt blasted them like the aftermath of an explosion. Camocroc had attacked, its three-foot-wide snout plunging into the ground right where they had been sitting.

He didn't stop to see if Camocroc had injured itself.

The creature wouldn't give up easily, and it could run. In fact, out in the open, it would likely outrun them.

He needed a plan. They were close to a place where the beast couldn't follow. They would have to be fast over open ground, but they might make it.

Using their downward momentum, he kept them rolling until a tree trunk came between them and the recovering creature. Camocroc had dropped its camouflage, the mottled green and brown skin dull in the sparse sunlight. Thank goodness it hadn't been directly above them when he had first put Oakley down. It had needed to move closer; otherwise, he probably wouldn't have seen it.

Now, as he watched, bits and pieces of its cloak were coming back in to place. Soon, it would be near impossible to spot again.

He pushed Oakley to her feet and took off after her. As he passed her, he waved a hand. "This way!"

He shoved through a curtain of vines to the left, then sprinted to the right. Zig-zagging through the trees would hamper the large animal's pursuit.

Sprinting headlong into the jungle was probably the worst survival strategy, but they had no other options. Racing ahead, he prayed Oakley could keep up and also that they didn't run into anything more dangerous on the way—like Red Grizzly.

He cringed at the sounds behind them. A snap of branches. The crunch of bark scraping off trees. He glanced back. Oakley was paler than before. At least, she had no problem staying behind him. If anything, he was slowing her down.

The trees thinned out as they neared the edge of the clearing. Decision time. They could skirt the open area and stay near the trees or dash full speed for the other side. He opted for the sprint, shoving Oakley in front before realizing she didn't know where to go. "Head for the rocky area. There's a cave."

She gave him a confused look. He didn't blame her. She couldn't see the cave because they were going to enter it from the roof.

Hot breath puffed against his neck. This is what he got for promising one girl she'd be safe. He should know better than to make impossible promises. He pushed his legs harder.

Halfway through the clearing, he chanced another look back. Camocroc had put all of its energy into a running gallop. The camouflage had completely faded again, leaving its mass of blotchy skin rippling with exertion.

The full out sprint may have been a mistake. Camocroc was slowly gaining on them. Plus, they were going to need several seconds to open the grate and drop down into the cave. Even more critical now that Oakley was in front, he had to keep her from running too far and falling off the cliff beyond.

He scanned the area ahead. The thick pile of granite rocks to the north could work in their favor. "Veer right, Hook! To the taller rocks!"

Camocroc's breath seared his neck as it crept closer. He smelled the rancid odor of rotting meat. His steps faltered.

He recovered quickly, pouring more adrenaline into his legs. In front of him, Oakley pumped her arms and churned her legs. Her long ponytail flew in the wind. Her trim waist twisted with each step. If not for the life-or-death consequences, this would have been a sexy race.

She was approaching the rocks fast. He'd have to make his move soon. Just another second of pushing hard to make sure the creature was fully committed.

Her pace slowed a fraction, probably from realizing he'd sent her running directly at a wall. It was time. He grabbed her by the waist, tucked her body into his, and jumped to the side. Their speed carried them a few feet in the air, buying him time to shift his shoulders. He hit the ground on his left shoulder, rolling like a tire to disperse the momentum. It was a move he'd done many times, just not with someone tucked under him.

Camocroc wasn't able to turn and smashed full force into the rocks in a loud, massive crash. It wouldn't kill the thirty-foot-long creature, only stun him. They had to move fast.

Once again, he hauled Oakley to her feet and dragged her by the wrist. Hopefully, he wasn't leaving any bruises on her tiny bones. They dashed to the flatter section of rocks.

He quickly found the metal grate. The crunching and splintering of the rock behind him warned that Camocroc would be up in a few seconds. He flipped the two latches open. The heavy grate creaked as he lifted it off and thunked when he tossed it aside.

Loud huffing. Thundering feet. It was coming.

He grabbed both of Oakley's wrists and swung her over the opening. She yelped in surprise. Quickly, he lowered her to her armpits, then dropped her. This was the back end of the cave and would only be about six feet tall. A long drop for her, but certainly not fatal. Hopefully, the rainwater collection bucket hadn't been in the way.

He shoved his feet over the edge and glanced up.

Camocroc reared on its hind legs, glaring down at him with black eyes, a snorting snout, and dripping teeth.

It lunged.

Kaleo dropped into the cave. His feet hit and one of his ankles rolled, shooting pain up his leg. His grunts didn't compare to the growls of frustration Camocroc made above.

Fortunately, the roof of the cave was a slab of solid granite. Camocroc pounded its nose into the rocks until streams of blood dripped through the opening. Kaleo backed up a few steps, wiping sweat from his brow. This time, Oakley grabbed his arm and drew him away. He knew what she was thinking. If Camocroc could smell them, it would keep trying to reach them.

He hunched over to keep from hitting his head as they walked down the tunnel. Around a bend, he stopped to stretch his sore ankle. Just a mild sprain.

The snarls faded and the roof gradually increased to about eight feet. He stopped again, this time to stretch the muscles in his back.

"Where did that come from?" she asked.

"It camouflages to the surroundings—"

"No, I know that was Camocroc. I'm talking about that insane evasion technique. Where did you learn it?"

He smiled at the hint of excitement in her voice, even though he wouldn't answer her. The defensive move had predated his arrival on the island. If he shared his past life with her, the innocent way she looked at him would change. "Later."

She scowled. "Always later with you."

On instinct, he reached up to brush back stray hairs that had fallen from her askew ponytail. She didn't stop him, but she fidgeted with one of her silver earrings until he took his hand away.

Did he make her nervous for good reasons or bad? Because she had his insides all twisted in knots. He hadn't fallen for a woman since he'd come to Extinction Island. In fact, the last woman he helped caused loads of problems because she'd fallen for him. Maybe these tangled feelings were a warning sign.

Voices echoed through the tunnel. The others were coming. Oakley ducked behind him, and he swallowed down a smirk of pride. At least for this moment, he could pretend to be all he might have been ... if the past hadn't happened.

Cane came around the corner first, a spear in his

hand. He would never allow any of his people to walk into danger before himself.

"Hey," Kaleo said.

Cane lowered the spear, then glanced behind Kaleo. He stepped to the side. Cane had met Oakley twice in two days but probably didn't know her name. "Oakley Laveau, meet Cane LeBlanc."

"Hi." She gave a half-wave.

"Laveau is French," Cane said in his smooth voice. "And your accent is distinctive. Are you by chance from Louisiana?"

She took a step forward. "Yes. I'm from a small town near Thibodaux."

"I'm from Chauvin, close to there." He smiled at her.

Suddenly Kaleo wanted to punch him in his perfect teeth. Instead, he spoke up to divert Cane's attention. "Sorry to crash into your home. We had no choice."

Cane shook Kaleo's hand. "Understood. Was it Red Grizzly?"

"No, RG hasn't been seen recently. It was Camocroc. I didn't think it would come this far away from a river. Apparently, it's expanding its territory."

"Then, you'll want to wait at least a couple of hours before you leave, even from the front entrance. Come have some mango juice with us."

Cane headed toward the living room area. Kaleo nodded at the two women behind Cane. Neve Torres smiled at him like a sister. She was a thirty-something local who'd refused to evacuate her home when the U.S. government took over the island. "Oakley, this is Neve."

Neve gave Oakley a nod and one of her shy smiles before she followed Cane. Kaleo put a hand up to acknowledge Hazel Collins, but she didn't look at him. She glared at Oakley with murderous eyes.

"And this is Hazel." When beautiful, auburn-haired Hazel came to the island, he'd done his best to protect her. She took his protection and asked for more than he could give. Once her feelings became obvious, he had to get her out of his bedroom. From the look of it, nothing had changed.

Hazel gave a mumbled greeting to Oakley before turning her gaze to him and completely rearranging her expression into something innocent and full of longing. "How are things back home?"

"Fine." He understood why she would think of the compound as her home. She'd lived there for a year, hiding in his room, refusing even to go out to the pool. Judging by her somewhat-tanned skin, she'd overcome enough of her fears to venture outside. Cane had been good for her. "Chubs still misses you."

Other than Kaleo, Chubs was the only one who'd ever spent time with her. She shrugged, then pushed her shoulders back, thrust her hip to one side, and stuck her chest out. "Just because I had to leave, doesn't mean you couldn't come stay here once in a while."

He avoided her eyes. Hazel was beautiful, but fearful

and needy were not his type. He couldn't handle the pressure of trying to be everything to her.

Oakley squeezed around him and pushed past both of them. He took the opening and followed, leaving Hazel standing there looking half irritated and half smug.

In the main area, the cave stood more than twelve feet tall. Several branching tunnels led off into darkness, most of them sleeping areas. Women on one side, men on the other. He recognized several men lounging in a corner, splicing arrows onto sticks to make spears. After nodding at them, he nudged Cane and pointed at a crimson woven mat on the floor, then a painting on the wall of the emerald jungle with a misty azure sky. "You've decorated."

"Thanks to Neve," Cane answered.

As the gracious host, Neve brought them both large cups of mango juice. Oakley took hers and shot Kaleo a curious look. "I don't get it. You two obviously know each other." She turned her knitted brows to Cane. "But when I first showed up on the island, you ran away."

Cane spread his hands wide as if to say he had nothing to hide. "Was there a question in there someplace?"

Kaleo expected her to fire back with her sarcasm. She seemed to think twice about it with Cane.

She turned again to Kaleo. "What's the deal?"

Behind her back, Cane shrugged. His way of asking, *Why not tell her?*

Though he wasn't ready to completely trust Oakley, he didn't have much choice after literally dropping in on

Cane and his crew. "Okay. Obviously, I know these guys, but I can't act like it in front of the gang." She crossed her arms over her chest and waited for him to explain.

Instead, Cane spoke for him, always the peacemaker. "Three years ago, I ran into Kaleo in the forest. Once I realized he didn't want to kill me, we started talking. About life, about hunting, about which dinosaur meat was best. Right now, I'd bet he's thinking *Saurosuchus* meat sounds good."

Oakley let loose a small smile.

Kaleo took the opportunity to speak for himself. "After I took over the gang, I had a lot of guilt about what I've done to survive. Talking to Cane helped me to move forward. He's a good person. Hanging out with him makes me want to be a better man." He took a deep breath. No going back now. "Oakley, meet Pastor Cane LeBlanc."

"Pastor?" she croaked. She looked at the ceiling as if mentally putting the pieces together. "What could a pastor do to be sentenced here?"

Cane bit his lip and shuffled his feet. "I wasn't sentenced. I came here voluntarily."

She dropped her hands to her sides. "So you're crazy, then."

He laughed. "No, just committed."

Kaleo put his cup down, placed both hands on her arms, and forced her to look at him. "You can't tell anyone. If the gang knew I protected Cane and the people here, they would assume I wasn't strong enough to lead them. Someone would kill me or I'd have to kill them."

"Please, heed his warning, Oakley," Cane said. "Hurting Kaleo endangers you both."

She looked wounded by his suggestion. "I don't want to hurt him."

Kaleo believed her, but she could change her mind in an instant. Hazel had professed the exact same statement, until he'd refused her advances. Then, she'd sought out Misty's advice on poisons. He understood how dangerous a woman's devotion could become.

CHAPTER SEVEN

THE CAVE FELT MORE humid than the jungle, but at least it was cool. Oakley sat awkwardly on a handwoven stool with her cup of juice. Shortly after Kaleo's introduction of Cane, Hazel had pulled him into a corner to talk. Her vibrant auburn hair swayed as she gestured, and her long graceful legs pranced around his stoic form. She stomped her foot, drawing Oakley's gaze to a small tattoo of a starfish on her ankle. A gorgeous woman who loved starfish should be on a yacht somewhere, not a cave hidden in the jungle. From Kaleo's expression, he was at a loss for how to respond to whatever she was demanding.

Cane dragged a matching stool across the rough floor to sit next to Oakley. Did she have to start thinking of him as Pastor Cane? Because the title didn't seem to go with his jeans, boots, and worn T-shirt look. Not to mention every pastor she'd met before—and Louisiana was full of pastors—had a way of making her squirm. But Cane put her at ease. It seemed he did the same for everyone else here. Well, everyone except Hazel.

Cane peered at Oakley with wide sea-green eyes. He seemed to be waiting for her to speak. She blurted out the crux of her confusion. "Why would you come here voluntarily?"

A brilliant grin split his face. "These people need help. Who else would come besides a preacher?"

He had a point. Most people on the mainland wanted to ooh and aah over the photos of dinosaurs in the wild and pretend the prison part of this place didn't exist. However, there were a few notable exceptions. Members of the media had talked about making Extinction Island a reality TV show about death row inmates—because, of course, the inmates wouldn't mind having their gruesome deaths televised. Recently, the activist group CADRE, Citizens Against Death Row and Execution, proposed that anyone who survived ten years on Extinction Island should have their sentence commuted. As if merely surviving would equip someone to safely rejoin society.

Whatever the legislature decided for this place, she would be forced to endure it, but Cane had come here for his own, unfathomable reasons. Much as she might be tempted to label him as psychotic, he didn't seem like a crazy cult leader.

He shifted on the stool. "Did you know the government decided to expedite death penalty cases mainly for monetary reasons?"

She shook her head. That could explain her fast-tracked conviction. Wasn't her life worth more than money? Perhaps not to the government. The prosecutor would have argued that Monica's life was the real cost in this equation.

"Rather than housing death row inmates for decades as they've done previously, it's cheaper to expedite the appeals and either execute them immediately or ship them here. They've convinced the voters it's more humane because they are giving the convicts a choice." He gestured toward the jungle, its verdant expanse visible through the open mouth of the cave. "For once, money caused the lawmakers to do the right thing."

She blinked at him, shocked that he thought this place was a good solution to the recent rise in crime.

"At least here," he continued, "people like you have a chance to live free."

People like her. She'd been convicted and the world considered her a criminal, but somehow she didn't feel like one. Not that she was a saint. She just didn't belong here. A glass-half-full kind of guy like Cane might see her as a work in progress.

His gaze stayed focused on her, waiting for something. She squirmed a bit. Why would he think Extinction Island was worth defending? Maybe she should be grateful for the choice between being executed right away and coming here, but at this moment, after barely outmaneuvering Camocroc, it didn't seem like a silver lining. "To live free would imply I have a choice of where to go. All the *lawmakers* have done is given me a bigger death row cell and packed it full of deadly creatures."

He twisted his lips to the side. "Point taken. Like so many things, it's about perspective."

Easy to have a positive perspective when you could leave the island anytime you wanted. She set her empty cup down on a nearby rock ledge. "You could have helped people on the mainland. Why come here?"

The white, toothy grin again. "Because God is here."

He said it so simply she almost believed him. Did God show up for dinner at the table nestled in the corner? Or maybe he tucked them in to bed every night? Cane's attitude seemed too naive to be realistic.

"If you're from Louisiana, then you know I've been to church before. There's one on every corner." She softened her tone. "I attended several churches with different friends. I never got anything out of it."

He went quiet for a long time. Did they teach this technique in seminary? Give someone enough time to ponder their own faults and failures, and they will beg God for forgiveness. It wouldn't work on her. She stiffened her posture and straightened on the stool.

When he spoke, his voice seemed to have a somber melody to it. "The only thing worse than being lost is wandering blindly, believing you know where you're going."

What in the world did that mean? Every place she went here, she wandered around blindly. She had no idea where she was going most of the time, much less where she wanted to go.

He paused to search her eyes for a moment. "When the jungle of life comes up around us, many people push through the trees, striving to get to a lovely meadow full of wildflowers just beyond their reach. Often, they glimpse the wildflowers right before they fall off the cliff in front of them."

Any response escaped her. Her conviction for Monica's murder had already thrown her over the cliff.

"What are your wildflowers, Oakley?" he persisted. "Where are you trying to go?"

She'd love to get out of this crazy place, though that probably wasn't what he meant. If she went searching for anything soon, it would be the dark-haired man. Who knew how long Jim Durham would stay on the island? A glimmer of an idea hit. If Jim had also come here voluntarily, maybe Cane would know where he was. She dismissed the thought. For now. She'd rather not explain her story to Cane when she hadn't even told Kaleo yet.

Kaleo walked up behind Cane and placed a hand on his shoulder. "Neve was asking for you."

"Of course." Cane took her hand and gave it a goodbye squeeze. "Nice to meet you, Oakley."

Before he left, he whispered something in Kaleo's ear, too quiet for her to hear. Probably about her. The calm and peace fled as quickly as they had come.

Kaleo extended a hand to pull her from the chair. "We should go soon if we want to avoid traveling at dusk."

At least he wasn't planning to leave her in this musty place. Although she might be physically safer here, emotionally she felt vulnerable. She took his hand and got to her feet.

With minimal good-byes from Kaleo, they made their way to the massive front entrance. The lip of the cave jutted out over a one-hundred-foot drop to the forest floor. The view was amazing, just like the painting on the wall of the cave, all turquoise sky and green-jeweled trees.

From the far wall, he grabbed a harness attached to a set of handlebars. He swung the handlebars over a swivel hook looped onto a wire. The wire was secured to the roof of the cave.

"Other than the back door entrance we used, the zip line is the only way in or out," he said.

A swarm of butterflies invaded her stomach. She'd never zip-lined before, much less over a jungle.

He must have read her skeptical expression. "It's perfectly safe, although we don't exactly have inspections every year."

"Why don't they build a bridge and use the sound frequency to keep the predators away like the compound does?"

"No electricity. They've been working on solar panels, but haven't found the materials yet. Besides, this is more effective and faster." He held the harness while she stepped in. His fingers brushed along the outside of her thighs, sending additional butterflies flocking to her stomach. She wiped a bead of sweat off her brow.

Spending time with Cane calmed her down, while Kaleo stirred her up. Right now, she could use a calming influence.

She hooked the buckle securely around her waist. Instead of words of comfort, Kaleo yelled one phrase before he pushed her off. "Pull the short rope to slow down at the end."

The wind whipped through her ponytail and raked over her body. She bit her lip to stifle the scream begging to erupt from her throat. No sense in helping Camocroc find them again. She glanced down once and ice-cold fear filled her veins. If she fell, she'd have a full twenty seconds of plunging helplessly, knowing she would die. The terror finally crawled out of her in a long guttural sound.

Gravity hauled her down fast. The trees grew more menacing as she raced closer. She had to slow down. With both hands, she grabbed the short rope and pulled hard, but a few seconds too late. The runner on the zip line hit the end, stopping her violently.

She sucked in a shaky breath. At least it hadn't broken.

With trembling fingers, she unhooked the harness. As she stepped out, she fell face first onto the ground, her hands barely keeping her head from hitting a rock. She rolled over to see the long rope taut and the harness already inching its way back up the zip line. She'd better move before Kaleo crashed into her.

Somehow, he made the trip look graceful. "Not so bad, was it?"

Rather than smacking the smile off his face, she muttered, "Let's go."

On the way back, she kept an eye out for anything suspicious in the trees. Their last experience had taught her something about Camocroc. It had distinguishing deformities—three copper dots on its neck, probably a birthmark, and a long dark scar cutting through its rib cage.

Kaleo shot her a look over his shoulder. His voice was low and deep, barely over a whisper. "Interested in studying any reptiles out here?"

She matched his volume. "Not up close again. Or alive. Although Camocroc's camouflage is stunning. I've never seen such detail. The geckos in my backyard couldn't have imitated the veins on the leaves like it did. Why haven't we seen pictures of Camocroc on the mainland?"

He shrugged. "We have no way of knowing if Camocroc was brought back naturally or if it's a genetically modified organism. I could see why Asperten, not to mention the government, might want to keep the specifics of the genetically modified ones confidential. Plus, I suspect the government keeps some stuff out of the press because they don't want people to repeal the death penalty act. If the public knew how stacked the deck was against us, it would seem cruel to send even criminals here."

"But haven't you survived for three years?"

Kaleo stopped, twisted around, and gave her a serious

look. "Don't underestimate the risks out here. Camocroc isn't the one I'm worried about. It might kill me, but that would be dumb luck. The truly frightening animal here is Red Grizzly. It's as smart as any of us and controls its pack better than I do."

He returned to hiking. She didn't ask any more questions.

By the time they reached the compound, the sun had started to set. Cody waited for them there, his little feet shifting as he bobbed up and down. She reached out to stroke his neck, and he nuzzled her. "Glad to see you're okay too."

After a dinner of tough meat and strawberries, they went back to the bedroom. She sat on the bed and crossed her legs, while Kaleo sat on his blanket on the floor.

She twisted her fingers, entangling them in the sheets. He'd proved to be trustworthy, but she needed to know who she was dealing with. "I'd like to make a deal with you."

He narrowed his eyes in a seductive way. "What kind of deal?"

Ignoring the niggling of worry, she patted the bed next to her. "You can sleep up here with two conditions."

"Okay, shoot."

She held up a finger. "One, it's still platonic. You must honor your original promise."

"Done."

She ticked off another finger. "And two, you have to tell me what you did to get here."

He ran a hand through his thick hair, then settled his elbows on top of his bent knees. At first, his expression appeared closed off. Just when it seemed he'd refuse, he let out a long sigh. "I suppose it's time." His caramel eyes met her gaze. "If you tell me first."

Her teeth worked her lower lip. Kaleo had trusted her with his secrets and saved her life more than once. He already knew the basics of her story anyway. "I had a feud with my best friend, Monica, who also happened to be a coworker."

He tilted his head, causing his hair to shift forward. "About what?"

"A guy." She waved her hand in the air dismissively. "It was stupid, but I'd been angry. The night Monica died, we met at a bar to work things out, even though I didn't want to forgive her just yet. This dark-haired guy was also there."

"*The* guy?"

"No." With a deep breath, she recounted the story of how she'd lost her two fingers to Blackie, including how Jim Durham had pulled the boy and her out of the water. "Jim was at the bar with Monica. They had just met. He called me a hero, bought me a drink, and dropped a gold coin in it."

Kaleo narrowed his eyes.

"Weird, right? He said I could have it once I finished my drink, that it was my reward for the bravery I'd shown. By the time I drank the last swallow of vodka and club soda, the room started to spin. The next thing I know, I woke up at Monica's apartment." She expelled a shaky breath as she remembered the unnatural quiet except for the solitary sound of the dripping faucet. "I found Monica submerged in the bathtub."

She fell silent for a minute. The white tub. Monica's foot sticking out. Her blank face. Fear and water mingled together, hinting at hazy memories of another tub ... of her mother. Only the vaguest thread of recollection spun across her mind. None of the memories would solidify.

She brought her focus back to the story. "I tried to get Monica out, even though she was much taller than me and too heavy for me to move."

Kaleo frowned. "You can't remember anything else?"

She shook her head sadly, prepared for his laughter. It didn't come.

He merely looked at her with confusion written on his face. "Why did they convict you of murder?"

"The prosecutor said I killed her out of jealousy and revenge for stealing my boyfriend." She sucked in a breath, some things were hard to accept. "Truly, I was jealous of her."

"But what evidence did they have?"

"They found my shoe under her body. I don't know how it got there. The prosecutor said it was from when I placed her unconscious body in the tub after I drugged her. She also had bruises on her arm, ones that matched my small hands, and my skin cells were found under her fingernails. Strangely though, she didn't drown. She was electrocuted in the water. The prosecutor claimed I electrocuted her with a hair straightener, then disposed of it, since it wasn't found in the apartment, to make it look like an accidental drowning."

Kaleo shifted on his blanket. "That's not a common method for murder. What did this Jim guy say at the trial?"

"Nothing. They couldn't find him."

His eyes went wide. "Convenient." He tapped a finger on his knee for several minutes. "So, you might not have done it?"

She shook her head again. "I know I don't remember what happened, but she was my best friend. I can't imagine killing her."

Should she tell him about Jim Durham being here on the island? Kaleo was the first person, besides her dad, who believed her amnesia. It meant more to her than she could express. If she told him about Jim, he would probably insist they hunt him down immediately. Suddenly, that sounded like a bad idea. If she was innocent, then Jim was probably a killer. She'd be walking Kaleo right into his path. Risking her life was one thing. She didn't want to be responsible for risking his.

Deep down, though, there was more to it. A part of her feared what she'd discover. It didn't seem possible for her to drink enough to black out while still killing Monica and disposing of the evidence. And yet, she'd blacked out only a few days before when facing Blackie, and he'd gone belly up. Could she have carried enough hate inside of her to kill Monica and then enough guilt to block it out?

The reverse possibility continued to nag at her, as well. If Jim had drugged her and then killed Monica, why? As far as she knew, Jim and Monica met the same night Monica died. They barely knew each other. And even more confusing, why would he have left Oakley alive? None of it made any sense.

She cleared her raspy throat. "Enough about me. Your turn."

Surprising her, Kaleo rose to his knees and leaned over to touch her cheek. His fingers rolled over her ear, stopping on one of her fleur-de-lis earrings. "Pretty. Like a flower, but tougher."

She raised an eyebrow. "They were my mom's. It's called a fleur-de-lis, very popular in the south. And you're stalling."

"Okay." He flexed his shoulders, settled on his blanket, and fixed his eyes on the ceiling. "I grew up in a violent house. My dad hit me a lot. Broken ribs, busted nose, that kind of thing. Sometimes, I was glad he beat me because it meant he wasn't beating my mom. Other times," his voice was filled with shame, "the beatings hurt so much I wanted him to go back to beating my mom so it would stop for me."

She fought the urge to comfort him. Instead, she hugged her knees tight. "How old were you?"

"It happened my whole life but grew worse the year I turned twelve. I think my dad saw my growth and knew I would be bigger than him soon." Kaleo took a long swallow. "Then I understood why he did it. My father beat me out of fear."

Her heart broke for the scared little boy he had been. "Did you ever hit him back?"

"No. I ran away when I was thirteen. The streets are dangerous for most kids, but I understood the rules. They were the same ones I had at my house—nobody cares, the strongest survive, all the rest get beaten down." He raised his eyes to meet her gaze. "I fell into street fighting and then my anger had an outlet. I got paid for it too. The beatings hadn't caused me to turn away from my father's violence, they'd made me just like him."

His admission about his past concerned her. Surely, he'd had some sort of morality. "Did you worry about your mom?"

"All the time. I abandoned her." He hung his head. "I never tried to help her. I guess I was angry at her too for not helping me." He blew out a heavy breath. "I found out much later that my father killed her a year after I left. The police went to arrest him and discovered he was already dead. He'd shot himself in the head."

"I'm so sorry." She'd had a loving, if a little distant, father. How hard this must have been for Kaleo to live in fear every day.

He pressed his lips together and focused his eyes across the room before continuing. "Close to my seventeenth birthday, I discovered mixed martial arts. I loved it, and I was ruthless. It made me an instant success in Hawaii and brought me to the mainland."

She scooted to the edge of the bed. He still hadn't told her what had brought him here.

"I won my first two fights, sending both men to the hospital with concussions and broken bones. My sponsor was thrilled, even though the organizers of the tournaments threatened to ban me. I was under a lot of pressure to tone it down, but I knew I couldn't. The anger was a toggle switch, all on or all off.

"I started drinking a lot. It only made things worse. One night, I was flirting with this gorgeous woman, Annabelle. I remember her big, green eyes. Her boyfriend told me to leave her alone. Instead, I grabbed her and kissed her long and hard right in front of him. As soon as I let her go, he punched me. Rightfully so, but I didn't care about what was right. We took it outside where I ..." He bit his lip and swiped a hand down his face before continuing. "I beat him to death while I listened to Annabelle scream for me to stop. If it would have ended there, I might not have been sentenced to death."

His breath hitched. She honored his silence while he fought for composure.

When he spoke again, his voice was raw. "Annabelle kept trying to pull me off of her boyfriend, even after he was dead. She jumped onto my back. I swung around, grabbed her wrists, and threw her off. It was a move which had won many fights. This time, she flew through the glass door of the bar. A shard of glass sliced into her throat. She bled out in seconds."

Oakley jerked back from the edge of the bed. What

he'd done was horrible. How could she reconcile the man he seemed to be with the man that he said he was? Which of those men should she give more weight to? Then again, maybe she shouldn't trust either of them.

For a moment, she tortured her lower lip. Then, she moved over and patted the bed again. A deal was a deal. "You can come up if you want."

He rubbed the heel of his palm against his chest. When he met her gaze, his deep eyes were tormented. "Maybe tomorrow."

WHEN OAKLEY AWOKE, Kaleo still snoozed on the floor. She lay there for several minutes, savoring the stillness. Despite his horrible admission last night, he had done nothing except protect her. Out of anywhere on the island, she felt safest here. She could go live in the cave with Cane and his followers, but that would be isolated and awkward, especially with Hazel there.

Staying here made the most sense. At least until she felt confident enough to leave to find Jim Durham. Problem was, after two full days of survival training—and almost dying twice—she was no closer to being ready to go it alone.

That left her with the same two choices: continue training with Kaleo or ask for his help in finding Jim. She mulled it over and came to the same conclusion. She'd give it another couple of days before asking for help. If she had hurt Monica, she'd rather not have Kaleo around when she found out. Better to let him believe the best about her.

But if he trained her well, eventually she'd need a clandestine way out of the compound. This morning was the perfect time to scout for one.

She crept out of bed and carried her boots to the door. She cracked it open, slipped outside, and silently closed it. Once in the hallway, she put on her boots. Now what?

As long as she didn't run into Daric, she'd be fine. The rest of the men wouldn't risk angering Kaleo by hurting her.

She wandered down the north wing of the resort to the area where the hallways converged, the main area where she'd entered just three days ago. A grand staircase led from the main area to a lower level where they usually grabbed food. She took the stairs down to the courtyard of tables. One table by the windows held dried meat, corn cakes, and berries, along with a pitcher of mango juice.

Before she could sit, an intermittent thumping noise came from an opening opposite of the hallway where she'd entered. A petite, older woman with smooth salt-and-pepper hair and baggy clothes emerged. She walked with a limp, her wooden cane smacking on the floorboards with every other step.

She waved the cane at Oakley. "Sit. Have some food. Don't mind me." She appeared to be in her mid-sixties. Certainly old for a place like this, though not elderly. Oakley didn't have to ask her name. This could only be Misty, the woman who'd poisoned her husbands.

"Can I get you something?" Oakley asked.

"No, no. I'll get my own."

She waited while Misty filled a bowl. Then, she grabbed a bowl for herself, filled it with blackberries, and nibbled on them while enjoying the view through the glass.

Misty seemed ready to head back to wherever she'd come from. Just before she disappeared down the corridor, she glanced back at Oakley. "Watch yourself, girl. Around here, looks are usually deceiving."

Oakley furrowed her eyebrows. Who was the old woman referring to? Kaleo? But he had saved Misty from brutal beatings. Perhaps she meant Daric?

Soft footsteps padded behind her. Violet walked over and took a seat at the next table. Had Misty seen Violet? Oakley already distrusted the beautiful blonde.

"Daric's still sleeping," Violet said.

"Good. Nothing worse than a serial killer who's also an early riser." Oakley clamped her mouth shut, biting her lip in the process. She really needed to get a better grip on her sarcasm. Though she wasn't afraid of Violet, she probably shouldn't purposely antagonize her.

Violet leaned on the table and shot a glare at her. "He told me you have a thing for him."

She nearly fell out of her chair. "What?"

"Don't even think about it. I won't give him up."

Oakley raised her eyebrows. "I'm sure you won't have to."

Violet sat up in the chair to her full height, probably

six inches taller than Oakley. "Maybe you should focus more on yourself. You know there's something weird about your boyfriend, right?"

She choked out a laugh. As if Violet had a smidgen of credibility regarding men. Any weird things about Kaleo were a lot easier to deal with than the many murderous things wrong with Daric.

Violet shrugged. "I wouldn't trust him."

"But you trust a murderous psychopath?"

Violet slammed a hand down on the table. "Daric didn't do the things they say he did. He was framed."

The woman couldn't possibly be that dumb. Oakley peered at her face. She didn't blink or back off. "How could they frame him for ten murders at the same time?"

Violet's posture wilted a little. "He thinks the lab messed with the DNA testing."

She couldn't hold in her biting response. "If you're wrong, then 'till death do you part' will come all too quickly for you."

Violet stood and stalked around the table, towering over her. Her fists were clenched. "You've got a big mouth for someone so small."

Oakley couldn't argue with that. Another sarcastic barb hung on her lips, one about the proportion of brain size to body weight decreasing as height increased, but she clamped her lips shut. She didn't want to fight a girl who had at least thirty pounds on her.

Her lack of response angered the woman. Violet swung a punch at her stomach. She barely had time to squirm out of her chair. Violet's knuckles skimmed her abdomen as she dodged out of the way. The follow-up punch connected hard with the right side of Oakley's ribs. She doubled over and fell to the floor, her muscles aching.

A piercing spike of pain shot through her head, eclipsing the pain in her ribs. The migraine drenched her in agony. Swaying under the pull of it, she reached out with a blind hand to block any more attacks.

"What did you do?" The low voice roared in her ears, too deafening to distinguish.

Someone knelt next to her, smoothing her loose hair off her forehead.

"Tell me where it hurts." It was Kaleo. His softer voice eased her headache a little.

"My head." Her muscles in her arms spasmed. "And I'm all twitchy."

"She's lying. I didn't hit her in the head." The high-pitched whine came from Violet.

Kaleo left Oakley, and the pain in her temples grew again with the sound of his raised voice. "So, you admit you hit her."

Oakley forced her eyes open. Daric swooped in between Kaleo and Violet, coming to stand toe to toe with Kaleo.

"If your"—Kaleo gave Violet a disdainful look—"*visitor* dares to damage my property again, she'll be kicked out."

Oakley's heart pinched at being called property, but he had to keep up the appearance of a ruthless leader. If only he'd come back and soothe her pounding head again.

Daric's eyes burned with defiance. The truth was written on his face. The more Kaleo staked his claim on Oakley, the more Daric wanted her.

After another minute of the stare down, Daric marched off and Kaleo knelt next to her again. Gently, he put his middle finger on each temple and rubbed soft, slow circles. She closed her eyes in relief. A small moan sounded. Had it come from her?

Her muscles stopped spasming, and her whole body relaxed. The sharp pain ebbed into a dull ache, then faded almost completely. Only a residual hum remained, wrapped around the back of her head.

"Thank you," she whispered.

"Let's get you back to our room." She moved to stand, but he swiped an arm under her legs and scooped her up.

Our room. She buried her head in his chest. He smelled of lemons, coconut, and leaves, a scent that left her longing for a safe space in the outdoors. He carried her through the main area and down the hall.

"Aw, come on, man. You don't have to flaunt it," Chubs growled as they swept past.

In the room, Kaleo placed her flat on the bed. He lay down next to her, propped up on an elbow, and brushed her hair back from her forehead. "Better?"

"Much better. Thanks."

"Where did she hit you?"

Oakley pointed to the ribs on her right side.

"Stay still. This might hurt." He pulled her shirt tight, then slid two fingers along each rib starting closest to her hip. The higher he went the more tension coiled in her belly. The sore ribs complained from the prodding, but her skin tingled at the contact. The weird mixture of pain and pleasure charged her body with awareness.

"I don't think any of them are broken." He rested his hand on her side, and the spark between them ignited and grew. His gaze fell to her lips.

Her body begged her to roll into him, invite a kiss, and see if he tasted like lemons. But if she did, his vow to keep his hands to himself would be over. Initiating contact would break open the dam of emotions between them, and then what would she do with the overflow?

Besides, she barely knew him. He'd admitted last night that he had a monster hidden inside. Sometimes, she felt like she did too. If their shared monsters drew them to each other, an actual relationship might be a disaster.

She scooted away.

"When I woke up and you were gone, I thought ..."

"What?"

He flipped his hair out of his eyes. "I thought you'd left. I was going to find you."

"So you could drag me back." Sometimes, she hated her sarcastic self-defense mechanism.

He let out a disappointed sigh. "So I could beg you to come back."

Whoa. She hadn't expected that answer.

He focused his intense eyes on her. "I don't want you to leave, Hook." His chest heaved as he blew out a breath. His expression turned sad. "There's just one problem."

She swallowed hard, unable to break eye contact. "What's that?"

"Daric. He wants whatever he can't have. Right now, that's you. Violet senses it, and she's acting out. It's not safe for you here."

He was right about Daric and Violet. The situation was volatile, though Oakley couldn't imagine leaving either. With nothing to say, she stayed silent.

"The only way out of the gang is to die." He shifted backward on the bed until he sat staring down at her with his shoulders resting against the wooden headboard. "You met Hazel in the cave. She came here, stayed for a year, and left about three months ago. To accomplish it, I had to fake her death. We spread blood around outside and told everyone Red Grizzly had killed her. I can't have another girlfriend die too quickly. The guys might get suspicious."

She let out a sigh of her own. "Why do you stay here? Why not go live with Cane and Hazel?"

He narrowed his eyes. "I'm not looking to live with Hazel, if that's what you're asking. I stay here because it keeps Cane safe. A different leader would hunt them down and either kill them or make them slaves. I'm sure Cane would say God would find another way to protect them. But sometimes God uses people as protectors. Don't you think?"

She nodded rather than debate the whole God thing. For certain, Kaleo's position in the gang had saved her life. Maybe there was some kind of plan in that. But if God was supposedly in control of it all, how had she ended up here in the first place?

▭

THE DENSE, grasping trees enveloped Oakley and Kaleo as they headed toward the small river. Their hunting trip had been fruitless up to this point. Even though fruitless was better than running for their lives, they needed to bring back meat.

For this trip, Kaleo carried a bow and arrow slung over his shoulder. His profile created a rugged, Robin Hood image she found hard to ignore. Maybe he really was a good guy. Or maybe she was fooling herself, like Violet.

Originally, he'd told her to stay away from the river. Today, he said hunting there was worth it when he couldn't find game elsewhere. Like everything else in this place, every rule had an exception.

At the edge of the tree line, he dropped to his knees and swept the bow off his shoulder. With one hand, he pushed through the center of a bush to peer at the muddy bank.

She adjusted the straps on her backpack and crouched behind him, keeping her voice at a whisper. "Wouldn't a gun be easier?"

He shook his head. "Last time I checked we didn't have a metal forge on the island. We can't waste bullets." He pointed with the bow across the water. "A small *Velociraptor* is a perfect target."

"Why?"

"The mother won't be around. Juveniles are left to fend for themselves. Plus, they aren't as dangerous as full-grown raptors. Don't get me wrong, these guys will do their best to rip your guts out. Usually, they can't quite reach."

She eyed the turkey-sized animal lapping water from the stream. "Speak for yourself."

He grinned at her while notching the arrow. Squinting one eye, he pulled back his right arm and sighted the target as it dipped its head to drink from the creek. A sharp twang. The arrow hissed, then thunk, it stuck in the tender part of the animal's neck.

The raptor backed up a few paces before it fell. Blood dripped from the wound into the water. Kaleo ran through the stream to scoop up the kill. She followed, soaking her boots in the ankle-deep flow.

He held the animal out to show her. She took a step toward him, but then a tingle of alarm stopped her in her tracks. Something was wrong.

On a tree near the bank, leaves faded from hazy to clear. The unusual swirling of colors moved in no particular pattern. Nearby, an image came into focus, never wavering—three copper dots, and only inches from those, the black slash of a scar.

Camocroc!

"Kal—" His name was cut off by her own scream as the creature lunged for him.

He ducked, narrowly avoiding the massive white teeth

swinging above his head like disembodied steak-knives sailing through the air.

He leaped to the side and pulled his bow up while quickly notching another arrow. Camocroc splashed into the water between her and Kaleo. It faced her and roared. Her heart pounded in her chest.

"Run!" he yelled.

She backpedaled up the bank, sliding on moist leaves.

He released the arrow. It hit Camocroc in the back of the neck, barely penetrating the hard, scaly skin. It roared again and charged at him.

He rolled to the side, just missing the swipe of its deadly mouth. Camocroc stomped at his rolling body with its front feet, leaving impressions in the dirt the size of serving platters.

"Oakley, run!"

Her name on his lips snapped her out of the shock. He couldn't concentrate on getting away until she was safe. She darted into the trees, listening for sounds of pursuit.

After she ran about thirty yards, she stopped and put her hands on her trembling knees. No sound reached her except her own jagged breathing and the distant thump of heavy feet. Had Camocroc pursued Kaleo?

Surely, he'd get away. She circled back from the other direction, her steps tentative. She'd never been alone out here before. Every blowing leaf or swaying branch seemed to hide a monster. *Don't panic.* With a little luck, she'd stumble into Kaleo after he'd shaken Camocroc.

At the creek, she leaned against a tree on shaky legs. Too much adrenaline had made her lightheaded. The dead raptor lay immobile in the dirt. She focused on searching for signs of Camocroc. Nothing moved near the trees. No birthmarks or scars stood out, floating in midair. It appeared to have moved on.

The sharp crack of a branch behind made her heart race again. She whipped her head around and scanned the foliage, dread coiling in her stomach. It couldn't be Kaleo, he'd be in front of her. Maybe it was Cody? She hadn't seen him all day.

Better to be safe. She stayed frozen for a few more crashing heartbeats.

Nothing.

She should find another place to wait anyway. Silently, she crept past the dead juvenile and moved downstream to shallower water before stepping out into the creek. On the other side, the sound of crunching leaves froze her steps in place once again.

A high screech came from behind her.

She spun around and sucked in a sharp breath. A five-foot tall *Velociraptor* crouched at the edge of the trees. Had it been drawn to the smell of blood from the juvenile raptor? This one, though, was an adult.

She held her breath captive. Maybe if she stood completely still, the raptor would take the easier meal. Did they eat their own kind? She avoided eye contact and didn't move a muscle. Not that she had any reason to move. She had no weapons and no real path of escape.

The raptor shifted on its feet for several seconds, its claws dipping in and out of the water. Then, it let out another echoing screech and ran at her.

She screamed and scrambled up the far bank, keeping one eye on the animal. Leaves and nettles slipped under her feet and hands.

The raptor leaped, its massive front claws flexed.

One claw missed. The other scrapped along the tread of her boot and dragged her foot backward. A little higher and it would have gouged her leg.

Jerking her foot back, she continued the mad scramble to get away from the animal. Up close, its claws were longer than her hand and curved to a deadly point. If this savage game of tag ended in her getting caught, the raptor would slice her to shreds.

Climb a tree. Raptor's advice from the boat might be her only chance. She focused on a large specimen Kaleo had called an Elephant Ear Tree. She darted for it and managed to get one leg draped over a branch when the raptor leaped again. Its heavy weight pressed against her backpack for a brief second before twisting her to the side and knocking her forward.

She hit the ground with both hands out. No damage done, but judging by the ripping and slashing noises, she had only seconds before the raptor realized her backpack wasn't part of her.

She tucked her arms in and pulled her legs underneath her body in a crouch. Springing up, she threw the raptor off along with her pack. As it rolled to the side, she backpedaled toward the trees.

Her head pulsed with a fast-approaching migraine. They were coming way too often lately and at the worst times.

She was ten yards from the trees. If she could get there, maybe she could hide.

The raptor charged and leaped again. Its claw pointed straight at her abdomen. As she twisted away, the vicious toe caught the flesh between her shirt and jeans. Pain flared through her as it sliced a gash from her belly button to her hip.

The animal landed and slid along the ground into a clump of bushes.

She stumbled into a tree trunk and fell. Her head throbbed as if the claw had struck through her skull. She briefly pinched her eyes shut, but she couldn't keep them closed. Not if she wanted to survive.

The raptor regrouped and stared at her with black eyes. It would attack again soon. Her fear-numbed brain gave her limited options. She had no other defense except to kick it. She raised her right leg and coiled it toward her body.

It screeched and ran at her. Squinting, she tried to judge its speed. The timing was crucial.

Following its previous pattern, when the animal was two feet away, it leaped at her. She rolled to her left and kicked out with all her might, forcing its momentum sideways. The animal hit the ground inches from her head. Not injured. Only stunned.

In desperation, she shoved at it with both hands. When her palms touched the raptor's scales, something powerful rushed through her chest and shot down her arms. Heat exploded out of her hands.

Painful spasms wracked her body. She squeezed her eyes shut and cried out.

Then, the agony eased. She tried to open her eyes, to fight again, but her muscles felt like stretched rubber.

The raptor would come for her. She had to move. But her body wouldn't obey. The pull of darkness dragged her down until nothing remained.

CHAPTER NINE

KALEO PERCHED on top of a hill strewn with granite boulders. Camocroc had pursued him until he'd climbed up. When the beast had realized it stood no chance of navigating the rocks, it gave up and left. Before Oakley arrived, he'd only caught a glimpse of the *Saurosuchus* twice, both times near a well-traveled game trail. What had made it more active? And why did it seem to find them everywhere they went?

A sharp scream broke through the still air. *Oakley!*

The sound had come from directly east of him. Though it was foolish—Camocroc had lumbered off somewhere in the same direction—he climbed down and bolted through the trees. Her pain, her fear, whatever had made her scream, stirred his most primal need to protect. He hadn't tried hard enough to protect his mom. He wouldn't make the same mistake with Oakley.

A vigorous rustling rose above the sounds of his slapping feet. The noise came from a nearby bush. He froze and swallowed his next breath. Hopefully, the curious animal would move on when it heard only silence.

A branch moved aside, and Cody came bobbing out of the brush. Kaleo blew out his trapped breath and began running again. The animal followed in his shadow. Come to think of it, Cody always seemed to know where to find them as well.

He broke through the trees to the creek where he'd left her. The scream had come from this area. He ran down the tree line for a few yards, then skidded to a stop. What he saw didn't made sense.

Oakley lay on her back, not moving. An adult *Velociraptor* lay nearby, twitching in death throes. Her uninjured hand connected the two of them. His heart shrank to a hard lump in his chest. Had she killed the raptor, then died of the injuries it inflicted on her? But how would she have killed it?

Blood dotted her shirt, though only a small patch of it. As he dropped to his knees next to her, the *Velociraptor* grew still in death.

He pressed two fingers to her neck. A faint pulse. Was he imagining it? He wiped his hand on his jeans and tried again. A small thump tapped against his fingers. She was alive!

Relief washed over him. He brushed the loose hair from her cheek. "Oakley?"

She groaned and rolled her head toward him.

"Are you okay?" He ran his thumb along her jawline,

stopping at her chin. He brushed her soft lower lip, fighting against the desire to kiss her awake. But if he did, even if she responded, he would've broken his promise. His vow was proving to be a massive challenge. He gathered her into his arms, sheltering her small form completely.

Slowly, her eyes fluttered partway open. "What happened?"

"I'm not sure. I was hoping you'd know."

How did an unarmed human, much less a tiny girl like her, kill a raptor? That kind of thing never happened. Except ... A chill ran down his spine. He'd seen something like this once before. Survival against all odds. Could she have the same traits?

She opened her mouth but didn't let another word out. Her eyes closed and her head fell limp against his arm. He lifted her gently into place over his shoulder. For the second time in two days, he knew where he had to take her.

OAKLEY WOKE to her whole body swaying. Was she back on a boat? She pushed her eyes open and almost fell out of a hammock perched ten feet from the edge of a familiar cliff. Somehow, she'd gotten to the cave hideout.

She rubbed her aching temples, trying to remember. The raptor had closed in on her. She'd kicked it, then shoved it away. Had she passed out afterward? A quick flash of Kaleo's concerned face. She must have woken briefly. The raptor had been dead beside her. Confusion twisted her insides into tight knots. A dead raptor. A dead gator. Her dead best friend. *She* was the common denominator in all of it.

Footsteps pulled her from the dark memories. She swiped a hand through her tangled hair, surprised to find it loose from her ponytail.

"You're awake." Cane's soft gaze filled her with warmth and relief. "How are you feeling?"

She twisted her head to the side to stretch out her stiff neck. "Like I wish my sore muscles were only make-believe." She swung to the side to put her feet on the rocky floor. At least her head didn't hurt anymore.

He chuckled. "Not surprising. Kal told me what happened."

"Well, maybe you can explain it to me, because I don't remember much." Her memory loss had developed into a habit lately.

"I think I can explain quite a few things. If you're up to a trip."

She swung out of the hammock and stood, testing her body's balance. No issues. "Where?"

He grabbed the zip-line handles and motioned for her to go first. "To talk about this, we need to go back into the jungle."

A flutter of fear passed through her stomach, but she wouldn't be controlled by it. She grabbed the handles, then caught a glimpse of Hazel in the corner, standing next to Kaleo and looking like a mouse who'd found herself alone in a cheese factory. Oakley met his gaze, but it was guarded and indecipherable. She turned away, stepped into the harness, and let gravity take over.

This time, the cool rushing air of the zip line invigorated her, driving the drowsiness away. A few minutes later, Cane stood next to her on the edge of the jungle. He took her hand, and a feeling both intimate and familiar trickled over her like an unforeseen rain. He gently pulled her into the trees. She glanced back at the yawning blackness of the cave. Could Kaleo see them?

When she turned back around, Cane was staring at her, his green, crystal clear eyes filled with kindness and compassion. Something inexplicable drew her to him. Perhaps his calm demeanor. Perhaps his easy self-assurance. He had nothing to prove and nowhere he'd rather be.

He smiled and tugged her farther into the jungle. She followed him for several peaceful minutes before the pangs of fear returned. No matter how beautiful this place was, every time she came out here, something attacked her. "Where are we going?"

"I have to show you something." He released her hand as if he could sense her hesitation.

They walked for several more minutes until she finally stopped and put her hands on her hips. "What are we looking for?"

He dipped his reddish-blond head toward a bush.

Small scuffling noises came from beneath the thick ball of green leaves. "That."

He pushed through the bush with her following warily behind. On the other side, two *Compsognathus* tumbled about, possibly play fighting or maybe real fighting, When the animals saw him, one darted into the underbrush and the other went as still as a statue.

She folded her arms across her chest and whispered, "Even at my size, I'm not scared of these guys, Cane."

He nudged her backward. "Stay several feet behind me."

What did he think? That one of them might bite off his big toe? With pursed lips, she backed up a step and pressed her rear end into a tree trunk.

Cane shuffled closer to the animal on light feet. "I'm sorry little guy. We need some meat, and she needs a demonstration. You understand, right?"

As if it did, the compy jumped up and down in place. Cane put his arms out in a strange pose like Moses parting the Red Sea, which might have been the only Biblical reference she knew. What was he doing?

The tiny hairs on her arms stood at attention. The air felt charged with expectation. She wrapped her arms around her body.

Nothing happened for several seconds. Cane didn't move except to thrust his hands closer to the creature.

A few more seconds ticked by. The creature's neck swayed, almost snake-like. Its head fell forward. Its body shook, then dropped to the ground. Sitting with its legs splayed out like a person, the animal appeared hypnotized. Cane was some sort of Dinosaur Whisperer.

She steeled her insides, waiting for the moment when he would pull out a weapon and kill the compy. After all, he'd said they needed meat.

He merely whispered again. "There you go. Just let it put you to sleep."

It flopped over onto its side. All movement ceased.

He stepped back and lowered his hands. With a grim smile, he swept one arm at the compy like a magician finishing a trick.

Her eyes went wide. What in the world? Was it dead? Had he really killed it with just his hands? She moved toward the compy. The faint smell of something bitter drifted to her nose.

He put an arm out to stop her. "Give it a few more minutes."

She stared at him, mouth agape. "You killed it?"

He nodded slowly, with regret. "God gives many gifts. But I'll be honest, I haven't come to understand why he gave me this one."

When Cane declared it safe, she ran to the animal. No pulse. No breathing. Stone cold dead in a matter of seconds, without even touching it.

An icy cold rush brought goose bumps to her flesh. While still squatting, she circled around to face him. "How?"

"My body makes a deadly gas. It smells a little like bitter almonds."

That was what she smelled, though the scent was fading fast. Almonds usually meant cyanide. Like the strange species of millipede she'd read about in her animal anatomy class. As a self-defense mechanism, the millipede would push hydrogen cyanide out of its pores in amounts capable of killing rodents and birds. Except Cane's level appeared far more deadly.

He opened his palms wide, exposing a network of webbing between his fingers. "It comes from here. Small doses knock an animal or person out. Larger doses and longer exposure are fatal."

Did he mean fatal to animals or humans? Probably both.

Equal parts fascination and fear warred within her. A quick glance at his expressive eyes allowed fascination to win out. She captured one of his hands to examine the intricate pores, delicate and tough like a finely braided rope, woven to create tiny openings to the center.

He closed his hand around hers. "Oakley, I believe we have these gifts for a reason."

We? Of course, he thought she could do the same thing. But her hands looked nothing like his.

"Close your eyes."

She balked, even though he'd shown no signs of wanting to hurt her.

"You're safe with me."

His soothing voice eased her nerves. She let her eyes fall closed as he rubbed the back of her hand. His fingertips were calloused and rough, like Kaleo's, but cooler. He examined the space between her fingers, his only comment, a faint *Hmm*.

"Think about something that makes you mad or frustrated. What happens to your body?"

She conjured up Violet's haughty gaze. "My heart races, my blood burns, and my head pounds."

He examined her other hand. "You get migraines?"

"Not normally, though I have lately."

"Interesting."

Her eyes popped open. He didn't have to treat her like a lab rat. She resisted the urge to pull away because she needed to know what might be inside her. The migraines and the rushes of adrenaline exploding through her veins were uncontrollable in the moment.

He took both her hands and held them to his chest. "Focus on the anger. Pull up another image in your mind."

"What if I hurt you?"

He cradled her hands more tightly. "The gas doesn't affect me much."

What did he mean by that? Rather than ask, she closed her eyes again. This time, Hazel's perfectly freckled face popped up, her red hair flowing in the breeze as she laughed at something Kaleo said. The charged hum thrumming through her veins was familiar, though she'd never stopped to notice it before. Her muscles were restless, like she had energy to burn.

She opened her eyes to see Cane wrinkling his brow. He seemed to feel it too. Maybe he was tracking her pulse. He nodded, gesturing for her to continue the exercise.

She pressed her eyes closed and brought up Monica's image. As much as she tried to forgive Monica, even in death, it hadn't completely happened. Their relationship had always been complicated. Monica, only a few years older, showered Oakley with compliments at first, then tried to control everything she did—something she would normally not allow. But Monica had this subtle way of drawing her in, making her think she needed the friendship and advice. Looking back on it, Monica served as a surrogate mother and that made the betrayal much worse.

The hum intensified as a fuzzy image came up of a woman with pale skin like hers, but lighter brown hair. The face was pulled from an old picture Dad kept in his desk drawer. Her mother's smile was wide, though an underlying rigidity hardened her eyes. She had a coldness no mother should have. For a moment, Oakley's eyes swam as if water covered her face, even underneath her eyelids. She gasped for air, but her lungs were clear. An electrifying jolt sped through her arms.

"Yikes." Cane let go of her hands.

Her eyes flew open. He stood several feet away, looking at her as if he were the one in danger. "What happened?"

He rubbed his hands together. "You gave me quite a shock."

"So? Static electricity is normal."

He took a step toward her, his green eyes earnest. "Not like this. The pressure built and built, throbbing through my hands, until one final jolt zapped me like I'd stuck a knife in a toaster."

She almost laughed, then stopped herself. He was serious. She examined her hands. Had they killed the raptor? She peered at her left hand, at the missing fingers. Could she have killed Blackie as the gator bit down?

She looked up to meet Cane's weighty gaze. She might be just as dangerous as him only in a different way. "I don't understand."

He shook his head. "I don't either."

A sick feeling crawled through her stomach as the distant puzzle pieces snapped together. No memory of Blackie chomping down on her fingers. The gator had rolled over dead. No memory of the raptor after she shoved it. It was found lifeless. And then there was Monica. Every time Oakley blacked out, something—or someone—perished.

A cloud of dread leached into her soul faster than the deadly gas Cane had released. No longer could she justify her innocence with her amnesia. What if there had never been a straightening iron? What if Jim Durham had nothing to do with it? Maybe she stuck her finger in the water, used all the rage she'd felt, and killed Monica deliberately?

No way. Even if she had some sort of electrical power, she wouldn't hurt anyone ... would she? With a shaky hand, she gestured to the dead dinosaur. "If this is a gift, that makes your god crazier than you."

Cane looked at her sadly. "Is it crazy to believe in purpose?"

"I've known plenty of Christians and you're all a little unbalanced, thinking you're the only ones who've gotten the whole god thing right?"

He took another step toward her, his hands outstretched as if pleading. "Trust me, I didn't get it right. Jesus did. I just listened."

She opened her mouth briefly before slamming it shut. As it turned out, she didn't have anything to say to that. Most of the religious people she knew were more than willing to debate, attempting to prove they were right rather than put the ball in Jesus's court. How was she supposed to argue with a dead guy? The fight drained out of her. She had no reason to lash out at Cane anyway. None of this was his fault.

She shoved her destructive hands in her back pockets. Until she found out what happened to Monica, she couldn't deal with what might be inside of her. Her terrible ruminations still came back to one place, or rather one person who would know. She had to find Jim Durham. "Cane, I need your help."

CHAPTER TEN

EVEN THOUGH OAKLEY and Cane had different abilities, they spent the trip back to the cave trying to find a common denominator. Other than being from small towns in Louisiana situated forty-five miles apart, they didn't discover a single connection.

Upon their return, Cane nodded at Kaleo, most likely confirming the expected results of their experiment. She bristled at the gesture. Keeping her ability secret made the most sense, although Kaleo probably deserved to know. He'd seen enough to suspect already.

After a few cursory good-byes, Kaleo took the zip line first. As he sailed down the wire, Cane came up and stood behind her. He reiterated his promise to search for Jim Durham, as long as she promised to talk to Kaleo about Jim and her unique ability tonight. Apparently, he hadn't given Kaleo any specifics and thought the details should come from her.

She trailed Kaleo on the return trip to the compound. Her hands fidgeted with the straps of the borrowed backpack Neve had given her full of women's clothing and hair ties. How should she broach the subject with him? *By the way, I might look harmless, but I could kill you in an instant?* Or maybe she should try something a little more subtle. *You know how I said I was innocent? I might have been wrong.* Oh, and surely he'd respond well to: *Can you help me track down this guy named Jim so I can find out if I shocked my best friend until she drowned?*

That last one could be the deal breaker. Kaleo had been willing to believe her amnesia meant she was innocent. If he thought she'd murdered Monica and blocked it out, he might not feel like protecting her anymore. Maybe he'd send her away to live with Cane, like he did Hazel. The idea twisted her stomach into a tight tangle of nerves.

In front of her, he walked with a rigid spine and purposeful stride. What was he thinking? Perhaps he was going over the questions he must have about her ability. Questions she also had. Questions even Cane couldn't answer. How did she keep from electrocuting herself? How much charge could her body hold? How did she get this way? None of the questions had answers, and the silent three-mile walk back to the compound didn't bring any new possibilities to mind.

As they came through the gazebo, Wyatt was searching the fronds in the courtyard outside the main entrance. "What's going on?" Kaleo asked.

Wyatt stood straight up, almost at attention. These

men respected Kaleo and would continue to, as long as she kept his secret. "It sounds nuts, but I saw the hind quarters of a big raptor. Maybe a *Utahraptor*."

"Worried about Red Grizzly?"

Wyatt gave a short nod. "I just saw the hind quarters. Could have been it."

"How would it get past our sound defense?"

Wyatt shrugged. "Maybe it went deaf?"

Kaleo laughed and punched him in the arm. "If it did, we'd be in luck. Another predator would take it out or it would starve if it couldn't hear any prey." He stepped toward the door. "Come back inside."

"Okay. I'll keep an eye out from in there."

As they left Wyatt in the entryway, she leaned close to Kaleo. "He seems so normal. Why did he kill all of those people from the highway overpass?"

He stopped to peer at her. "What does normal mean to you?"

The question caught her off guard. "Well, he doesn't give off a serial-killer vibe. Although, now that I think on it, when I first met him, I had a gut instinct to stay away."

"Good. Guys like him have urges they can't always control. He was taught to kill in the military and decided he liked it. Once a week, we send him out to hunt for challenging game so his urges don't get out of control. Plus, he knows he doesn't have enough bullets to take us all out. I ration how many he gets."

He resumed walking down the hall. She caught up to him. "Do you think Red Grizzly is out in the courtyard?"

"Not likely, but not impossible. Most *Utahraptors* are good problem solvers. RG ranks above them all. When I've run from it, sometimes it circles around and tries to trap me. Just when I think I've lost it, it jumps out where I least expect. And when it looks me in the eyes, I can tell it's trying to predict what I'm going to do." Kaleo stopped again to force her to look at him. "If you see Red Grizzly, don't try to kill it. Even if you have some sort of"—he cleared his throat—"gift, RG would cut you to pieces before you had a chance to kill it."

She straightened to her full height. "Then at least I'd take it down with me."

Frustration darkened his eyes, followed by a flicker of amusement. "Easy, Hook, I'd like to keep you around for a while." He lowered his voice to a husky whisper. "Besides, I'm looking forward to sleeping in my own bed tonight."

Heat pooled low in her abdomen. Thankfully, he turned away and missed the blush rising up her neck.

At the door to the room, he tilted his head and cupped her cheek. "Why so flushed?"

So he hadn't missed it. "Uh ... must be sunburn." Some of it probably was.

"Yeah." He smirked and opened the door.

She stood behind him for several seconds, waiting for him to enter. Finally, she peered around his shoulder and let out a gasp. The comforter lay on the floor, along with the pillows. The sheets were half off the bed, and the dresser drawers were hanging askew. Someone had ransacked their room.

"Who did this?"

He fisted his hands. "I know only one person who would dare."

Daric. The enemy she'd made on the boat ride over wasn't going to leave them alone. With no proof, Kaleo probably couldn't do anything about it, and tonight, she was too tired to care. "Hopefully, he left our toothbrushes."

She headed for the bathroom. The pleasant flush from earlier morphed into an erratic tangle of nerves. She was about to be alone in a bed with Kaleo who slept in only his shorts. What would he expect of her? She splashed some cold water on her face, changed into a pair of running shorts and a loose tank top, and brushed her teeth. By the time she came back out, he had straightened the bed and put most of the clothes back in the dresser.

He went to the bathroom for his turn while she crawled into bed, tugging on the tank top to keep it from riding up. Were these clothes scavenged from the stuff people had left behind when they evacuated? Or had they belonged to some of the other women Kaleo protected? He hadn't given her an exact number of women who'd passed through his bed. Perhaps he'd used his rugged white-knight charm on all of them.

The bathroom door opened, and he fixed her with a heady stare. Her insides melted into a hot mass of lava. His gaze never straying from hers, he walked around to his side of the bed and stripped off his T-shirt. She'd always turned away before. This time, she couldn't have looked away unless she gouged her eyes out. The deeply bronzed skin, toned pecs, and stomach muscles that flexed and contracted with every breath—his entire essence screamed Hawaiian warrior. He wasn't overly muscled. He was powerful. What would it feel like to run her hands down those rippling abs? To feel him pressed against her?

Whew! She pulled the comforter up to her neck. He smiled. The man knew the effect he had on her. She expected the pursuit, even anticipated it. Instead, he climbed under the sheets and propped his head on one arm. The pose was no less enticing.

She couldn't risk reaching out to him though. Given what she had just found out about herself, they had no idea what would happen if her pulse skyrocketed. She took a deep, steadying breath.

He glanced at her lips, then looked away as if he'd thought better of it. It would be too easy to lean his way a few inches, give him permission to kiss her, get lost in his arms. She had to tell him about her ability, before the temptation of his nearness overwhelmed her. "I gather you know about what Cane can do."

He nodded, his expression unreadable. With the tips of his fingers, he gently rubbed up and down her right arm. The exploratory move sent tingles flowing over her skin, making this confession much more difficult.

"Mine is different. Apparently, I can create my own—" She swallowed hard as his fingers grazed her ear to brush a strand of hair behind it. "I can create an electric shock."

His hand returned to her arm, though he kept it still. He gazed up at the ceiling for a long moment. She gave him the space he needed to process her words.

Once focused on her eyes again, he shrugged a shoulder and gave her a big grin. "Maybe if you shocked Daric you could fix him. Like electroshock therapy."

She stiffened. "How can you joke about this?"

"Oakley, my whole life is insane. Running from dinosaurs, including their farts. Hoping not to be exposed to the other gang members as a good guy. Feeling more alone than when I lived on the streets. What's one more insane thing?" He began to stroke her arm again. "Besides, it doesn't change who you are."

She wasn't so sure. "It may have changed Monica's life."

A grim, realistic glint entered his eyes as he grasped what she'd insinuated. Another long moment of silence crept by, his gaze never wavering from hers.

Finally, she asked, "Are you afraid to sleep in the same bed as me now?"

A quirk of an eyebrow. "I'm going to ask you the same. Are you afraid to be in the same bed as me?"

She had to concede his point. He was just as capable of killing her.

He rolled to the side and clicked off the bedside light. In the dark, his fingers brushed her cheek. "I told you, I'm good at keeping people under control." His gruff voice made heat flow through her core. Her thoughts slowed as his gentle touch carried her restraint away on a wave of desire. The faint light coming from under the door illuminated his grin. "We could give you something new to focus your energy on."

He put a hand under her chin and drew her toward him. His grin faded as his lips parted. She leaned in, anticipation building in her stomach. Would those lips be firm or gentle? Maybe he would taste like the mint leaves from his toothpaste.

Then, the hum came, buzzing through her head. It didn't hurt, yet. The pain usually came next. What if she shocked him like she had Cane, only harder? What if she did to him what she might have done to Monica?

She pulled back. "I can't."

The disappointed shadows of his face just about broke her resolve. To keep from bridging the distance between them again, she rolled to the other side of the bed and kept her back to him.

In a quick motion, he scooted to her side of the bed and pressed himself against her back. He swept his arms around her midsection. She fought, trying to push him off. He hung on, not injuring her, but not letting go. When he whispered in her ear, "I won't hurt you," she gave in and let herself relax.

His strong arms wrapped around her torso, warm and comforting like her weighted blanket from home. Within a few moments, his breathing became slow and rhythmic. All her reasons for pushing him away faded. For this moment, in his arms was exactly where she should be.

Except it couldn't last. Her power made her a natural-born killer. Eventually, that would drive him away, maybe even for his own survival.

CHAPTER ELEVEN

THE SWAMP across the street from Marcel Laveau's house had coughed up a ten-foot-long alligator. He watched the beast lumber on the asphalt and silently hoped the reptiles his daughter encountered were just as slow. But he knew better. Oakley's mother, Lillian Hebert, had told him stories of the terrifying genetic modifications she had made to some of the dinosaurs. What would Lillian say if she knew their baby girl was fighting those same prehistoric predators in their home territory?

Marcel's relationship with Lillian had been a tumultuous love affair lasting ten years. They met while enjoying the ocean air on the outside deck of Asperten's floating headquarters in the Gulf of Mexico. Though they worked in two different divisions of Asperten International—Lillian in Biological Research, and he in the Chemical Division—they both held the same fascination with jazz instruments and the science of nutrition. On their days off, they spent time picking berries at organic farms or jaunting down to New Orleans for slow jazz in a nightclub.

On the day Lillian told him she was pregnant, he immediately proposed marriage. She refused, saying one mistake shouldn't determine their future. Of course, it already had, but she was stubborn.

The following January, he got his first glimpse of Oakley's chubby baby face. No mistake had been made. She was meant to be his daughter.

For years after he'd first met Lillian, he'd only guessed at the purpose of her research at Asperten. Even when she confessed to the manipulation of the dinosaur DNA, he didn't suspect human subjects were involved. Not until the night he found Oakley crouched on one side of the bathtub next to Lillian's unconscious form. When he asked what happened, Oakley couldn't remember anything. A few weeks later, Lillian died at the hospital, never having regained consciousness. He was still in the dark as to how it happened. But one thing was clear, Lillian's research had affected their daughter.

He turned from the window to glance at his computer, sitting lonely on the other side of his office. This was his week to work from home, instead of flying out to the headquarters, but he couldn't concentrate on his work. Oakley had been gone for five days. Five days with no bright smiles. Five days with no bubbly phone calls recounting her latest tangle with a gator. And five days of wondering what might be happening to her. It was killing him, literally sucking the life out of every long, torturous day.

Even worse, he had no idea who to blame. He'd scoured the criminal investigation reports without finding any clues or any hope of proving Oakley's innocence. Had she actually killed her friend? Strange how the possibility didn't shake him up. His need to protect her rose above whatever she might have done.

Then again, she could be innocent. The prosecutor had pushed hard and fast to convict her. The trial had seemed rushed. Why would the prosecutor be so eager to send a young woman with no criminal record to Extinction Island?

The doorbell chimed, and he checked the camera feed on his phone. An unfamiliar balding man in a black suit stood on the porch.

"What do you want?" he asked through the microphone on the doorbell.

"Sir, my name is Special Agent Noah Brooks with the FBI. If you are Marcel Laveau, then I need to speak with you about a Miss Oakley Laveau."

He sucked in a sharp breath. This man had news, but what kind? His stomach clenched into a mass of tight dread. "I'm coming."

Calm down. Whatever he conveys has already happened. Nothing can be done to change it.

Even so, his hands shook as he locked his computer—Asperten was paranoid about security—left the office, and opened the front door. He ushered the man into the living room.

Agent Brooks sat on the edge of the love seat. His dark suit stood out against the cream-colored cushions. "Sir, may I ask, where is your wife, Felice Laveau?"

Marcel rested on the matching love seat arranged perpendicular to the one where Agent Brooks sat and folded his hands in his lap to keep them immobile. "Felice is at the grocery store. She's Oakley's stepmother, and they're not close, so you can tell me what you need to say about Oakley."

Agent Brooks pinched his lips together and nodded. "Sir, there is no easy way to say this."

Marcel's stomach roiled at what the agent hadn't yet said. He shut down the physical reaction, focusing instead on the movement of the agent's lips. If he could just find out what had happened.

Agent Brooks pulled out a small notepad and flipped to a page. "On September 26th at 1:14 pm Central Standard Time, Oakley Acadia Laveau's biological tracker registered an error code. Afterward, all biological activity ceased."

A cold wave of horror washed over him. "All activity ceased? You mean she's dead?"

Agent Brooks opened his mouth to answer but hesitated. Marcel also let his mouth drop open as he waited for the words that would change his life forever. Was his daughter gone?

"Truth is, no inmate's tracker has ever transmitted an

error code prior to shutting down. This particular code signaled an electrical overload." He rubbed at his jaw. "Of course, she could have been electrocuted, but I find it unlikely in the middle of the remote jungle. Normally, upon encountering an error code, we would run a diagnostic test by satellite, except, as I said, the tracker is unresponsive."

Marcel twisted his hands together. "What you're saying is, you don't know if the tracker malfunctioned or if my daughter is dead."

Agent Brooks nodded while flipping the notebook closed and stowing it in his breast pocket.

The tension rose from his stomach into his chest. Something about this visit seemed askew. "Why did you come here? It certainly wasn't to tell me you don't know anything."

Agent Brooks narrowed his eyes and leaned forward as if trying to provoke a reaction. "After this incident, I checked Oakley's transfer files. On September 20th, she was scheduled for surgery to install a government-issued tracking implant with Dr. Denison. At the last minute, Dr. Denison had a family emergency. The official record states Dr. Sheridan Miller took over to perform the minor surgery. Do you have any knowledge of this?"

He didn't bother to curb his sarcasm. "They didn't inform me. I'm just her father."

"Problem is, no doctor under the name of Sheridan Miller is registered in the state of Louisiana. I spoke with Officer Lewis, who had control of the prisoner during the stated time period. He indicated she was moved from the operating room she was supposed to be in—the one he had been told to guard—and was missing for thirty minutes. He didn't realize she was missing until Dr. Miller's nurse brought her out from a different operating room. The nurse claimed the operation had already been performed. The tracker registered as operational with the website so Officer Lewis didn't pursue the matter." He shifted closer to the edge of the cushion. "You knew nothing about this?"

Marcel stood and began to pace the room. "Unbelievable. You lose my daughter while trying to tag her like a head of cattle, and this is somehow my fault?"

Rather than acting offended, Agent Brooks took on a sympathetic expression. "Sir, I can only imagine what your daughter's conviction would have done to you emotionally. I would completely understand if you had some absurd idea to get a faulty tracker installed in hopes of getting her off the island. I'm aware of your connections to the biological research company, Asperten International."

The mass of tension in his chest exploded into a hot ball of fire. "If you're suggesting I attempted to fake my daughter's death, that's ridiculous."

Agent Brooks rose stiffly to his feet, hands clasped in front. "I apologize for my insinuations. I had to ask."

The angry fire in his chest dissipated, leaving him an empty shell. "Since her sentencing, all I do is think about her and what she might be going through. I haven't been sleeping. Heck, I can barely eat. I'm in a living nightmare. Please find out what has happened to my daughter."

Agent Brooks nodded and moved to the door. "I will, sir. I know someone who visits the island regularly. He is already tasked with checking on Miss Laveau's status."

Marcel took a deep breath. He had a feeling that someone was Ogden "Raptor" Greene—one of the few men who could handle himself around the dinosaurs—but he wouldn't ask to confirm his hunch. If the agent discovered Raptor was her old boss, it might make him think Marcel had colluded with him to save Oakley.

He closed the door behind the agent, then dropped to his knees on the hardwood floor and sobbed into his hands. "Oakley, are you still out there?"

The mournful emptiness of the house answered him with silence.

He had no choice except to wait for Agent Brooks, or possibly Raptor, to find information. But waiting was all he'd done for the last five days.

As he wiped his nose, another alternative came to mind. Every sixty days, the families of inmates were allowed to visit their loved ones aboard a special ship. Most didn't go for either financial reasons or lack of time. If he remembered correctly, the next departure date was tomorrow. He hadn't planned on going because Felice insisted Eric needed him here for emotional support to cope with Oakley's absence. But if Marcel could make the ship, he would get his answer. Surely, Oakley would come. If she was still alive.

CHAPTER TWELVE

THE MORNING SUN slipped through the patio doors and landed like a spotlight on Oakley's smooth, fair skin. A slight sunburn reddened her cheeks. This was the first time he'd woken before her, and his first chance to stare unabashedly. It was after eight o'clock, and she still slept peacefully. Her body must have finally shut down due to the continual stress.

Eventually, she'd get used to the close calls and constant fear. Then again, maybe his upbringing had prepared him for this life of chaos. Oakley hadn't shared a lot about her background, certainly not anything to explain why a jury would think she murdered someone, but her confession last night demanded that he confront the truth. Whether she was guilty of murder or whether her friend's death was an accident, this beautiful, sweet, sarcastic woman carried a violent streak inside. If nothing else, the electrocuted *Velociraptor* testified to it.

He let a tortured sigh leak out the corners of his mouth. None of the other women who stayed here had tempted him, including Hazel, who willingly offered herself to him. But with Oakley, he fantasized of running off to a tree house and spending the whole day in bed together. Problem was, his position as leader meant no permanent relationships. If she stayed here for more than six months, she would be one more pawn for the others to use to take him down. He didn't care about the power. The longer he stayed in charge, the longer he could protect Cane and the others. And after what he'd done, he was compelled to protect any woman who came off the boat, not just Oakley.

As he rolled over, his long hair flopped over his eyes. Chubs was falling behind in his duty as chief hairdresser. Come to think of it, he'd let quite a few of his duties go in the last few days. The garbage in the corner hadn't been taken out. The pool had clumps of leaves floating in lazy circles. And he'd let someone destroy their room yesterday.

Better to go deal with him than lay here, dreaming up ways to spend time with a dangerous woman he barely knew. He slipped out of bed in just his shorts and grabbed the trash can on his way out.

Chubs wasn't in his room next door, so he walked down the hall. Voices drifted from around the corner.

"I'm behind on the laundry. I'll get it done soon." It was Chubs, sounding plaintive.

Daric's low, rumbling tone responded. "Mine comes

first or the deal is off. Without my help, you'll never get a woman. Kal isn't offering up his girl, is he?"

"No."

No surprise to hear Daric treating a woman like a bargaining chip. In fact, the real wonder was that Daric had kept Violet alive for two whole days.

As he rounded the corner, he dropped the trash can at Chubs's feet. He shot Daric a hardened glare. Time to find out what kind of bully he was dealing with. "Chubs won't be doing any more stuff for you at all." He pushed his shoulders back and strode to within six inches of Daric. "We have a ranking system here, and I'm at the top. Chubs works for me. You work for me. Every person in this compound works for me. Those who have a problem with the ranking are eliminated, one way or another."

Daric's face ballooned, turning red with rage, even while his eyes continued to work the situation. Kaleo recognized the same calculating personality as himself, always evaluating, always weighing the cost of action. It made Daric the most dangerous man in the compound.

Kaleo flexed his hands and biceps to punctuate his threat. "One more thing, never come into my room again."

The knife registered as just a glint in Daric's hand. On instinct, Kaleo swiped his arm down to shove the knife to the side. Then, he swept Daric's arm back around and spun him. Before he could complete the move and lock Daric in place, Daric kicked backward, hitting him in the tender area of the upper thigh, and dislodging one of Daric's tennis shoes.

Kaleo grunted and backed away. Good thing the kick wasn't a few inches to the left or he would have gone down for the count. Not many men were fierce enough to aim for the groin.

Daric stood awkwardly off balance with just one shoe. He raised his fists and fixed a hateful glare on Kaleo. This would be a fight to the death in the hallway.

From the corner of his eye, Kaleo saw movement down the corridor. Chubs was charging away from the fight, but there was someone else.

"Kal!" Oakley had run to him.

"Stay back," he growled.

Now he had to keep Daric in front of him to prevent the man from getting to Oakley. Daric surged forward and lunged at him with the knife. He grabbed Daric's wrist, twisted it, and plastered him to the wall.

But Daric didn't stay pinned long. Using the extra leverage from six more inches of height, he shoved Kaleo backward.

Kaleo spun to the side, allowing Daric's momentum to carry him into the table where Taye constructed arrows. A stray shaft clattered to the floor. Daric picked it up, brandishing it in his left hand. Great, two weapons to none.

"What the hell?" Violet distracted them briefly.

Both men quickly focused again on the fight. Daric fisted the shaft and swung at Kaleo, leaving a bloody gash across his chest. He let out a low growl and charged at Daric.

They both tumbled to the floor. Daric continued to

swing the shaft. Kaleo deftly avoided it. The bigger threat was the knife. He kept his left knee on Daric's knife arm while Daric jabbed the shaft at Kaleo like a blunt instrument. Eventually, Daric swung low with the shaft, and Kaleo captured the arm beneath his other knee.

Daric struggled, but couldn't free himself. If Kaleo let him up, he'd likely stab him in the process. In a quick move, born during his street fighting days, he released Daric's shaft arm and punched him twice directly in the bicep. The battered muscle released the shaft.

As soon as Kaleo let go, Daric yanked his arm to his chest. Kaleo shifted backward so he couldn't aim for the groin again. With the change in leverage, Daric brought the knife up.

Before Daric could get a good swing in, Kaleo punched him in the nose. His hands flew up to protect his face, and he dropped the knife. Kaleo landed several more blows to his face, stopping only when his fists began to ache. This was it. The time when he had to make a choice —pull back or kill.

If he pulled back, the others would see him as weak, and Daric would always be a threat. Kaleo had to kill him. Some men didn't deserve to live. Just as he reared back for his hardest blow yet, a voice cried out.

"Stop! Or I'll kill her."

The desperation in Violet's tone struck a nerve in him. He slowly turned his head. Violet held Oakley in front of her, one hand circling her chest, the other holding the discarded knife against the pale flesh of her neck.

Oakley had her eyes squeezed shut. Was she trying to summon up enough electricity to injure Violet or trying not to? No matter which, he couldn't take the chance with her life.

"You've made your point." Violet's voice was tinged with hysteria.

He had no doubt she'd hurt Oakley, if necessary. His words were as hard as flint. "If you kill her, I'll kill you."

Her expression never changed. "Get off of Daric and I'll let her go."

He climbed off Daric's limp body and stood over him. Blood seeped from the man's nose and his bottom lip was swollen. No permanent damage done, though he would hurt for a while.

He fisted Daric's shirt and lifted him to his feet. Voice low, Kaleo spoke directly into his face. "I'm not finished with my girl yet so you get a pass this time. But if you threaten me again, I'll let both girls die just for the pleasure of killing you. Got it?"

A shaky nod. Kaleo shoved him back down the hallway.

Violet eased away from Oakley and dropped the knife on the ground. She refused to look at Kaleo as she ran after her boyfriend.

He moved to Oakley, catching her just before her legs gave out. "You're okay," he whispered.

Taye came running down the hallway. "What happened? Daric looks messed up."

"Next time will be worse." With a nod to Taye, he

scooped Oakley into his arms and headed for his room. He should have stayed in bed watching her sleep after all.

Back in the room, he placed her on top of the comforter, then lay down next to her. She sat back up and hovered over him. "You're bleeding."

Blood smeared in a wave across his chest. The wound stretched from the center of the breastbone and along his right pectoral, ending just before his armpit. It seeped small amounts of blood. Nothing to worry about.

"It's fine." He lay his head back before realizing she also had blood on her. Red stains, turning brown, coated the blue of her right sleeve. "You aren't cut, are you?"

"This is yours." She jumped out of bed and headed to the bathroom.

He saw the stains extended to her back. "I'm sorry. I bled all over your shirt."

"That's what you're concerned about?" she called from the bathroom. She came back with a towel and a makeshift first-aid kit.

"On second thought, making Chubs work extra hard at getting blood stains out sounds like a perfect punishment."

She held the towel to his chest. "Don't blame him for running away. He was scared."

He pressed his hand over hers, holding it tight to his skin. "You didn't run."

The corner of her mouth lifted. "Yeah, but I might have questionable judgment."

With his thumb, he drew slow circles on the back of

her hand. Her shoulders relaxed, and she gave him a little smile, though she wouldn't look him in the eye. Something else was wrong. "I wish the court's judgment hadn't brought you here, but I'm grateful for it."

With his other hand, he caught her chin and forced her to look at him, hoping she would open up about what was bothering her. And she'd better do it soon because if he stared into those lagoon-colored eyes for too much longer, he would break his promise and steal a kiss.

When she stayed silent, he tipped her head to the side to look at her neck. A two-inch-long scratch marred her perfect skin just below her chin. Not deep enough to bleed, but enough to make a statement of her vulnerability. He leaned in and brushed his lips along the wound. She shivered and sucked in a breath. An invitation for more?

He pulled back to assess her intentions. She bit her lip and slowly raked it through her teeth. Did she have any idea how seductive that was? His pulse pounded in his ears as heat rushed through him.

She brought her gaze to meet his. "There was something I didn't tell you last night. Jim Durham is here."

It took a few seconds for her words to make it past the passion muddling his brain. "The guy from the bar is on the island?"

"I saw him when the ship docked. Given what I found out yesterday, I can't wait any longer to find him." The blue of her eyes shimmered with longing. Her soft voice held notes of hope and fear. "But I don't want to leave."

He captured her hand and kissed her palm. "I don't want you to leave either, but ..." Reality sucker punched him, driving away the desire, and squashing the fantasy of happiness. He dropped her hand and forced his gaze from her lips. Kissing her would only make this harder. "You can't stay. That fight was too close. You'll either be killed by Daric or Violet or your abilities will be discovered."

She wrinkled her delicate brows. "Maybe if they knew, they would fear me like Misty."

"No." He smoothed a lock of her hair. "This is different from their superstitions. They would use you for your power."

She scooted to the edge of the bed and wrapped her arms around her torso. He reached out, then stopped himself before touching her. Nothing could make this better. He needed to keep her safe, but he couldn't do that here. The incident with Daric confirmed it.

He forced out his next words with steely resolve. "It has to be tonight. At dusk, we'll fake your death."

CHAPTER THIRTEEN

CANE GLANCED sidelong at Hazel as she tiptoed through the kitchen area. He dropped the soapy dish he'd been cleaning into the plastic bucket, sending suds splattering over the side, then wiped his hands on his pants and turned to face her.

Slung over one shoulder, Hazel wore the muddy backpack Kaleo gave her when she left the compound. Cane hadn't seen her with it since that first day. "Where are you going?"

She stopped, her back to him, and cleared her throat. "Nowhere."

Obviously, she'd hoped to pass by him without explanation because her answer was lame. "Hazel, wherever you want to go, someone should go with you."

She didn't turn around. "I want to be alone."

He switched on his most patient, pastoral voice. "You know I'm concerned for your safety."

She swiveled her head around. "You say that, but what about my mental safety? I'm going crazy in here."

"I know it's hard. We're safer here together." He softened his voice more. When she was in a rebellious mood, most anything would set her off. "Is this about Kal?"

Before this recent visit, Kaleo hadn't come by the cave for months. It must be hard for her to see him again, especially with another woman. Even though there hadn't been a real relationship, sometimes faking one brought up genuine emotions. What she'd felt, what she still felt, for Kaleo was real enough. Too bad he didn't return the sentiment, though Cane understood why. Hazel had demons she'd only begun to address.

"He can't possibly love the little tramp." Venom poured from her voice.

"Hazel." She knew the rules about name calling.

"Sorry. It's just .... She's not even a woman. A fifth grader could beat her up."

Oakley might be tiny, but to call her childlike was slanderous. Her curves alone had kept him up at night. Not to mention her expressive aqua eyes, the fluid grace of her hands, and the softness of her skin—right before she shocked him. Her body held a spark capable of knocking any man to his knees.

Hazel turned all the way around. "Do you think he loves her?"

He cleared his throat to buy time. How was he supposed to answer that one? *I wouldn't blame him?* Or worse, *I hope not because I may be falling for her?*

He met Hazel's gaze. "What I believe doesn't matter. If Kal had wanted to pursue a relationship with you, he would have already done it. You have to let him go."

Her face fell. She looked like a lost little girl for a moment. Then, her characteristic stubbornness hardened her eyes. "He might come to his senses if she wasn't around."

She wouldn't really try to eliminate Oakley, would she? He flipped the gentle pastor voice to righteous indignation. "If you hurt someone to get to Kal, it won't work. He will hate you for it."

She blinked and gave a slow nod. Maybe his logic was getting through.

Don't let her go. The small, familiar voice in his mind was insistent. He'd come to believe it was the Lord speaking softly to his soul. He always tried to obey that voice. "Hazel, please stay here. It'll be dark soon."

She took a backward step toward the wide opening and the zip line. "I need to get out of here. This place is suffocating."

He spread his arms wide. "It's safe."

She walked a few more steps.

Don't let her go.

What was he supposed to do, hog-tie her? "Hazel, please—"

She threw the words over her shoulder. "You always say I'm not a prisoner. You can't stop me. I'm just going to pick some berries. Alone."

Yeah, sure. Berries. But she was right. The cave was a sanctuary, not a prison.

He followed her to the entrance and watched mutely as she strapped on the zip-line harness. Just before she pushed off, she whispered, "Thank you."

It felt like a goodbye.

Should he follow her? She was probably just blowing off steam. If she showed her face at the compound alive, the other inmates would know Kaleo had deceived them, and they'd both die. Surely, she wouldn't risk it.

He let out a weary sigh. Hazel had no way of knowing this, but the confrontation between her and Oakley would happen sooner rather than later. He'd received the coded message from Kaleo just a few hours ago. After dark, Cane would head to the designated spot by the canyon, where Oakley would be alone and waiting for him in the jungle.

TEN YARDS AHEAD OF RAPTOR, the rustling noise continued as he slowly slid his feet, following behind the sound. Whatever was up there moved stealthily, purposeful. He'd tracked all kinds of predators in all types of terrain. This one was most likely human. Of course, that didn't make the situation less dangerous, only less predictable.

Raptor had run across this trail on his way to the large resort occupied by the Cazador gang. Usually, he tried to stay away from the place, but this afternoon—only an hour after he arrived on the secure dock used by government personnel—he'd gotten a satellite call to check on Oakley's status. He'd followed her tracker's last known coordinates to an area near here and found nothing, except disturbed dirt from a struggle.

The resort compound where the Cazador gang lived—which he affectionately called the Sociopath Sanctuary—was nearby so he planned to check there next. No matter where he found her, he only hoped to find her alive. Every other status check the government had requested ended in finding a body, or parts of one.

The noises ahead ceased. Had the person heard him or had they reached their destination? Raptor slunk through the trees several yards to the west of where the steps had halted. He squinted through the branches. From here, the person would have an unobstructed view of the resort compound across a wide canyon. Why would they want to spy on a violent gang?

Out of habit, Raptor pulled out his cell phone. It didn't work for calls on the island, but he used the camera to document every person he had contact with. The photos had eased more than a few family member's minds when they saw proof that their loved one was still alive. The government gave death notices, just not in a timely manner, and no civilian had access to the government tracking website.

He moved a few feet closer before peering around a tree trunk. Dressed in khakis and a green, short-sleeved shirt, a dark-haired man with a prominent, thin nose stood three yards away, holding a polished .22 caliber handgun. A nice weapon. This was no convict. They were lucky to have guns at all, much less a well-maintained, expensive one.

The man whipped his head up and caught sight of him. Fortunately, the man kept the gun pointed at the ground. "Who are you?"

Raptor rubbed at his jaw. "I was about to ask you the same thing." He moved forward and stuck out his right hand. "My name's Raptor. I'm an animal behaviorist."

The man hesitated as if he were trying to think of a reason not to shake hands. Eventually, he relented. "Jim."

"What are ya' doing out here, Jim?" A full-zoom camera sat at Jim's feet.

"Paleontologist." Jim tapped the camera with the side of his foot. "Taking pictures of dinosaurs in the wild. I'm hoping to do a paper on the comprehensive differences between the genetically modified dinosaurs and the fossil record."

"Uh-huh." Sounded reasonable, except Asperten International wouldn't want a paleontologist documenting their genetically enhanced dinosaurs.

Jim gestured over his shoulder at the resort. "What's that?"

"Not a place you want to go."

He shrugged sheepishly. "I guess I was trying to be a little chivalrous. It looked like a place I might find Oakley Laveau. I followed her trial on television. Such a beautiful woman. I hated to see her sentenced to live here. Since I was coming anyway, I thought I'd see if I could help her."

Raptor leaned his back against the tree and crossed his arms, hiding his phone underneath. "You're looking for her, but you haven't seen her?"

He shook his head.

Something about this man as a lovesick stalker didn't ring true. The stalker part, yes. Not the lovesick part. And despite his friendly words, everything about him said *back off*. He wouldn't likely let Raptor get a picture voluntarily. "That's sweet, Jim. Better to just do your job and get out of this place in one piece. You can't save everyone."

He looked around as if danger lurked on all sides. Slowly, he bent down to retrieve his camera. "Yeah, you're right."

As he stood, Raptor quickly took the picture, then pushed off the tree and slipped his phone into his back pocket. If this guy was looking for Oakley, maybe her dad would know him. His heart pinched at what Marcel must be going through. Had they told him his daughter's tracker had gone out and what it might mean?

Raptor took a deep breath and corralled his emotions. Oakley was like a little sister to him. No matter how long it took, he would find her and get answers for both himself and Marcel.

When Jim disappeared into the forest heading the other direction, Raptor made his way quickly toward the compound. The sun was setting, throwing shadows over every leaf and branch. He needed to avoid being caught in the open in the dark. Plus, he'd rather not put the guys on edge by showing up too late. Most of the men were friendly to him because he brought luxuries like chocolate, batteries, and clean socks, but the convicts could turn on him in an instant.

He circled through the trees to the head of the chasm. Just before the arched gazebo, he froze, his senses on high alert. It took a few seconds to figure out what had set off his internal alarm. A small scratch, like a nail scraping on the wood of the gazebo.

His eyes strained in the fading light. Shadowy motion drifted behind the foliage hanging from the archway. He didn't dare try to move.

The shadows stilled. He focused on silent, even breaths.

No sound came for a time, then a quieter scrape.

Choosing his steps carefully, he silently slipped to the side of the gazebo where most of his body would be hidden, but where he'd have a view of whatever came out. He tugged his tranquilizer pistol from his pocket.

A few more seconds ticked by. Then, a large dinosaur poked its head out of the gazebo, complete with dark-green scales and a red tuft of feathers on top. *Red Grizzly.* The largest and smartest *Utahraptor* in this jungle. How did it get in the courtyard? The convicts used sound to deter dinosaurs from scouting the property.

Red Grizzly sniffed the air, its wide nostrils huffing. Good thing Raptor had put on a fair amount of eucalyptus oil to mask his scent and to act as a repellent. The animal stopped sniffing and turned its head. Mud and leaves were stuck to its ear holes. Dread rippled in hot waves through Raptor's stomach. Red Grizzly had figured out how to defeat the sound threat.

He held his breath. With his arsenal of weapons, he rarely feared dinosaurs anymore. This would be the one exception. Its intelligence continued to expand, turning it into a foe with the brain capacity of a human and with weapons no human possessed—teeth meant for tearing flesh and an eight-inch claw to eviscerate its prey.

Red Grizzly pulled its head back inside the gazebo. A small shuffle as it moved again toward the compound. Could he warn the people inside? No matter what they'd done, no one deserved to die so brutally. But if he made any sound, he might be the first victim. Silently, he slipped away into the darkening forest.

CHAPTER FOURTEEN

TO MAKE the event more credible, Kaleo insisted they fake Oakley's death inside the compound. In their room, as a matter of fact. He thought the gang members would be more likely to believe it if some of them were witnesses.

They spent their last day together lounging by the pool, talking about meaningless things, but the small talk did nothing to ease her nervousness. During breaks in the conversation, she stared through the patio doors at the bedroom. How would they accomplish it? Kaleo hadn't given her any specifics, and she was afraid to ask.

Their banter also hadn't kept her from staring at his muscular waist as it tapered into his swim shorts or the water sliding over his firm shoulders and down his defined chest. Ever since this morning, when he kissed the wound on her neck, she could barely look at him without sweeping her gaze over his lips. As if not being able to stay had sent her awareness of him soaring to new heights.

Would he try to sleep with her now, given that it would be his last chance? Perhaps he made a habit of seducing the women he protected and then kicking them out. What would Hazel say about him?

She picked at the salad he'd had delivered to their room. He hadn't pressured her for anything so far. He'd kept his distance and his promise. By this time tomorrow, she'd be gone. Would she ever see him again?

After cleaning up their light dinner, Kaleo leaned close to whisper in her ear. "Lock the door."

Despite her fears, the slightest breathy word from him shot heat through her body, but she couldn't indulge these feelings. Better to wonder what kissing him would be like than to deal with the ache of remembering every day. Besides, who knew what a kiss from her could do to him. She'd never felt such powerful chemistry before. Her previous relationship had been more affectionate than passionate. What if she freaked out and electrocuted Kaleo in the middle of a steamy kiss?

She focused on the slash wound across his chest. Staying here wasn't worth the risk to either of them. He caught her staring at his chest, and she blushed. His dark eyes turned turbulent. Playfully, she reached up and ruffled his unruly hair.

He captured her hand, pressing it between both of his. "This isn't how I wanted it to be. Cane will help you find Jim and get some answers."

Words wouldn't come. She needed answers, but what if Jim didn't have any? Or worse, what if he confirmed the one thing she didn't want to believe—that she'd killed Monica? Oakley gently tugged her hand away. Any answers she got would have to be dealt with on her own or with Cane. It would be too dangerous to see Kaleo after she "died."

To set the scene, he threw to the floor the bloody towel she used earlier to stop his chest from bleeding. She would wear her blood-soaked shirt.

"We need more blood." Before she could protest, he slipped a knife from his back pocket and quickly sliced it down his palm.

She grabbed another towel and wrapped it around his hand. "Haven't you lost enough blood for one day?"

He shrugged. "No way I'm cutting on you. And it's not like we have a DNA lab out here. They won't know it's not yours." He stripped the towel from his hand and let the blood drip on the comforter, then smeared stains across the wall near the patio doors.

He spread another blanket on the floor—the one she'd be wrapped in.

"The blanket needs some blood too." His false cheeriness added to the somber mood as he flipped the blanket over and put some blood on the outside.

"What if it stains the hardwoods?" she asked.

"More realistic that way."

Oh, yeah. He'd done stuff like this before. What else might make it more realistic? Her hair. Letting it fall wild and loose would suggest that Kaleo had grabbed her by the hair. She ripped out her ponytail holder and threw it to the floor.

He dropped the bloody knife near the blanket. Next, he knocked over a few unlit candles and dumped the trash can. "Your shirt looks good, but you need some in your hair and on your face. Sorry."

She stepped toward him and put her hands on his chest, carefully avoiding his wound. His heart rate quickened under her fingertips. He'd left his shirt off, insisting he wanted it to look like he was trying to force himself upon her when she defended herself.

"Well, maybe just your face. Your hair is dark enough they won't be able to tell." He palmed her cheek with his injured hand, his thumb skimming her jaw line.

Her heart raced, matching his for a brief second as if they beat in unison. He pulled away much too quickly. She glanced out the patio doors. The sky had deepened to a hazy lavender. Dusk was about an hour away. They were out of time.

With a heavy sigh, he met her gaze. "Okay. Scream for me, Hook."

She took a deep inhale and let loose, expelling all the frustrations of the past months—Monica's death, her conviction, the dinosaur attacks, this uncertain spark between her and Kaleo, her terrible power—her lungs voiced it all. By the time she finished, he was wide-eyed. But he quickly sprang into action. He punched a hole in the wall where he'd placed the blood, probably injuring his other hand. His loud grunt didn't sound forced.

He cleared off the dresser, slamming the contents into the opposite wall, then pounded on the door to rattle it. "One last yell and choke it off."

She pitched the scream high, pretending to choke in a throaty gasp.

A knock sounded on the door. "Kaleo, are you okay?" Chubs's nervous voice.

"I'm fine." He motioned for her to get on the blanket.

She lay down with her arms askew, turned her face away from the door, and held her breath. The door unlocked with a click and opened with a whoosh of fresh air.

"She grabbed the knife while I was taking a nap." Kaleo gave a low chuckle. "She won't do it again. Ever."

A brief moment of silence followed. She let the air slowly seep from her lungs.

"Too bad. She was nice to look at." The sad lusting in Chubs's tone caused a cold sweat to break out on her forehead. Hopefully, he couldn't see it.

"I'll need you to clean the room while I take her out for the dinosaurs to eat."

"Sure." Chubs sounded eager, probably wanting to make it up to Kaleo for running away this morning. "But—"

"But what?" Kaleo snapped.

"Can I just touch her hair? I have to know what it feels like."

A frustrated grunt. "Fine. I'll wrap while you touch."

The blanket flopped on her face. At least he'd picked

out a soft one. She let the last air in her captive breath leak out and took in another, slowly so the blanket wouldn't move with her chest. Strong hands rolled her body one turn.

Something tugged at her scalp. If only she could squirm to keep Chubs from touching her. She held perfectly still.

A sharp pain in her scalp almost made her yell. She bit her lip to stifle the cry. If she had her way, she'd smack Chubs. How dare he rip hair from her dead body?

"Dude, that's gross. Give it to me." Kaleo's tone commanded instant obedience.

Strong hands rolled her one more time. She had to be at the end of the blanket—a human burrito ready to be served to the first available carnivore. Kaleo hoisted her off the ground, and she allowed herself to flop forward like a sack of rice. A dead body had to show no resistance. Her stomach rested over his shoulder, and her face pressed into his thick back muscles.

She took slow, even breaths. Best not to think of the firm pressure of his hands resting on her upper thighs just below her buttocks. Her insides had already begun to heat up, and it was hot enough inside the blanket. She hadn't developed a headache yet, but she couldn't afford to accidentally shock him and give their plan away.

Her whole body swayed as he walked down the hall. Good thing she hadn't eaten much for dinner or she might have spewed it all over the inside of her cocoon.

"Had a little accident?" The voice was deep, perhaps Taye's.

"Yep. This one was too fiery for her own good. I'm going to dump her in the canyon."

"Want me to do it?" Chubs again.

Kaleo laughed. "She's small, but you still couldn't handle her."

She'd be quite insulted if she really were dead and they discussed getting rid of her like the inconvenience of taking out the trash. More movement, then a slamming door. Fresh air filtered into the blanket. He'd already cautioned her to remain mummified until he put her down, just in case someone from the compound was out walking.

For many nausea-inducing minutes, she swung and bounced on his back. At the same time, his stamina impressed her. His steps never faltered or slowed. She was nothing more than a heavy backpack to him.

Finally, all motion stopped. She breathed deep, steadying her stomach for what came next. In a fast move, he flipped her up, swung her legs to the side, caught her back, and laid her gently on the hard ground. She struggled against the inside of the blanket while he unraveled it from the outside.

When her head broke free, she sucked in the musky smell of fallen leaves. The earthen scent faded as he leaned over her, bringing his own scent of lemon and coconuts with a faint undercurrent of hibiscus from the ones he grew on the patio.

"Are you okay?"

"Fine." She moved to sit up, but had nowhere to go. His body and the roll of blanket on the other side held her in place. The heated look in his eyes kept her from fighting him. Instead, she met his gaze and enticement stirred inside her. *It's better not to know*, played on a loop in her head. But she wasn't listening. Her eyes were fixed on him—his full lips, his hair caught by the wind, the cocky smile creasing his perfectly tanned skin.

Her breath hitched when his hand moved to her waist. His smile widened. He was toying with her, enjoying the effect he had on her. The snarky side of her reared its head for a brief second. She squashed it. His touch set her on fire, and she wouldn't say anything rude to make him stop.

But two could play this game. She drew her lower lip in and slowly let it out. His gaze was riveted on her mouth. She curled her hand around his uninjured one and placed it on her cheek. He ran his thumb along her cheekbone. The texture of his rough hand against her skin caused her blood to simmer.

His thumb moved down to caress her lower lip. "Do you want this?" His tone held none of the cocky expression she still saw on his face. He knew she wanted this, and yet he willingly gave her the power to decide. He'd meant it when he said he wouldn't cross the line until she gave him permission. That gift more than anything else tipped her over the edge.

She gulped, then nodded.

"This probably isn't a good idea." He leaned closer until only a breath separated them. "But I'll regret it if I don't."

His lips met hers in an explosion of desire. Heat shot through her veins in fast pulses, making her lightheaded. She entwined her hands in his hair, pulling him closer, kissing him deeper.

He scooped both arms around her back and angled her to press against him. Goosebumps erupted across her skin as their bodies melded together. Waves of longing flooded through her from top to bottom, drowning her senses.

Keeping one hand in his hair, she brought the other to his strong chest and ran her hands along his hard muscles. He groaned, igniting a spark of lightning within her. It burned white hot before exploding out of her.

"Whoa." He pulled back, surprise etched on his face.

"I shocked you, didn't I? I'm sorry."

He gave another cocky grin. "Don't be. I liked it."

His mouth covered hers again. She let the feel and taste of him sweep her away. Just as she noticed the spark within her amplifying, he slowed down, giving her a chance to catch her breath.

She could have kissed him all night. To her dismay, he leaned back and gave her a soft peck on the forehead.

"Now I regret not kissing you a hundred times since you got here." He pressed something into her hand before he pulled away.

Her fingers curled around the handle of a knife. He

stood, and as he looked down at her, a smile spread across his face. "I would have given you back your taser, but … you know, what would be the point?"

A breathless laugh escaped from her lips. Their gazes met and held for several intense seconds, then he disappeared into the dark terrain. He'd left her with every nerve tingling and the craving for his lips nearly tearing her heart into pieces.

CHAPTER FIFTEEN

OAKLEY SQUIRMED on the hard ground and brushed her hair from her face. A scant amount of moonlight filtered through the trees, leaving her in murky darkness. How much longer would she have to wait? The signal had been sent out at about lunchtime—a small bag traveling along a miniature zip line to a spot in the forest supposedly checked every day. The bag contained two marbles: one dark red and one yellow. Kaleo said Cane would recognize the color of death and the location indicated by the yellow marble. Still, she didn't like the idea of waiting in the dark with the smell of blood all over her. What if Cane had forgotten to check today?

At least she hadn't been cold as the dew dropped around her. The memory of their kiss had kept her warm for hours. What girl wouldn't have an intense physical reaction to a guy like Kaleo? And that only made him more dangerous. The greater the attraction, the greater the devastation if it all fell apart.

A shuffling noise came from the bushes to her right, from the direction of the compound. She let her arms and legs go limp and held her breath. It might be someone who didn't believe Kaleo's story about her death.

More shuffling rattled through the underbrush, followed by a familiar high-pitched squeal. *Cody*. She almost jumped up to grab him in a big hug, but in case someone had followed him, she stayed still. She lay motionless on her back, even when Cody bobbed up and down on the blanket and squeaked in her face. Eventually, he settled down and curled up beside her, his tail touching the tip of his pointy snout.

After twenty minutes with no other visitors, she rolled over and cuddled his leathery-soft body against her chest. He smelled like leaves and his cooing noises reminded her of a purring cat.

"If I only had a camera—" Cane's voice startled her.

She shot into a sitting position, accidentally shoving Cody into a nearby bush.

Cane laughed as he knelt down beside her and set his bow and quiver on the ground. "Just when I think you're a real-life Snow White, you toss the cute critter away."

She scowled at him, though he had no way of knowing Daric's nickname for her. And truly, it sounded completely different coming from Cane's lips. "You scared me."

He raised his brows. "So, you threw him away for self-preservation?"

Rather than answer, she searched under the bush for Cody. He'd disappeared into the forest. She'd probably scared him as much as Cane had scared her. She pointed at the quiver. "I'd rather be a female Robin Hood. Will you teach me sometime?"

He winked at her. "Sure. I'm a sucker for fairy tales."

She rolled on to her knees. "Can we go?"

"Good idea. From what Kaleo tells me, your pet will show up again eventually. Plus, I've learned when the nice dinosaurs disappear it's usually because the mean ones are around the corner."

"Lovely thought, thanks."

He grabbed his weapons and walked into the jungle. She followed his lanky silhouette. He moved quietly for someone with such large feet. His hands swung by his sides. His long, slender fingers looked harmless, but were just as lethal as hers, in a different way. He seemed to accept it as fact. It wasn't so easy for her. "Cane?"

He faced her with one finger to his lips. When she gave him a disappointed look, he flashed all ten fingers at her. Be quiet for ten more minutes, but why only ten? It would take them much longer to reach the cave entrance.

Almost exactly ten minutes later, he stopped walking and reached up to a nearby tree. He pulled down a ladder, letting it unfold until it touched the ground. When it locked into place, he gestured for her to climb.

She looked up at a large, shadowy structure encased in a massive treetop. A tree house?

At the end of the shaky ladder, she flipped a latch to open the trap door in the floor of the structure. The door gave a thump as it came to rest against hardwood planking. She scrambled in, noticing a faint glow inside even though the wooden shutters were closed tight. The glow came from three potted plants spaced around the room.

"What are these?" she asked as he peeked through the opening in the floor.

He climbed all the way inside. "I don't know, actually. They're found in only a few places in the forest. We keep some here in case we have to spend the night."

"We're sleeping here?"

"It's too far to travel to the cave at night. Not worth the risk. I know this isn't as luxurious as your recent accommodations, but it's probably nicer than the cave." He pointed at a cot with a blanket on the far wall. "For you."

He moved to sit on another cot resting against the opposite wall. She scrutinized him. His manner of speech, the fluid way he moved, his peaceful expression—none of it belonged in a damp cave, much less the death-shrouded jungle. Other than what he'd already told her, was there another reason he'd come here?

Did you see Hazel at the compound?" His quiet question pulled her out of her thoughts.

"No, but we stayed in the room all day. Why?"

Cane twisted his mouth at her statement, though he refrained from asking what they did all day inside. "Last time I talked to her, she wanted to return to the compound. She believed she needed to claim Kaleo again."

Oakley dropped to the cot and threw the blanket over her feet. "Again. As in, they had a relationship before?"

"Only in her mind." He picked up a watering can and filled it from a basin by the wall. Slowly, he watered the glowing plants. "I tried to stop her from leaving, but I couldn't."

"What's her story?"

For a moment, his expression shuttered. Just when it seemed he wouldn't answer, he released a heavy sigh. "I'm telling you this so you'll understand and be careful. When she comes back, the two of you will be living at the cave, and we've got to make it work."

"Okay."

He rubbed a hand down a day's worth of stubble. "Hazel has a problem with authority. She killed both of her parents because they kept her from seeing her boyfriend."

Oakley twisted her hands together. "And now she's decided I'm a threat to her desire for Kaleo."

He put the watering can away and dropped to the cot again. "Exactly."

Just great. All she needed was another person trying to kill her. One of these days, she might have to defend herself. With her new ability, self-defense took on a whole different meaning. "Would you use your power against someone else?"

"I'd like to think I wouldn't. I believe God always provides a way out without killing." He stared at the wooden ceiling. "Though, I can't say with certainty. Self-preservation is a powerful motivator."

"Does Hazel know what you and I can do?"

He shook his head. "You, Kaleo, and Neve are the only ones who know."

Which meant Hazel had no reason to fear her. Whether that was for the best or not remained to be seen. Hopefully her power would stay secret until she figured out how she ended up with it.

Cane tilted his head. "You're wondering why we have these abilities?"

"Are you telepathic too?"

He shrugged. "It's weird. I get feelings from you. I've always been good at reading people, but with you, it's more enhanced."

He might as well have taken the words right out of her mouth. Since the day she'd met him, she'd trusted him and never once questioned his motives. It wasn't like her.

"So why do *you* think we have these abilities?" he pressed.

She wrapped the blanket around her legs, hugging her knees to her chest. "One person is a fluke of genetics. Two people are a pattern. Even though our abilities aren't the same, I think it's likely someone did this to us. Someone created this part of us."

"I agree. At one time, I thought I had a freak DNA mutation. After meeting you, I can't understand how it would happen to both of us differently." He gestured to his tall frame, then swept a hand toward his strawberry-blond hair. "And somehow, I don't think we're long lost cousins."

She laughed. It *was* extremely unlikely.

His features softened into a scholarly expression. "I've been thinking hard about this. Man can't create something new. We can only work with what God has already given us. Our DNA won't accept any kind of crazy modification and still create a functioning person."

"What are you trying to say?"

He blinked as if he'd just discovered it himself. "God knew this would happen. He left room for the possibility inside our DNA. People may have tinkered with us, but I truly believe"—he captured her gaze—"we were still created by God, even if by the hands of man."

"But we don't know what they changed. What if the person who created us is evil? We might be evil deep down." He started to speak, but she held up a hand to stop him. "You see it all the time with serial killers. They're born with sociopathic tendencies. Less likely to feel empathy. More likely to hurt people. Psychologists don't believe they can be rehabilitated." An image came to her unbidden. Daric's pitch-black tennis shoes looming beside her, just before he tried to assault her. She pressed the memory down. "In reality, some people are just born bad."

Cane pushed out of his cot and knelt down in front of hers, placing his hands on the edge of the blanket. Next would come the platitudes, the empty words about how those made by God couldn't be all bad.

In a voice so low, she almost couldn't hear him, he whispered, "Those are my fears exactly."

His words stunned her into silence. She gave a shaky nod. To have her fears laid bare and to share them with him doubled her anxiety, even as it eased her burden.

He smoothed the blanket over her feet as if trying to brush away the worry. "If we're not capable of change, if we're strictly bound by our genes, then God help us."

A sudden coldness washed over her. Did she believe they were beyond hope? That they were destined to act out any evil inside them?

She stared down into Cane's eyes, shadowed in the low light. He was a man who didn't pretend to have all the answers. A man she could be real with and not face judgment.

He let out a soulful sigh that seemed to blow away his dread. With one finger, he tilted her chin up and skimmed his thumb lightly along her jaw. The smallest gesture, but one look in his eyes, and it was clear he'd done it on purpose. He wanted her to think of him as a man, not just the leader of the cave people. A sweet warmth spread through her, a tamer version of the feelings Kaleo had kindled. "Good night, Oakley."

She whispered good night as he pulled away. When she dropped her head onto the cot, she stared up at the timbers on the ceiling. Her life had been on hyperdrive since she'd arrived on the island, flipping her emotions back and forth like a pinball machine. Kaleo sparked her nerves with desire, literally, but he was unpredictable and untamed. The exact opposite of Cane whose calm demeanor soothed her. A man like him would commit and never waver. The two of them were working their way into her heart, and she couldn't sort it all out.

Maybe she shouldn't trust anything she felt.

WHEN KALEO RETURNED to the compound, the lights were on full brightness in the courtyard. Granted, the moon occupied only a small slice of the sky tonight, but he'd have to lecture Wyatt for depleting their power reserves.

As he approached the door, his steps slowed. Coming back to this place without Oakley felt wrong. Even though she'd spent less than a week here with him, her absence shriveled his heart into a dried-out apple core. He breathed a heavy sigh and pushed open the door to find Wyatt staring at him.

"What's with all the lights?" Wyatt asked.

Kaleo folded his arms. "I was going to ask you the same question."

"Chubs said it was your call. He also said to watch the tree line. Is there something I should know?"

Without answering, he pushed past Wyatt and went in search of Chubs. They needed to get a few things straight.

When he found Chubs's room empty, he entered his own. Chubs sat on the bed, his expression strangely flat. "Where have you been?"

"Disposing of the body away from camp." Also, walking around aimlessly. He'd been stupid to fall for a woman he couldn't have, but he wouldn't tell Chubs that. He planted his feet. "Since when do you question what I'm doing?"

Chubs bent at the waist and, with one finger extended, circled the area on the floor still stained dark red. "It didn't all come out of the wood."

Kaleo shrugged, then walked to the bedside table to get a glass of water. As he lifted the glass to his lips, Chubs grabbed his other hand and turned it over to expose the knife wound.

"Is some of this blood yours?" he asked.

"She pulled a knife on me, so yeah, a lot of the blood is mine." He yanked his hand away and took a long drink of water, keeping his eyes locked onto Chubs, who hadn't gotten up from the bed. The sharp tone of voice, the fidgeting hands, and the challenge in his eyes—something had gotten under Chubs's skin.

"You should have told me." Chubs's voice was disappointed, tinged with anger.

Uh, oh. Told him what? He had more secrets than Chubs would ever know. So which was he referring to?

"I'm the one who cleans it all up." Chubs searched out his gaze. "I do everything you say. Why would you lie to me?" Chubs waited for an answer, his fingers drumming the white comforter.

Kaleo could only guess at an appropriate response. Best to go with something vague that might cause him to give a hint as to what he knew. "I wanted to protect you."

A deep throated scoff. "More like you wanted to protect her."

Did he mean Oakley?

He scooted farther from Kaleo, while staying on the bed. "And she ended up dead anyway."

Dead. His stomach bottomed out. It couldn't be her. He had left her only hours before. Had Chubs followed him? Nausea rolled through his gut. "How?"

"After I cleaned up in here, I went out to throw the rags away. That's where I found her." Chubs swallowed hard. "In pieces."

He dropped the glass, ignoring the high-pitched crash and the prick of shards on his legs. Had Oakley come back to the compound? He sank to the bed with a gruff whisper. "Red Grizzly?"

"Probably. She was just outside the trash pile. Her scalp and both arms were gone. I could only identify her by the starfish tattoo on her ankle."

The starfish tattoo. A blender of emotions churned inside him. Misery, fear of exposure, guilt, relief. It wasn't Oakley.

It was Hazel. Her jealousy must have caused her to risk coming back to see him.

"Where has she been all this time?" Chubs swiveled

on the bed to face him. "No, actually just tell me why. Why did you lie to me?"

This was the constant battle within him. Keeping secrets was one thing, lying was another. Street Kaleo would have lied again without blinking, but new Kaleo found lying painful. Chubs deserved the truth or at least part of it. Kaleo wouldn't betray his friends at the cave.

"A year ago, I decided to change my life. I don't want to be the same selfish person who made the mistakes that landed me here."

Chubs's mouth dropped open. "You mean, like you're getting religion or something."

"Not exactly. I just want to be better."

He cursed. "You can't change the past, Kal. There's no making up for it. That's a bunch of crap meant to make people feel better about being awful." He hit his chest with a fist. "We are horrible, terrible people. No one can make it okay. We just have to be who we are."

Kaleo held his head high. "I need more."

"But it isn't reality. In reality, Hazel killed her parents while they slept. Why didn't she deserve whatever we would do to her?"

Kaleo hardened his stare. "Do you really want to compare our pasts?"

The anger faded a bit from his eyes, replaced by sadness. "You're just like Teresa."

Kaleo flinched at the accusation. Teresa was the teacher who'd abused Chubs. The thirty-five-year-old woman had convinced him to sleep with her when he was only thirteen. He killed her in her classroom, along with seven students and two other teachers.

"She was a church-going woman. She told me the sex was okay because we loved each other and God is all about love. At first, I didn't care so much if God was okay with it, I just wanted the sex. Later, she used it all against me. She said God would be angry with us for what we did, and we had to keep it a secret. I was fine with that, until she said God told us to stop." Chubs pushed at his too-long bangs. "God is love or God is judgment. It doesn't go both ways. People just make this stuff up to suit themselves."

Kaleo kept his voice even. "Isn't that what you're doing? You make up whatever rules benefit you."

"At least, I'm honest. I'm real." He looked down his nose at Kaleo. "I can't help you anymore." He turned to go, then turned back as if he'd forgotten something. "You did the same thing with her too?"

Now he definitely meant Oakley. Kaleo remained silent, an action that in itself spoke volumes.

Chubs pinched his lips together. "It's dangerous to go soft in this place."

Kaleo bolted to his feet, ready to show how not-soft he was, but the fight quickly left him. It wouldn't do any good at this point. Chubs had to decide where his loyalties would lie.

After Chubs left, Kaleo grabbed a backpack from under the bed. If Chubs ratted him out to the others, he had to be ready to escape. Previously, his plan had been to fight to the death and either perish or lead whoever survived. But Oakley had given him reason to want to escape.

After throwing a few necessities in the pack, he lay down in bed alone. As he tried to sleep, the stress of the day still lingered. Was Oakley safe? Had Hazel suffered much? Would Chubs make the right decision? Even as clueless as Chubs could be, he had to realize how much blood would flow if he spilled Kaleo's secrets.

CHAPTER SIXTEEN

RAPTOR ROLLED over on the twin-sized bed and almost fell to the concrete floor. His wide frame probably would have been better off on the floor, but he couldn't resist sleeping on a mattress. He didn't stay at Asperten's underground facility often, only when he needed a good night's sleep. This time, even the mattress hadn't helped. Images of past trauma had invaded his dreams. Velociraptor, T. rex, the genetic freak dinosaurs—he'd escaped them all. The near misses left plenty of scars, both physical and psychological. Usually, this concrete bunker served as his safe room, but last night, his brutal dreams were of Oakley. She was out there somewhere. He had to find out what happened to her.

Raptor's FBI contacts had convinced Asperten to give him limited access to the bunker since he routinely risked his life to check on the well-being of the dinosaurs Asperten had created. Even so, most of the rooms here were restricted because Director Lumas Verret didn't trust him.

It was mutual. Arrogant and entitled because his grandfather had founded the company, Director Verret was the kind of man who held a position of power simply to exercise control. On the few occasions they'd met, Raptor would have expressed his dislike for the man if it wouldn't have jeopardized his chances of working with the dinosaurs. Thankfully, the director spent most of his time in the main Asperten research facility located in a floating building offshore from Louisiana.

Raptor sat up and placed his feet on the cool concrete. He might have another bone to pick with the director soon if the Utahraptor lineage continued to progress in intelligence. As much as Raptor loved predators, he would recommend to his government contacts that the specialized highly-intelligent branch of the species be destroyed. Pitting any human against such a smart Utahraptor simply wasn't a fair fight.

Most senators continued to uphold this version of the death penalty as more humane since they gave the criminal a choice, but those pompous men had never seen the results of a dinosaur's work. They'd never seen a person's insides strewn across the jungle floor in a bloody stripe or heard the wretched scream of a man being eaten alive. The average life expectancy on the island was a mere three years and only stayed that high because of gangs who banded together for survival.

Despite his distaste for the death penalty, Raptor

hadn't argued against it until they'd sent Oakley here. No matter what the court decided, she didn't kill anyone. He'd supported her decision to come to Extinction Island, given the alternative, and believed he'd be able to keep an eye on her.

Now, he might be too late.

The failure weighed him down like a sauropod standing on his back, making him sluggish. With a deep breath, he stood. He owed it to her father to find out what he could. Over the years, Marcel had been a source of influence due to his position with Asperten, and more than that, he was a friend.

Raptor went to the tiny bathroom and scooped some water from the basin that was filled by a rain reservoir on the roof. He scrubbed his hair, his armpits, and his face.

After he checked his supplies and strapped on his boots, he walked up the sloped hallway to the thick metal door. It opened with a few twists of a wheel, similar to the ones on a submarine. From the outside, a manual keypad shifted tumblers to allow access to the wheel. No one could get in without the code, which was changed every week.

The jungle at this elevation held a cool vapor. Not hot, but still sticky from the humidity. He turned toward the Sociopath Sanctuary. He'd go there first, again, hopefully without running into Red Grizzly this time, and if the men there weren't any help, he'd check with the other smaller groups in the area.

An hour hike brought him to the edge of the cliff

where the compound sat. He surveyed the area from a distance, as he had yesterday. No large movements, no rustling trees or bushes. Not even a dark-haired stalker.

Just to be cautious, he retrieved his pistol from his backpack and stuck it in the back of his jeans. He pulled a short machete from the bungee straps on his pack, then crept quietly toward the compound.

He hesitated at the gazebo. The foliage was calm. The birds still chirped their carefree songs. After listening for several minutes, he edged through the area on his toes. No sign of the cunning animal.

As he approached the front door, it flew open. He jumped back. A man he'd met several times trained a weapon on him for a brief second before lowering it to point at the ground.

Wyatt gave him a suspicious look. "Did you bring us something?"

Raptor smiled. "You know it."

Gifts had won him many friends down here, but he remained on guard. Most of the convicts would take what he had and slit his throat because he didn't have more to give. He only interacted when absolutely necessary, and he usually came to this group first because something about Kaleo was different. He had a cooler head and didn't encourage random violence.

Raptor pulled a handful of batteries from his pocket along with a package of matches, some Twizzlers and Swedish Fish. "Is Kal around?"

"Yeah." Wyatt balanced the gun under his arm while

scooping the prizes into both hands. "Daric, go get Kal," he yelled at a blond-haired man, who was almost the same height as Raptor, although much thinner.

Raptor raised his brows in surprise. Kaleo had let the San Diego Slayer stay here?

Daric scowled at Wyatt's order, but he went back into the compound, presumably to do as Wyatt had asked.

As Raptor followed Wyatt inside, he asked, "Have you seen anything strange by your front door?"

"Now that you mention it, I saw the right flank of a dinosaur's hindquarters the other day. I wondered if I'd imagined it. Also, I've noticed some clumps of muddy leaves where people don't usually walk and a few feathers within the perimeter. I figured the feathers blew in. The leaves I wasn't sure about."

Kaleo rounded the corner, his confident expression belied by the bags under his eyes. Raptor nodded in greeting and out of genuine respect. Kaleo always kept his guys under control, and if a guy didn't fall in line, he kicked him out to live on his own. "I was just about to tell Wyatt. You've got a problem. I came by here yesterday about dusk. I didn't enter the courtyard because it was already occupied. By Red Grizzly."

Wyatt's mouth dropped open. "What?"

Kaleo looked concerned, though not exactly surprised. "Thanks for the info. Wyatt, go check the sound emitters."

Raptor shook his head. "No need. I'm sure they're working fine. I saw RG with clumps of muddy leaves stuck to its ear openings. It's figured out how to defeat your sound at the source of impact."

Again, Kaleo didn't appear surprised, just mildly interested. The man had quite a poker face. "That sucks. So why did you come here yesterday?"

"I'm doing a well-check on a girl who arrived almost a week ago. Her name's Oakley Laveau. Seen her?"

Wyatt barked out a laugh. "Kal's done more than see her."

A white-hot ball of fury rose in his chest. She'd been here at their mercy the entire time. Had they killed her? Every ounce of respect drained away. Raptor wanted to kick Kaleo's ass, but couldn't do it here. He put on his own poker face and kept his voice calm. "Where is she?"

Kaleo's Adam's apple bobbed, barely noticeable. "She was here, staying in my room, until she came at me with a knife. I left her body at the head of a ravine west of here, unless the dinosaurs have taken it."

Something about his story and his tone didn't ring true. It wasn't the part about Oakley coming at him with a knife—he could see her doing that—it was his bearing because it ran contrary to the hardened killer impression he was trying to give. The small tic by his left eye, the slight reddening of his neck, and the flattening of his voice like he was trying too hard to be nonchalant. He was lying. He had a reputation for being ruthless, yet fair. If she had come at him with a weapon, he would have disarmed her, maybe beat her up. He wouldn't have killed her.

Daric took a step forward. "How did you get the call to check on her so quickly? This happened last night about the same time you said you came here."

Last night definitely didn't fit since he'd gotten the call to check on her yesterday afternoon. He ignored Daric, instead focusing on Kaleo and answering the question as if he had asked. "The higher ups claim it happened two days ago."

Daric drew his brows tight. The suspicious gesture reinforced Raptor's own suspicions. The timeline didn't add up.

Raptor took a step backward. Time to get out of here and check out Kaleo's story. "Perhaps her tracker malfunctioned a couple of days ago, before you had the fight with her."

"Makes sense." Kaleo narrowed his eyes as if he could sense the barely restrained emotions inside Raptor. "Did you know her?"

A long bleat from a ship's horn came through the windows. Another one quickly followed.

"What's that?" Daric asked.

"A signal from the visitor's ship," Raptor explained. "Every two months a ship brings visitors who want to see their loved ones."

Daric's eyes lit up. "Great! We could hijack it and get out of here."

He laughed. "Only if you can overpower five guards armed with automatic weapons and cut out your own tracker, then of course, you'll have to disable the tracker embedded on board the ship. Otherwise, no matter where you go, they'll find you."

Daric spread his arms wide. "All of us could do it together."

"Not gonna happen. The metal access door is closed, overseen by the guards I mentioned. At least two guards aim machine guns down from above. One prisoner is allowed into the ship at a time, and only those who have visitors on board. If your name isn't on the list, you don't get to board." Daric probably didn't have too many people coming to see him. But it did give Raptor an idea. If Kaleo was lying and Oakley was still alive, she'd try to get to the ship in case Marcel had come to see her.

"They'd probably allow you on board." Daric looked over at Kaleo. "Let's grab this guy and force them to give us the ship."

Raptor took another step back toward the door, his fist clenching on the machete, his other hand skimming his hip, ready to reach for his pistol. "They wouldn't care enough about me to give you a ship."

Kaleo stretched taller and pushed his shoulders back. "Back off, Daric. Like he said, it's a ridiculous idea." He nodded at Raptor. "I appreciate the heads up about RG. If you see him out there, put a bullet in his brain for me."

"Will do," Raptor said, even though they both knew he couldn't. His government contract forbade him from killing any dinosaurs except in the case of self-defense. He retreated slowly, not turning away from the men until the door closed completely. Despite his grudging respect for their leader and his growing conviction that he hadn't killed Oakley, Raptor wouldn't come here for a while. Kaleo had his hands full with Daric, and the situation was bound to get violent.

He left the compound and headed in the direction of the ship. If Oakley wasn't there, he'd still have time to check the nearby creeks later. His stubborn streak wouldn't allow him to quit. She wasn't dead until he found her body himself.

▭

AFTER THE CRAZY naturalist guy left and Wyatt went to check the sound emitters, Daric stood alone in the entryway. What kind of guy would take a job running around with dinosaurs and checking on dead convicts? Raptor had to have a screw loose, but he seemed to have a soft spot for Oakley—just like Kaleo.

Daric peered out the front door. Wyatt was now searching the bushes for evidence of the *Utahraptor*. Kaleo had already retreated to his room, though his body language had given Daric good reason to have serious doubts about Oakley's death.

What were the chances her tracker would malfunction, and two days later, Kaleo would kill her? Pretty slim, especially when the timing of her death came right after Kaleo and Daric had fought. Pretty convenient.

What if she wasn't dead? Chubs had seen the body, although not for very long. Kaleo could have pretended to kill her and instead stashed her in some secret hideaway so that he alone would get to enjoy her.

It was worth checking out. Daric would send the one person he could trust to investigate further.

He found Violet reclining on a tattered lounger at the pool, working on her deep brown tan. He dropped to the cracked cement beside her. "I need you to do something for me, babe."

She gave him the sappy, loyal smile she'd given him the first time they'd met—in prison with plexiglass between them. From the letters they'd exchanged, he knew her type: attracted to bad boys and convinced only her love could turn him good. Women like her were useful, if not a bit annoying. But Violet made up for her irritating traits with her other attributes, as shown off in the skimpy bikini they'd found in the back of the old gift shop.

He ran a finger up her thigh. "I need you to go on a quick trip for me."

She swung one arm toward the trees draping over the roof. With the other, she lifted her sunglasses. "Out there?"

He nodded gravely. "I think Oakley might still be alive."

"No! You told me the bitch was dead."

"She might not be. You heard about the person they found in pieces yesterday?"

"Yeah."

"Chubs told me it was a girl he knew. Not Oakley. I

asked some of the other guys, and there was a girl who used to stay with Kaleo named Hazel. She died while on a hunting trip with him three months ago." He waited for comprehension to dawn, but Violet stared at him blankly. He sighed. "If this girl, Hazel, died yesterday, then Kaleo lied about the hunting accident."

"Which means he probably lied about Oakley too."

He tipped her chin up with two fingers. "We need proof. You're the only one I trust." He leaned forward to plant a sweet kiss on her lips. "I need you to find Oakley's body or the bones the dinosaurs left."

"Why can't you go?" Her voice whined like a squeaky violin.

He pulled back. "I have something here I need to do."

It wasn't a lie. His next move would be to undermine the guy Kaleo relied on most. It would take targeted manipulation to turn Chubs.

A small huff, followed by a kick of her heel on the wilted fabric of the lounger.

He jumped up, straddled her, and lowered himself down until their hips were pressed together. "You have to be strong, babe. If we get rid of Kaleo, I'll take over the gang and we'll be set." Sliding a hand along her back, he guided her up closer, pressing their chests together. He claimed her lips in a slow sensual kiss. "Imagine living in the suite with the private pool just outside your bedroom door."

She bit her lower lip. Her wall of fear was crumbling.

"You're the girl who jumped out of a plane to get to

me. You can do this." He rubbed his thumb against her chin. "And I can't do it without you."

One more long kiss, and she gave the answer he'd expected. "Okay."

"Good. And if you find her alive, bring her back so I can kill her."

Her eyes widened in surprise. This was the first time he'd suggested he was a killer. Up until this point, he'd played the innocent, framed patsy. No matter, she had to be all in now. It wasn't like she could go anywhere.

"If she's still alive, we need to get her out of the way." He caressed her cheek. "Bring her back to me."

Jealousy darkened her eyes. He'd gone too far, but getting out of trouble was his specialty. He leaned down to press hot kisses along her neck.

"Why are you obsessed with her?"

He glanced up. The pouting lips at least outranked the petulant whine. "This isn't about her at all. With both Kaleo and Oakley dead, the two of us will be king and queen." He grabbed both of her cheeks in his palms and gave her a big smile. "Then, let's get married."

Marriage didn't mean anything here. Still, his declaration worked. She entwined her fingers in his hair and kissed him hard.

After she pulled back, she said, "King and queen of Extinction Island. I like the sound of that."

They went back to the room to pack a few things for her. An hour later, he sent her out the door with food and water for several days, and a small handgun he'd swiped from the security detail. The gun especially seemed to embolden her. She'd hefted it in her palm a few times and practiced pointing it out the window.

It was too bad he couldn't have simply used the gun to kill Kaleo. He'd never get near Kaleo's room. The man had too many friends in the compound. Daric needed to turn them all against him first.

He headed to the other side of the resort, to the room next to Kaleo's. Chubs wasn't around, so he placed a candy bar on the dresser and settled against the headboard to wait. It didn't take long before Chubs sauntered in, looking like he'd been in the kitchen. A hint of red berries surrounded his mouth. The dude wasn't big by any standard, but he was as glutinous as all teenagers.

"What do you want?" His voice also held the wariness of a teenager.

Daric sat up and dropped his feet to the floor. "I want to give you a choice. Seems like you don't get many of those around here."

Chubs squared his shoulders. He was softening already. This kid didn't have a bit of common sense. Come to think of it, he and Violet had a lot in common.

"What choice?"

Daric stood and locked his hands behind his back in a professorial stance. "The power to choose your enemy."

Chubs threw up his hands. "Would you just get to the point?"

"Fine, I know something is up with Kaleo. I want you to tell me what's going on."

A shifting of his feet. Fear flickered through his eyes. Then he shook his head. "There's nothing weird going on."

"Bad choice." He smacked Chubs on the back of the head, then returned his hands to the small of his back. "This place is full of enemies. You don't want me as one."

"Problem is there are no friends in this place."

"Not true." Daric strode to the dresser and grabbed the chocolate bar he'd lifted from the naturalist's pack. "When was the last time you had some of this?"

Chubs's lips twitched. "Feels like forever."

"I know how to share." He slowly unwrapped it, broke off a piece of the half-melted candy, and handed it to Chubs.

Chubs snatched it, threw it into his mouth, and clamped his lips closed. A long moan sounded as he swallowed.

Daric popped a piece of chocolate into his own mouth and gave his most bored sigh. "Kaleo is soft. You know I'm going to be the head of this crew sooner or later. If you don't want to help me, I'll just kick you out whenever my takeover happens. Could you survive on the outside alone?"

His hands twisted and turned, all remnants of ecstasy gone. He stared at the chipped wood floor. His mouth stayed clamped shut.

No worries. Chubs wouldn't hold out for long. Daric placed the rest of the chocolate bar on the dresser. "I thought you might have something to say. Guess I was wrong. Hope you enjoy the company of Red Grizzly."

A few seconds of silence to let the picture of reality he'd painted become Chubs's view of the future, then he took a slow step toward the door.

No response.

He took another step.

Chubs's head popped up. He darted to the dresser and grabbed another piece of chocolate. Any second now.

Another step, and he was almost out the door. He grabbed the door handle and gave Chubs one last look.

Chubs swallowed the chocolate, then wet his lips. "You're right. I have something to say. Just don't tell anyone *I* said it. Especially Kaleo."

He resisted the urge to smirk. How little it took to get information when using the proper motivation—the promise of protection. Unfortunately for Chubs, once he got the information he needed, he wouldn't have any reason to keep his end of the bargain.

CHAPTER SEVENTEEN

OAKLEY SLIPPED through the trees behind Cane, his tall form moving gracefully. Much different than traveling with Kaleo, who, while still light on his feet, carved a wide trench through the forest.

Shortly after reaching the cave this morning, they'd heard two long blasts from a boat horn. Cane said it signaled an approaching visitor's boat. She'd completely forgotten the prospect of a visit from her dad. In truth, she hadn't expected to live long enough.

Please let him be on this boat. She'd been following Cane for an hour, and her innate sense of direction told her they were getting close. She'd give anything to see Dad's face, but what would he see in hers? She'd aged a thousand years in a mere five days, not just from what she experienced, but also from what she discovered.

Cane brushed aside a low-hanging branch and held it for her as she stepped through. The risks of coming to the landing area set her nerves on edge. If she ran into anyone from the compound, Kaleo's life would be in danger. But Cane had assured her that few of the convicts received visitors anymore.

"Do you ever get visitors?"

"No." He answered without turning around.

His tone closed the subject so she tried a different question. "Why did you come here? Other than Neve, you're probably the only innocent person on this island."

He stopped walking. His shoulders slumped a bit. "Nobody is truly innocent, Oakley." His voice turned to gravel. "I understand that more than most."

He didn't elaborate, simply resumed walking. What could the calm, strong, preacher man have done to mar his innocence? Curiosity nagged at her, but she wouldn't pester him. He deserved his privacy. Last night, he'd cracked open his heart and allowed her to see beyond the man-of-God shell to the real man underneath. Today, though, the religious veneer kept her at a distance.

They broke through the tree line and stepped onto the concrete landing platform where a tall ship had docked, almost identical to the one she'd arrived on. A familiar ebony face turned in their direction.

She should never have left the safety of the trees. She angled her body behind Cane. But it was too late. Taye had already spotted her.

Cane walked forward, exposing her again. What was he doing? They needed to get out of here fast, before anyone else spotted her. If Taye was the only witness to her being alive, maybe the others wouldn't believe his word over Kaleo's.

She searched the landing way. They were alone. Perhaps he intended to bargain with Taye to keep his silence.

Warily, she trudged behind. If bargaining didn't work, how far would Cane go to protect her and Kaleo? How far would she go?

When he reached Taye, he swept his arms out and gave him a hug. Her hesitant steps halted.

Cane glanced over his shoulder at her. "Don't worry, he's one of us."

One of us. Weird, and yet the way he said it didn't sound cultish, more familial.

"I mean, he's a good guy," Cane clarified.

Taye caught her gaze and winked. "My condolences on your loss."

She smiled at his dark reference to her fake death. Hopefully, it meant he wouldn't rat her out to the rest of the gang.

An officer holding an automatic weapon opened a heavy iron door in the hull of the ship. "Taye Turner, you're next."

He stepped through the door and disappeared into the blackness inside. The door slammed closed with a heavy clang.

Cane nudged her in the ribs. "Scared you there for a minute, didn't I? Sorry, I forgot he might be here. His mother still comes to see him anytime she can."

She tried to play off the incident, even though her heart still pumped faster than a sprinting raptor. "How often do the ships come?"

"About once every two months, only if visitors want to come." He gestured to a manifest taped to the side of the ship, too far away for her to read. Only three names were listed on it. "Most of the relatives and loved ones eventually give up. It becomes too hard to witness the pain this place inflicts on a person."

Oakley ran toward the list. A loud click sounded from above, like part of a gun sliding. She froze and craned her neck to the sky. A man pointed a machine gun at the crown of her head.

Cane yelled from behind. "No running. It makes the guys up there nervous."

"Thanks for the tip." Her sarcasm made the guy above twitch so she stayed put. No need to go farther anyway. She could read the list from here. Her heart leaped as she read the name on the bottom—Marcel Laveau.

Dad!

Her whole body felt lighter. She slid backward to stand near Cane. They had to call her name soon, right?

By the time the heavy metal door opened again, impatience had almost worn through her every nerve. Taye walked out with a big smile on his lips. "Next."

An officer behind him called, "Oakley Laveau."

She burst toward the door, then slowed her pace, in deference to the man holding the weapon above. Cane didn't try to come with her, probably couldn't.

The officer led her through a second metal door and into a bathroom-sized room with two chairs and a faded wooden desk. "Arms up," he ordered.

She complied, wincing when he frisked between her legs and under her breasts. When he was satisfied she had no weapons, he guided her roughly toward one of the chairs, then left.

Sitting on the edge, she fidgeted with a loose piece of wood on the corner of the desk. She practiced some deep breathing without much success. Her heart rate just wouldn't slow down.

Several minutes later, a door on the opposite side of the room swung open. A guard came through first, retreated to the corner of the room, and stared straight ahead. Behind him, Dad entered, wearing jeans and a light blue polo shirt with the Asperten logo on it. His fluffed up brown and gray hair was exactly the same, his wrinkles deeper set in his forehead and mouth. His eyes met hers with a sheen of grateful desperation. "You're okay."

Looking down, she gave her appearance a once over. At the cave this morning, she'd changed into a clean, slightly-too-big, yellow T-shirt, a color that reminded her of Monica, but her jeans were streaked with dirt. She brushed a hand over the soil on her legs. "I'm fine."

His eyes misted over. She'd never seen his spirit so broken. "Dad?"

"They told me you were dead," he said under his breath.

This place had tried to kill her many times over, but still, "Why?"

He put a hand on her arm.

"No touching." The guard came to life for a few seconds. When her dad moved his hand away, he went back to his impassive stare focused on the far wall.

Dad kept his voice to a low whisper. "An FBI agent came to the house to tell me you were dead." He reached out like he wanted to touch her face, stopping just short. "Your tracker ceased working two days ago."

Two days ago? About the same time she'd electrocuted the *Velociraptor*. She rubbed at the spot on her shoulder where the tracker had been implanted. Could she have shorted it out? Without thinking, she also rubbed at her right eye, which had begun to twitch, probably just her body remembering all of the pain after the implantation procedure.

Dad stayed focused on her as if waiting for an answer. She couldn't tell him much. Certainly not the truth. He either wouldn't understand her new ability—she refused to call it a gift no matter how much Cane insisted God had orchestrated their creation—or he would think she was crazy. Besides, what if they were recording this? She couldn't afford to announce her ability to anyone who might be listening. "I guess the tracker must have been faulty."

"Shh," Dad whispered. "I got on this boat last minute without telling the FBI." He glanced over his shoulder at the guard. "These guys have no orders regarding you right now. Your situation could change soon."

It took a few seconds for her to decipher his cryptic words. After discovering her alive, the government would want her tracker replaced. No way would she go under the knife again.

Time to change the subject before the guard got suspicious. "How is Eric?"

"Eric and Felice are fine. He misses you a lot."

She nodded and swallowed past the lump in her throat. "Dad, I need to ask you some strange questions. Please, bear with me." Her shoulders tensed, and she forced them to relax. She needed these answers. "Was I adopted?"

He reared back in his seat. "Of course not."

"You and Mom are both my biological parents?"

His tense look made her cringe. "Yes, Oakley. What's this about?"

She folded her hands in her lap. "It's just ... well ... I've noticed some unusual traits about myself. I'm wondering where they could have come from."

He looked like he might bristle again, then he slumped, his face sagging into those well-worn wrinkles.

When he stayed silent, she pushed ahead. "Tell me something about Mom that I don't know."

He gave a too-quick smile. "Your beautiful eyes are hers."

"I know that much."

He pinched the bridge of his nose. "She was brilliant, a thinker. She loved to talk about everything. It was how she made connections, not just with people, also in science. She'd be talking one minute about the lasagna and the next about the layers in the human genome." He ran a hand through his hair causing it to stick up even more in front. "And she couldn't organize anything to save her life. I was forever searching for her stuff. Car keys, paperwork, her driver's license. One time, she lost your chocolate bunny between the time she bought it and Easter. We got you a new one, though we never did find where she hid the first one. It's probably still in the house somewhere."

She smiled at him. "You obviously loved her. Why didn't you get married?"

"I wanted to, especially when we found out about the pregnancy. She was too into her work. She kept saying we would think about it once things slowed down for her. Years went by, and then ..."

She waited for him to go on. When he didn't, she prodded, "Then, what?"

He crossed his arms over his chest. "She died."

An image of her mother hovering over her flooded into her mind, her mother's expression twisted in agony. She pushed the vision away and squeaked out her next words. "Was it because of me?"

His face registered resignation, not the shock appropriate for the question. "What happened to her was complicated. I know she loved you."

Complicated. What did that mean? The shift in his

eyes and the twitch in the corner of his mouth gave him away. His expressions were as familiar to her as her own. He was lying.

She tried to remember the little bits he'd told her over the years. Her mother died at Thibodaux Regional Medical Center after a year in a coma. He'd never told her what caused the brain injury.

Another image swamped her, pulling her under. Her mother with hair askew and a blurry face, unfocused, as if she were underwater. Just as quickly, the image shifted position. Rather than becoming more focused, the face morphed into her father, also murky, his mouth turned down in a scowl.

She pressed her fingers to her temples. *Focus.* "What did Mom do at Asperten?"

Dad shifted in the seat, averting his gaze. "I don't know."

Most often, he was her father, not a researcher at a genetics company. Now, his upright posture and defensive air made it clear she was talking to the Asperten loyalist in him. "How could you not know? You both worked at the same place."

"We worked in different divisions. I was in Chemical Research. Your mom headed up the Biological Research Division."

Biological research sounded like a veiled term for DNA manipulation. "What kind of biological research?"

She fingered one of her mother's silver fleur-de-lis earrings. With a start, she focused on the emblem on her father's Asperten shirt. The fleur-de-lis held a prominent place in the logo. Her mother had also been an Asperten loyalist, even down to her earrings. Had her mother used the labs there to change her at the most basic level—her genes?

Dad pushed his fingers through his hair. "I just don't know."

It didn't look like that to her. But what had she expected him to say? *Yes, Oakley, your mother messed with your DNA, made you deadly, then left me to deal with it all.*

"Did Mom talk about goals for the research?"

He pressed his eyes shut. When he opened them, their green hue looked less like the first buds of spring and more like an approaching storm. "I know it's your way to push and push until you get answers. I can't go there."

She leaned forward in the chair. "Dad, I *have* to go there."

He looked at her—really looked at her—for the first time since she'd sat down. "There's something going on with you, isn't there?"

She nodded mutely.

His mouth fell open, and she wanted to take her admission back. He shot another look over his shoulder at the guard before returning his gaze to her. "I can't give you anything."

The door from which she'd entered swung open behind her and banged into the wall. The guard drew his weapon and pointed it over her shoulder.

She spun around.

Raptor stood in the doorway, both hands up, one hand holding out his government identification badge. "Easy. I'm one of the good guys. Never even had a parking ticket."

After looking at the badge, the guard reholstered his weapon and resumed his passive position. "Five minutes left," he grumbled.

Raptor dropped the ID on the table, grabbed her by the upper arms, and hauled her out of the chair, capturing her in a massive hug.

"No touching!" The guard put a hand on his holster for emphasis.

"Oh, right. Sorry." Raptor released her.

She fell back into the chair like a rag doll. From the huge smile on his face, he'd thought she was dead as well.

He leaned down to whisper in her ear. "The whole parking ticket thing was a lie. Don't tell him, but I once ran over a meter maid. Accidentally, of course."

She laughed in spite of herself.

He shifted his gaze to Dad. "Marcel. Guess what? Oakley is alive!"

Dad's smile was forced. "Yes, Ogden, it's a good day."

Raptor looked back and forth between them for a minute. "I get the feeling this conversation has been serious. Along that note, I've got something to show you both." He pulled his cell phone from his back pocket, opened the screen, and held it out for her to look. "Do you know this guy?"

Her heart thundered in her chest. "It's Jim Durham. He was with Monica and me the night before she died."

"Yeah. He said his name was Jim." Raptor peered closer at her. "He was looking for you."

Why would he be looking for her? It was supposed to be the other way around. Did he also want answers as to what happened to Monica?

Raptor turned the picture to face her father. His skin blanched and his lip trembled. For a moment, he said nothing, and then his voice came out in a thin stream. "His name's not Jim."

"You know him?" she asked.

"That's Adler Calais. He works in security." Dad swallowed hard. "At Asperten."

Raptor swept the phone into his back pocket. "He told me he was a paleontologist who happened to see Oakley's trial and wanted to check on her. Why would this guy lie to me and obsessively follow Oakley?"

The question was directed at her dad, but the unintentional accusation cut her deep as well. Somehow Jim—or rather, Adler—had to know what she could do. But how? Had he seen her electrocute Monica? If so, that should have made him fearful, not obsessed. Unless he was obsessed with her in the same way Violet was with Daric. And then there was the convenient fact that Adler worked for the same company as her mother and father. Too much of a coincidence.

She smacked her hands on the desk. The guard flinched. "Dad, you have to tell me what Mom was doing."

"Oakley, I love you." A halting breath came from his lips. "I just can't help you right now."

She held a frustrate scream inside, mostly because of the officer in the corner. "You mean, you won't help. Why not?"

"I have to think of Felice and your brother."

Eric's freckled, smiling face rose in her mind. Dad thought talking about her mother would jeopardize Eric? "I don't understand."

He scooted his chair back, preparing to leave. "You need to stay here, Oakley."

Her stomach flipped over and rolled with nausea. How could he tell her to stay here? She'd probably die here. Didn't he care? Even if she had killed Monica, she didn't deserve this. It would have been an accident, wouldn't it? She opened her mouth, but all of her arguments died on her lips. Since she couldn't remember, the truth remained a mystery.

The guard moved away from the wall. "Time's up."

Dad stood and shuffled toward the other door. "Stay away from Adler. He's dangerous."

Apparently, he thought she was too if he felt she needed to stay here. "But Adler's here. How can you leave me here with him?" The little girl whine preceded the tears burning her eyes. It was ridiculous to think Dad would show up and whisk her away. He couldn't, even if he'd wanted to, though she'd expected him to at least want to.

As he disappeared through the door, Raptor put an

arm around her shoulders. Behind them, the door opened to reveal another guard waiting to escort them out. If she refused to leave, they would literally throw her out of the ship's hull.

Raptor took the lead, pulling her along by the wrist. Her insides were burning to ashes, but she would do what she always did, stay strong and move forward.

When they emerged, Raptor introduced himself to Cane. They'd known of each other, even though they had never officially met. Cane's cave of refuge was a closely held secret. For a moment, she opened her mouth to spill *her* most closely guarded secret to Raptor. Something held her back. Maybe it was because he'd look at her differently when he realized she had likely killed Monica. Or maybe it was to spare him from hiding information from his government contacts.

He gave her another huge hug. "So does Kaleo know you're not dead?"

"Yes, we faked my death to get me out of the compound."

"Ah, good. I knew I liked him." Raptor crossed his arms, causing his muscles to bulge. "I'll hunt for Adler to get some answers as to why he's here. I wish I could take you back to the research station, but I'm not supposed to have anyone there, and they have cameras." He waved a hand at Cane. "Are you safe with him?"

She didn't hesitate. "Yes."

"Okay. Promise me you won't wander around more than necessary."

"I promise. And thank you for coming to look for me."

He tilted his head and gave a sardonic smile. "Anytime. If you need to find me, I'll keep close to the research station for a while. It's near Lemon Creek. Do you know where it is?"

She shook her head.

"I do," Cane said.

Seemingly satisfied, he disappeared into the trees on their left. As Oakley and Cane slipped into the jungle to head back to the cave, she filled him in on everything: her dad's visit, her connection to Raptor, and Adler Calais.

"Should I tell Raptor about my ability?" she asked.

Cane stopped so abruptly she ran into his back. "Absolutely not."

"I trust him."

He gently squeezed her arm. "It's not about trust. If this Adler guy is here looking for you, it could be because of your ability. Telling Raptor might put him in danger. It's the same reason my adoptive mother never gave me any answers."

She took the opportunity to ask more about his background. "What do you mean?"

He released her arm and resumed walking next to her. "My biological mom gave me up in a private adoption to Amy LeBlanc. Amy raised me as hers and was an amazing mom right up until the day she died from breast cancer. When she knew the cancer would beat her, she sat me down and told me what she wanted me to know about my real mother. Until that day, I didn't know I was adopted."

Wow! His pain didn't soften the blow of her own dad's betrayal, but at least she'd had him, and her mom, in her life.

"Amy and my biological mom forged my birth certificate stating Amy was my mother. Presumably, Amy had gotten pregnant out of wedlock, and thus they didn't name the father. She told me they did it to protect me."

"Protect you from what?"

"I don't know. I've always assumed my father was abusive and they were hiding me from him. If he abused me or my mother, then I didn't care to know who he was, but I did want to learn the name of my biological mother." He let out a prolonged sigh. "Amy wouldn't tell me. She took my mother's name to her grave. For a year, I couldn't forgive her."

"How did you get past it?"

He shrugged. "I loved her too much to stay angry. Now, I just miss her."

Oakley tried to focus on her own mother. The images were too blurry to make sense. She had missed her presence in a way, though not because of shared memories.

He swiped a hand down his face. "All this to say, no one knows about my ability. This guy is here for you, and we're at a disadvantage because we don't know why."

She stopped, forcing him to stop as well. "Maybe Adler has answers. Somebody had to create us this way." The more they learned, the more it looked like Asperten was the common link.

He gave her his full attention, saying nothing.

"Don't you want to know who did this to us?"

A sad shake of his head. "It doesn't matter to me. If they messed with my DNA, God created that DNA. He knew this would happen. Whoever did the twisting of the gene itself is inconsequential."

She mimicked his head shake. "I really don't understand your faith."

He chuckled at her imitation of him, though the intense sea-green of his eyes was somber. "Believe me, if I could pluck my faith right out of my heart and give it to you, I would."

Cane wanting to share a part of his heart with her caused a warm rush to flow through her. Calm, confident Cane. His quiet peace was so different from Kaleo's passionate stubbornness. Why was she drawn to both of them? Or maybe what tugged on her heart was the one thing they had in common—their innate goodness.

CHAPTER EIGHTEEN

KALEO PUSHED ASIDE a clump of leaves to check behind a thick bush. Rummaging through the courtyard first thing in the morning to look for evidence of Red Grizzly wasn't his brightest idea.

In fact, Chubs had accused him of having a death wish. But ever since Oakley left, just two nights before, he'd lost interest in keeping up appearances. Some of the guys were starting to whisper behind his back. If he didn't pull himself together soon, he'd face life or death consequences in his own domain.

Problem was, he'd finally let down his guard to show someone the real person underneath. Now, he couldn't stomach the lie any longer. Even the time he spent hunting with Taye yesterday hadn't eased his sense of isolation. He was alone in a jungle prison with twenty men who would judge his every move and kill him if he made a mistake. Strange how it had never bothered him before.

Behind a tangle of vines, a smudged footprint caught his eye. Fresh, made within the last twenty-four hours, and from a large raptor. It fit within the timeline of Hazel's death. A tiny prick of sorrow pierced his chest. Hazel was pushy and irritating, but she hadn't deserved to die. He'd sent her away to protect her, just like he had with Oakley.

What was Oakley doing now? Was she curled up next to Cane? The traitorous thought stole his breath. It didn't matter. As long as she was safe, let her stay close to Cane. But his hypocritical heart wrenched at the image.

Movement in his peripheral vision caused him to spin around and grab his whip. The length unfurled in a swoosh to the ground. Adrenaline shot through his veins as a *Velociraptor* jumped from the bushes, landing five feet in front of him. It swayed side to side, sizing him up. Had it been patrolling the same bushes?

Patrolling. The word struck a chord.

Could Red Grizzly be smart enough to leave a guard in its newly discovered hunting territory? It's what Kaleo would have done if he'd found a whole mass of prey in one location. On the other hand, maybe this guy just happened to come around, lured by the smell of recent death. But this raptor hadn't been deterred by the high frequency sound either. As the animal swayed, he noticed thin pads of mud covering each ear hole. He blinked and checked again. There was no mistaking the ear plugs. Not only was Red Grizzly capable of learning, it was teaching other raptors ... teaching them to hunt humans.

A tight knot coiled in his gut. At least this animal wouldn't be around long enough to hurt anyone. Kaleo cracked the whip on the ground. Leaves and dirt flew up from the impact.

The raptor crouched in an attack position, concerned, though not alarmed.

He snapped the whip inches in front of the raptor's toes. It jumped. Instead of jumping backward, it leaped at him.

Kaleo sidestepped, avoiding the attack, but he had only seconds to finish this. Raptors didn't typically kill on the frontal assault. They charged to get a sense of the speed of their prey, then hit the ground, pivoted, and made the kill with a faster rear attack.

Keeping his front facing the raptor, he repositioned to hold the whip high over his head. When the raptor leaped at him again, it wouldn't have time to sense the downdraft coming from overhead.

But this raptor did something unexpected. It pivoted and rushed at him from the ground—no leaping. It ran with claws extended, mouth open, and muscles twitching.

His whip would take a fraction of a second too long to slam down on the animal. The claws would reach his belly first.

Instinct deep in his gut took over. With the flick of his wrist, he adjusted the strike to swipe sideways.

The whip curved in a tight arc, slicing through the air, heading for the raptor's neck.

The raptor covered the distance between them in less than a second—its hooked sickle claw only inches from the tender flesh of his abdomen.

This would be close. He held his breath as the thick part of the whip struck its neck, penetrating the skin enough to stun the animal and knock it to the side by several feet. The claw sailed just past his side.

Before it could recover, he jumped backward and swung the whip again, this time aiming with the more deadly, thinner portion of the whip.

A crack sounded as the cord sliced clean through the raptor's already damaged neck. Blood gushed from the stump as its head flew into the bushes. The bulk of the animal lay bleeding on Kaleo's feet.

He drew in a slow breath to ease his racing heart. Too close.

When his pulse returned to normal, he cleaned the whip by swiping it through a bush. Then, he grabbed several large banana leaves and wrapped them around the body of the raptor. He hoisted the bundle to his shoulder. This sixty-pound animal would provide fifteen pounds of meat for the men.

He walked up to a small bush where the head had come to rest. The black eyes stared up at the sky, just as menacing in death. He brought his leg back and kicked the head a dozen yards into the jungle. If this dinosaur was some sort of guard, let Red Grizzly discover what happens when its prey escapes the cage.

▭

CANE WATCHED Oakley's hips sway to the rhythm of her steps as she walked in front of him. *Avoid ogling; keep your eyes down; the ground is the most dangerous part of the jungle.* The self-talk wasn't working. Oakley wore one of Neve's gauzy shirts, a light green one, and his attention kept drifting to how it clung to her in all the right places.

Built tiny, but curvaceous, she carried herself with an easy grace. Though he wouldn't call her feisty, she exuded a compelling inner strength. Not unlike Princess Leia from *Star Wars*. Oh, how his mom—a five-foot-ten-inch-tall stocky woman—had loved Princess Leia's character. One year she'd bought the white filmy costume, a material similar to the shirt Oakley now wore. When she tried the costume on, she ripped the fabric down the length of the side. Her reaction still made him smile. *We weren't made to wear costumes anyway, Cane. God wants us to be who we are.*

He'd always tried to follow that advice, but maybe Oakley had a point. How could he know who he was if he didn't know where he'd come from?

Who am I? Pastor of hidden sheep, sinner making amends, and killing machine.

Except knowing where the killing machine part came

from wouldn't change his struggle. It would only give him a target to blame.

A wet leaf smacked him in the face. He'd better focus his sleepy mind and pay more attention. Last night—Oakley's first night in the cave—had left him nearly sleepless. He tossed all night thinking about her. Was she comfortable? Was she struggling with nightmares like she did when Kaleo brought her in unconscious? That day, she'd whimpered and mumbled something about her mother before she woke up. Perhaps there was more buried in her subconscious than she suspected.

Shifting the bow and quiver on his shoulder, he blinked and scanned the foliage. He'd allowed Oakley to take the lead to give her more experience surveying the jungle, but if he didn't concentrate, she might lead them astray or they might get ambushed. "Take the left fork in the path. It will keep to the highlands where there are fewer dinosaurs and take us to the area where you saw Adler. Plus, it's cooler."

The weather near the cave stayed in the upper seventies, although the humidity made it feel warmer. At the higher elevations, like at the resort compound, the humidity turned into a cool cloud. The cloud forest, with its panoramic views and mild temperatures, was his favorite place in Costa Rica.

They traversed a small creek, no more than six-inches deep. He tapped her shoulder and pointed along the waterway. "Raptor is staying somewhere along here, probably much deeper into the jungle. This is the headwaters of Lemon Creek."

"Okay, thanks."

As they continued on, the shimmy of her hips again distracted him as she squeezed around a vine curtain hanging between two trees. He followed, also turning his body and looking above to scan for any threats. Snakes and poisonous spiders tended to drop down when least expected. He twisted straight again, and a blur of movement out of the corner of his eye brought him to full attention.

The blur vanished, leaving only dark foliage. His blood went ice cold and survival instinct kicked in.

No time to grab his bow and notch an arrow. Not a moment to explain. He grabbed Oakley and rolled her up in his arms. She let out a surprised yelp, but gave herself over to him quickly.

He sprinted downhill, cradling her in his arms.

From over his shoulder, a faint swoosh, then the click of snapping jaws. A low growl rumbled as the creature chased them along the slope.

She sucked in a quick breath, her arms clamping around his neck. He ignored the seductive feel of her and focused on their escape. The ground shook behind them. He tightened his thighs to keep his balance and continued running. Camocroc's stubby front legs couldn't handle the strain of a steep slope.

They had almost gotten away, but then the terrain leveled out. They came into a small clearing with one large tree in the center. He let her down as he tried to orient himself.

From upslope, thunderous steps continued to charge down. No more incline and very little time until Camocroc would be upon them.

A set of familiar trees sat at the edge of the jungle. This was a clearing he'd come through about six months ago, while being pursued by a territorial *Triceratops*. As he tried to escape, he stumbled into a trap and almost killed himself.

He grabbed Oakley's hand. "This way."

She pulled back, her head shaking vigorously. "I've got an idea."

The ground beneath their feet vibrated. He glanced back. Small trees splintered a dozen yards up the hill. They didn't have time for this discussion.

He returned his gaze to her. She was inspecting the forked trunk of the large tree in the middle of the clearing. "It's strong enough."

He grabbed her hand again. "We have to go."

"We can stop that thing right here." She stripped her stretchy ponytail holder out of her hair. "All you have to do is stand behind the tree and wrap this around its mouth."

"What?" He took the ponytail holder, then hesitated. The elastic hair tie was larger than most, but how was this supposed to hold Camocroc's mouth closed? He had to make a choice: trust her or drag her away.

A small cedar tree at the edge of the clearing fell with a snap. They'd run out of time.

"Go," she whispered and shoved him around the tree.

Just before his sight line would be cut off by the trunk, he looked across the clearing. The mottled image of a not-quite-camouflaged *Saurosuchus* barreled toward Oakley. His feet shifted to race back out there, but he would be too late.

The creature opened its massive jaws, teeth glistening with saliva. His heart clenched in fear. It would bite her in half before he could yank her from its path.

She remained passive, seemingly relaxed. He reached for her arm, knowing it was futile. Before he could touch her, she leaped to the far side of the tree.

Camocroc missed her by inches, its momentum carrying its body smack into the V-shaped fork in the tree. Its head lodged between the two sections of the trunk.

His mouth dropped open. She'd intended to trap the animal. He scrambled to the rear of the tree, stretched the ponytail holder as far as it would go, and flung it over the flailing jaws.

The jaws snapped closed as if forced by the hand of God and didn't open again. The creature struggled, its jaw muscles tensing, but the mouth didn't open. He couldn't explain it.

She touched his arm. "Now, we should go."

He nodded mutely, following her until they were a hundred yards away, where he stopped and stared at her. "How did that work?"

She smiled, and he found himself caring less about the explanation and more about keeping the smile on her face. "I figured a *Saurosuchus* would be similar to modern crocodiles. Crocs have a bite strength of several tons per square inch; you don't want to be on the closing end of their jaw. But the muscles to open their mouth are weak. You can hold a crocodile's mouth closed with a rubber band. That ponytail holder is somewhat stronger than a rubber band, although Camocroc is much bigger than a regular crocodile. It will escape eventually."

"I'm impressed."

She gave another small smile, then let out a growl not much different from the reptile. "I don't understand it. That crocodile freak-show seems to follow me everywhere. There's no way I still smell like gators from my old job."

"Guess I'm not the only one who's attracted to you." The shocking words popped out before he could stop them. He laughed to play it off as a joke. The sound fell flat. Kaleo's presence overwhelmed the moment. Any fool could tell they felt something for each other. He shouldn't even be looking at her out of respect for Kaleo. He cleared his throat. "At least, your pet dinosaur is safe. Good thing you left him in the cave. I think Neve is in love with him."

Oakley playfully pushed at his arm. "Come on. I saw Cody curled up next to you after dinner last night."

"Busted." He tapped his chin. "Sometimes I have the same problem, where a dinosaur takes a special interest in me."

"How do you handle it?"

"Usually I have to kill it." With his outstretched arm, he gestured for her to continue leading the way. "Are you sure you want to find this Adler guy? What if he's dangerous, like your dad said?"

"I think it's worth the risk. I need to talk to him." She raised her eyebrows, probably expecting him to guilt her into turning back because she'd promised Raptor she'd stay inside as much as possible. But guilt wasn't his style.

He also hadn't missed the other unspoken question implied by her expression—the one she'd voiced yesterday. *Don't you want to know?* The answer was complicated.

"Are you afraid we'll find out something bad?" she asked as she started to walk.

"Like what?" He tried to play it casual, but her insight was spot on. Seemed they both could read each other easily.

"I don't know. Bad family history, maybe." She paused and looked over her shoulder, a hint of amusement lightening her baby blues. "Maybe we really are related."

He groaned and raised his eyes to the sky. "Please, Lord, don't let the most beautiful woman I've met in ages be related to me. That would be cruel."

A lovely blush crept up the back of her neck. He smiled in satisfaction until her gaze fell to the ground. "You won't end up with someone like me."

She had to be referencing the dark stain of murder coloring her past. But she had no idea about the awful things he'd done. Besides, the past was history. God could make all things new.

He captured her hand. "Oakley, I think you're very special."

When she turned her eyes up, they flashed fear.

He grinned to lighten the mood. "Don't be afraid of me. I'm not afraid of you."

She tugged on his hand, not seeking escape, but more likely seeking answers. Her voice was a hoarse whisper. "What did you do?"

"Excuse me?"

"There's something hidden in your eyes."

His breath caught in his throat. How could she tell? *A bloated face. Legs immobile in death. The hint of almonds.* The flashbacks still threatened to paralyze him. He pulled his hand away.

Rather than look perturbed at his silence, she merely took the lead again.

As she spun away from him, he whispered, "I can't."

CHAPTER NINETEEN

OAKLEY PUSHED her loose hair away from her face as she examined the rocky edge of the cliff. Several areas of flattened grass provided clues to where a person might have stood. Not quite a week ago, Adler stared at her transport ship from this exact spot, but no evidence pointed her toward where he might be now. What had she been expecting? Certainly not a painted sign saying Adler went this way. It had been a long shot, but she had to try something. Hopefully, Raptor was having more luck with his search.

After scrutinizing the area one more time for any sort of path with no success, she turned to Cane. "Let's go."

He gave her a strained smile and took the lead this time. Ever since she'd brought up his past, he'd gone quiet. No longer playful or flirtatious, he was deep in thought.

When he'd called her beautiful a few moments ago, she'd kept her stoic veneer on the outside. Inside, her pulse had quickened. Tall, muscular, funny, and so unbelievably good, just about any girl would love to make him happy. But was she that girl?

She shook her head to clear it and took a deep breath of the cool air. Her messed-up insides didn't matter. Finding Adler had to be her first priority. She followed behind Cane, while brainstorming other places to look. She could only hope Adler had stayed on the island and away from the dinosaurs.

A loud ricochet reverberated through the trees ahead of them. It sounded like a gunshot.

Cane took a few steps toward the sound, then turned to her, motioning for her to stay put. She nodded. If it was someone from the compound, she couldn't be seen. As he disappeared from view, she glanced around at the dense trees. Was she safer away from the person who'd shot the gun or alone out here with the dinosaurs? Not to mention the terrifying possibility of another attack from Camocroc, who appeared to be following her.

After checking the branches for hanging snakes, she leaned against the nearest tree, ready to climb at a moment's notice. Several frogs chirped and croaked from a small wetland just down the hill. She crossed her arms and waited. The soothing sounds caused her heartbeat to slow, though the tension in her shoulders remained.

Maybe she needed to rub some reptile deterrent on her clothes. Lizards hated the smell of garlic or eggs, but she might not be able to stand being around herself if she smelled like one of them. There was another substance she'd learned about in class that repelled reptiles. What was it? She delved deep into her brain to pull up the information from her Ecology of Reptiles class. It was coffee.

She didn't normally drink it, but she could tolerate the smell. Neve tended a few coffee plants near the cave. She would have to grab some when she got back.

A soft footstep sounded behind her. Had Cane circled around?

She pushed off the tree to investigate, sliding between a set of hanging vines. Avoiding any sticks, she padded quietly on the leaves. The birds continued to chirp. The frogs croaked. No other sounds interrupted them.

When she didn't find anything notable, she headed back to where Cane had left her. Quick, loud steps crunched behind her. Before she could spin around, a hand clamped over her mouth.

She tried to scream. The sound came out muffled. A small, strong arm wrapped underneath her armpits and dragged her backward into the leaves.

She scrambled to get her feet under her, but the person kept pulling, keeping her off balance. Her feet pinwheeled, useless in the brush.

Whoever it was had several inches on her and therefore, better leverage. Yet, this person didn't seem as tall and wide as most of the men around here. She struggled for at least thirty feet before the person dropped her on the ground. She hit her shoulder on a fallen log and groaned.

Pressing a hand against the log, she lifted her torso.

"Stay down." The voice was gruff, female, and vaguely familiar.

She flipped her hair out of her face and looked up.

Violet. A gun rested in her left hand, pointed at the ground.

Cold fingers of alarm tripped down Oakley's spine as she put the pieces together. Violet had fired a shot ahead of them to lure Cane away, then circled around to grab her. Why was she searching for her? Had something happened to Kaleo?

"You look pretty good for a dead girl."

"How did you find me?"

"Patience and good ears. You thought no one would question Kaleo, and if they did, they would find the place he dumped you and believe you'd been taken by a dinosaur. Not all of us are blindly loyal or stupid."

"Daric sent you after me." Oakley paused for a second to give emphasis to her next words. "By yourself."

Violet blinked, a small crack in her tough facade. She quickly pasted on another haughty look and tightened her grip on the gun. Oakley had misjudged her. She wasn't so much fooled by Daric, she wanted to be just like him—strong, cold, and in control—but deep down, she had to know he didn't care about her.

"Let me guess. He had something else he had to do, so he sent you into the dangerous jungle alone to bring me in. Sounds like love."

The gun trembled in Violet's hand. "More like a test."

"Of what?"

She raised the gun a few degrees. "My loyalty. My ability."

The word *ability* resonated inside Oakley, triggering the cascade of shame and fear. But her misgivings about using her ability didn't seem relevant. Electrocution wouldn't do anything against a gun. "Seriously, how did you know I wasn't dead?"

A smug smile played across Violet's face. "Daric suspected the other dead girl was one of Kaleo's women from before you came along. He just couldn't prove it. There wasn't enough left of her."

"Other dead girl?"

"After you left, a woman was killed by Red Grizzly."

A swell of nausea ran through her. Cane had been looking for Hazel when he arrived. Obviously, she didn't make it to see Kaleo. Even Hazel didn't deserve to die so cruelly.

"You can only blame yourself," Violet continued. "If you and your other boyfriend hadn't been at the top of a hill chatting away, I might never have found you." With her free hand, she brushed the bangs off her forehead. The jagged outline of a scar cut through the pale skin by her hairline. Perhaps she had experience with violent men other than Daric. "When the gang sees you're alive, they'll kill Kaleo and hunt down your other boytoy. Then, Daric will take over, and he'll owe it all to me."

Oakley couldn't let that happen. She examined Violet's stance: rigid, inflexible, and straight up. Not unlike the stiff-legged alligators she had wrestled at the

Lazy Lizard while helping Raptor take blood samples. Taking Violet down shouldn't be much harder. Yes, she had the height advantage, but if Oakley could get on top, she could use Violet's leverage against her. Plus, she had her own key advantage—speed.

If Violet was the alligator, then the gun was the sharp teeth. Oakley needed to get in her blind spot and avoid the teeth while pinning the woman. Simple. In theory.

"Get up and walk," Violet demanded.

As she stood, Violet followed her movements with the barrel of the gun. This presented a problem. She couldn't attack Violet with the gun pointing right at her. Alligators had several blind spots, but Violet would have only one, behind her.

Oakley faked left, then spun in a circle to the right. The gun tracked left. By the time Violet realized she had spun in the other direction, she was already behind her.

With a vicious kick, she took out Violet's knees, sending her falling to the ground. She swung the gun wildly, aiming backward.

Oakley dropped one knee into her back. The other knee landed hard on her elbow, pinning her to the ground. The weapon slid from her hand and along the carpet of leaves.

Not far enough. With her arm held tight, Violet still struggled to get closer to the gun. Bucking and lurching against Oakley, inch by inch, she would win the battle by sheer weight. Better to get rid of the weapon completely.

Oakley flipped her knees out to roll over so they were

back to back, then she swung her leg and kicked the gun into the forest. It clattered through branches and under-brush until it disappeared.

The move had cost her valuable leverage.

Violet twisted her hips and managed to throw Oakley off her back.

She jumped up just as Violet did. They faced each other, arms out, fists clenched. In a straight up fight, Violet would win easily. Oakley hesitated for a long moment. She could make a run for it. But if she escaped, Violet would go back and confirm Daric's suspicions. They'd never stop hunting her or Cane until they took Kaleo down.

Maybe she could stall the fight. They weren't far from the place Cane left her. He'd have to come back soon. But if he did, what would they do with Violet? The cave had no means to keep someone prisoner. Capturing her meant risking her escape—and risking the lives of Kaleo and Cane.

Violet lunged at her and missed. They faced each other again, both cautious about their next move.

"Would you like a little sneak peek into what will happen when Daric takes over?" Violet asked. "You and your boyfriends will be slathered in blood, tied up, and left for the raptors. I hope Red Grizzly gets all of you."

Heat surged through her blood. Only an evil person could wish that on someone. "Who were you before all of this?"

Keeping her body poised to strike, Violet took a step

back at the question. Several seconds went by before she answered. "A medical examiner."

Made sense. Violet must have been obsessed with death before Daric came along and gave her a glimpse of the killing side. The Daric-is-innocent line had been a complete act.

A slug of bitterness and anger bubbled up from within Oakley, chilling her veins and freezing her heart. She didn't have to lose this fight. She had more control over her life than she'd ever had. More control over other people's lives. But could she live with what needed to be done?

Violet dove at her, arms grasping for her waist.

She leaped out of the way, barely avoiding contact. Violet quickly regained her footing, centered on her again, and snarled.

In only a few minutes, they had come to a stalemate. Violet wouldn't give up. Oakley wouldn't let herself be killed or taken. No matter which way she dissected the situation, only unacceptable options emerged.

Her silence and inaction continued to anger Violet, whose face contorted into a wrinkled mass of rage. Oakley braced herself for another attack.

Then, Violet shifted her stance and ran past her into the bushes on her right. Oakley eased toward the bushes on the opposite side, keeping an eye on the area where Violet had disappeared. Surely, she hadn't given up so easily.

Too late, Violet's plan became clear. She had entered

the bushes at the same spot where Oakley had kicked the gun.

Before Oakley could get lost in the foliage, Violet darted back out, weapon in hand. "You're coming with me."

She froze in place. No doubt Violet would kill her if she didn't comply. Worse, if Cane came looking for them, she would kill him too.

Time seemed to slow with every second punctuated by a crashing heartbeat. Her head ached and pounded in sync with her pulse. Her tortured brain struggled to come up with other options. Eliminating Violet was the only way to protect the men she cared about.

She sucked in a deep breath, then let it out slowly. "Fine. You win." She held her hands together in front.

Violet stared at her, her eyebrows quirked skeptically.

"Here, I'll make it easy for you." She turned around and held her hands behind her back.

Violet grabbed her wrists, entwining a rough cord around them. Oakley concentrated, nurturing the painful spark of bitterness until it grew into a blazing fire of hatred. How dare Violet threaten the two best men on this island? How dare she hunt down Oakley when all she wanted to do was survive? Violet could have let this go, returned to Daric without searching for long, but she'd escalated the situation.

No way out.

The migraine pressed against her eyes. Sharp tingles crawled along her scalp, raced through her chest, and along her arms. She pushed the fiery voltage through her hands.

Her vision faded in and out like black and white static as her head continued to pulse in pain. Violet's hands clamped down, her muscles seizing in response to the electricity. Their bodies rocked back and forth together for a long moment, the current vibrating between them.

The crackle of something sizzling. The sickening smell of fried skin. Spikes of pain jabbed through her fingertips.

Finally, the pulse ebbed away, and with it, the rocking slowed. Violet fell to the ground with a thump.

Oakley dropped beside her. She didn't pass out, but her vision spun and clammy goosebumps trailed down her arms. She pressed her eyes closed briefly. When she opened them, her gaze met the sightless eyes staring up from Violet's dead shell. Her eyeballs still sat in their sockets, yet they bulged like a grotesque cartoon animal. Patches of her skin had blistered and smoke drifted from the ends of her hair.

Oakley covered her nose and mouth, taking shallow breaths. She needed to leave, but couldn't make her legs move. The muscles in her arms and torso shook uncontrollably as the current dissipated.

In a flurry of leaves, Cane broke through the trees in front of her. He took in Violet's dead body as he knelt beside Oakley. "Are you okay?"

She nodded, her throat too dry to form words.

He ran his hands down her arms before he leaned back, apparently convinced she was unharmed.

She moistened her dry tongue. "How did you find me?"

"I followed the smell."

After another glance at Violet, he leaned forward again. With gentle fingers, he brushed stray hairs from Oakley's cheek. She searched his eyes for disappointment and saw only sadness mixed with compassion.

"You're in a precarious position, Oakley."

"How? She's dead."

"That's not what I mean." He cupped her chin, forcing her to keep staring into his soft green eyes. "You have godlike powers with no spiritual compass. It's a dangerous place to be."

She pulled away and pressed clenched fists to her chest. Was he trying to say she shouldn't have killed Violet? Right or wrong, she'd do anything to protect the people she cared about. "*Someone* created me to kill." At the start of his objection, she shook her head to silence him. "And it wasn't God."

CHAPTER TWENTY

"SHH. I'LL BE BACK SOON," Oakley whispered, rubbing Cody along the crest of his head to keep his squeaks to a minimum. The last thing she needed was for him to wake the rest of the cave, especially Cane.

"Where are you going?" The voice came from a side tunnel off the living room.

She would never get used to the shadowed, tight corridors here, illuminated largely by what came through the main opening. Neve's tanned face was barely discernible in the hazy dawn light.

She took a step toward the zip line at the entrance. "I have to go back to the resort."

"Why?"

Neve knew about their abilities, but Cane obviously hadn't told her what happened yesterday. Oakley followed his example and hedged a bit. "Kaleo's in danger. I have to warn him."

It was mostly true. Together, Cane and Oakley had thrown Violet off a steep cliff into a ravine. Hopefully, no one would find her and no dinosaurs would desecrate her body. However, if Daric was suspicious enough to send Violet out in the first place, he might become more suspicious when she didn't return. Oakley needed to warn Kaleo.

Neve frowned and faint worry lines encircled her almond-shaped eyes. "If you're caught, they will kill you both. Why not let Cane deliver the message?"

Good question. Why not?

Because she had this overwhelming need to see Kaleo. He would know how to handle the situation, or more precisely, he would know how to handle *her*. She'd taken Violet's life. Not an innocent one, but a life nonetheless. He knew what that felt like—except this wasn't quite accidental, like his rage gone wrong. She wouldn't fool herself. She'd made the calculated decision to kill Violet because it benefited the people she cared about. She'd needed to defend them, so why couldn't she erase the image of Violet with charred hair and bulging eyes?

Maybe she should have yelled for Cane. Or tried again to take Violet down by hand. Maybe it would have made a difference.

She'd never know. Violet had threatened Cane and Kaleo, and she had chosen the simplest path—eliminate the threat.

Was she different from any other predator? How much good would it do for a cheetah to swear off killing antelope or a black widow to vow never to eat its mate? Some things were inevitable.

When she expressed her fears to Cane, his eyes had brimmed with mercy and grace. She didn't deserve his compassion. Instead, she wanted understanding.

"I just need to see Kaleo," she finally answered.

After only a few days away, much of their experience together seemed like a dream. She needed to throw her arms around his waist, rest her head on his chest, and let his strength comfort her.

She took another step toward the zip line, away from Neve. "Don't worry. I'll take Raptor with me for safety. Cane won't need to come after me."

Neve shrugged. "Cane does what God wills." She tilted her head, her expression unreadable in the dim light. "With you though, he often seems to be confused about what God wants."

Oakley mumbled a goodbye and hooked herself up to the harness. As the zip line flew her away from the cave and toward the forest, something nagged at her. She'd forgotten to ask Neve for some coffee. Hopefully, Camocroc with his super-sniffer was taking a nap. But that wasn't likely. Camocroc didn't follow the pattern of modern crocodiles, which were nocturnal.

At the other end, she unhooked the harness and entered the twilight of the jungle. Every noise spiked her nerves. But she wouldn't be alone out here for long. She'd find Raptor and convince him to come with her to the compound.

After a tense half hour of walking, she found the tiny stream of Lemon Creek. As she followed the water for another hour, the stream grew to moderate size. Around a bend, she discovered a small metal door dug into the side of a hill. A keypad restricted access to the area. This had to be it.

She knocked on the door several times. No answer.

Should she continue alone or wait out here for Raptor? Cane would tell her to play it safe and return to the cave. She wasn't ready to give up yet. Before she'd made a final decision, a rustling in the distance put her on edge. She ducked behind a large bush.

The rustling drew closer, probably headed to the research station. She peered between a couple of branches and got a glimpse of two men walking toward her. One of them was Raptor. The other man was taller, yet slim with dark hair—Adler!

"Unbelievable." She stepped out from her cover and gave Raptor a smile. "You found him."

Raptor returned the smile, though it was tight lipped and stilted. "He wasn't easy to find, but he came willingly. That counts for something."

Adler focused his greenish-brown eyes on her. "I came because I wanted to talk to you." His voice held a strange mix of calmness and aggression.

"Good, because I have a lot of questions."

Adler hooked his thumb toward Raptor. "Not with him around."

He planted his feet. "I won't leave the two of you alone."

Adler continued, unperturbed. "We have private things to discuss. Including, one way in particular where you are unique. I imagine you might not want muscle-man to overhear."

Was he referring to her ability? How could he know? Maybe they did need to do this alone. "Raptor, give me your knife for protection, and then please give us a minute."

He squinted at her. A few seconds later, he handed over his long knife and moved to a position twenty yards away. He would barely be able to see them through the foliage, but they had to keep their voices low. Raptor had excellent hearing.

"All right, spill some answers. Why are you here on the island? Why didn't you show up for my trial? You were there the night Monica died. What happened?"

Adler swiveled his head away. "So many questions. Isn't there a more pressing one on your mind?" He returned his focus to her, a snake ready to snatch up dinner. "Like 'how am I able to electrocute people?'"

Her mouth dropped open. She reeled back a step and almost tripped over a rock. He *did* know. She meant to answer yes, to demand an explanation for how he knew. All that came out was a muffled moan.

"There's an entire division of the company dedicated to people like us."

"Us?" she choked out.

His stare drilled into her. "Our genes were manipulated by someone who worked at the company. Someone who disappeared fifteen years ago."

"What company are you talking about?"

He flattened his lips. "Come on. You're not that dumb."

Asperten. Dad's company.

"I'm here because I need to find the scientist that created us. It's why you're here too."

Her brain stutter-stepped through this new flood of knowledge. Adler was somehow like her and Cane. Did he know about Cane? Was their creator here on the island? "Why would this scientist be here?"

"We didn't know for sure she was until trackers started disappearing from the genetically-modified dinosaurs in this area. It was sabotage."

We. Who did he mean, more people at Asperten?

With a quick glance at Raptor, who had started to move back toward them, Adler turned to leave. She only had time to ask one more question before Raptor would come close enough to overhear, and there was something else she had to know. "What about Monica?"

Adler twisted back around. "Yeah, I was there. What do you want to know?"

Her lower lip trembled as she whispered the words. "How did she die?"

Adler tapped his chin, pretending to think. "You mean, did you kill her?" He scoffed at her. "If only you'd been strong enough to do it. Even after I pushed him into the water to awaken your power, you still wouldn't use it on Monica."

Her breath caught in her throat. On the tour boat, a dark shape bumped into the boy just before he fell. Adler endangered him just to see what Oakley could do. The rest of his words took longer to sink in. She hadn't killed Monica.

The corner of his mouth lifted. "I dropped her flat iron into the tub and took it with me when I left."

A clammy sweat broke out across her chest. He talked about murdering Monica as if he'd completed a simple item on his to-do list. *Pick up bread. Stop at Post Office. Kill promising young woman.* "Why?"

"To get you here. You can track the genetic freak dinosaurs better than I can. Plus, I'm sure you want to know where you came from. Find the creator, Oakley."

The truth filtered through her confusion like water through sand. Monica's murder had sent Oakley here, right where Adler wanted her to be, so she could help find the scientist who'd created them. *Them?* If Adler had the power of electrocution, he wouldn't have needed the straightener to kill Monica. Perhaps, like Cane, Adler had a different ability.

Adler moved to go, but she grabbed him before he could slink away. "I won't let you leave."

He laughed. "You should be more worried about what I could do to you."

She glanced in Raptor's direction.

"He can't protect you." He wrenched his arm away,

walked a few feet, and then glanced over his shoulder. "Don't worry. You'll see me again. We tend to find each other. It's probably the pheromones they pumped into us. Or maybe it's because we're the same deep down." He winked. "Programmed to kill."

AFTER ADLER'S DEPARTURE, Raptor stared at her for a long moment. The confusion and suspicion in his eyes nearly broke her heart. But she couldn't find the words to explain, to tell him she was a killer. It hadn't been Monica whom she'd killed, but that didn't change the reality of what she was inside.

Following the awkward silence, she pleaded with Raptor, and he reluctantly agreed to come with her to the resort compound as long as she stayed fifty yards away from the front door. She trailed behind him while his steps fell quietly and his ear seemed attuned to every forest sound. Briefly, he put up a hand to stop her before leading them in a wide arc away from the path. She peered into the trees and spotted a baby *Triceratops* blocking the way. The frill reached as tall as her shoulder. It munched without concern on a short tree. The mother had to be nearby, and upsetting her would cause problems.

Oakley tried to focus on the hike, even as her strained conversation with Adler replayed in her mind. He had come here—orchestrated her conviction to get her here—

all in order to find the person who had manipulated their genes? As if it would be so easy to find one person in the middle of thousands of acres of dangerous jungle. Then again, he'd said something about them finding each other. Through pheromones? In one of her classes, probably Animal Reproduction, she learned pheromones were hormones that acted on other individuals, usually through scent. Often they were used to warn against predators or indicate food trails. Some even attracted mates. Could those types of chemicals draw people together?

Come to think of it, she seemed to read Adler's emotions with uncanny certainty. The same was true for Cane, except on the opposite end of the spectrum. And Adler did appear to be able to find her at will. Were they somehow sending signals through pheromones? Perhaps this was the key to finding the scientist who'd manipulated her DNA.

Through the trees, the familiar canyon came into view. They were close to the compound. Her heart raced in her chest. Would Kaleo be happy to see her or would he be upset that she took the risk of coming?

Raptor stopped a hundred yards short of the gazebo entrance. "I'll go in and bring Kaleo out to you, after I skirt the perimeter. I've seen Red Grizzly here once." He pointed up. "If you encounter trouble, climb this tree and wait for me."

Of course he would assume she was helpless. She flexed her slim fingers, so innocent-looking and yet so deadly. Little did he know she could take care of herself.

After a few minutes, jungle noises crowded in around her, and her confidence began to wane. Maybe she actually was helpless. Her ability to shock might not work on something as large as a one-ton dinosaur.

The cacophony of jungle noises continued with the calls of macaws, loud squeals from monkeys, and the buzz of insects as she waited for his return. He'd been gone only ten minutes when her attention latched on to something different. A heavy footfall came from behind her.

Adrenaline shot through her as she grabbed the lowest branch of the tree and swung her legs up. From a low perch, she peered down. Her ponytail swayed with her momentum, acting like a beacon.

Chubs put his fists on his hips. "Can't say I'm surprised to see you."

Crap. If the intruder had been a small animal, she would have evaded detection, but the tree's sparse branches couldn't hide her from an observant person. She let go of the branch and dropped to the ground. Could have been worse. At least he wasn't Daric. "Why not?"

"Kaleo told me he faked Hazel's death." He rolled his eyes. "Now she's really dead, so I guess it evens out."

The callous comment set her nerves on edge.

He wiped his hands down his stained shirt and through his dark hair, causing it to stick up at odd angles. "He's resourceful. I assumed he faked yours also." He shoved his hands in his front pockets. "Since you're here, I want you to answer a question for me."

He talked about Kaleo in present tense. That probably meant the rest of the gang didn't know about Hazel's fake death or hers. Chubs was keeping the secret, but was he on Kaleo's side? Something about his haunted eyes made her squirm.

"Why did Kaleo change? I know someone talked to him. Who? It wasn't you because you weren't here then, but he must have told you something."

She held her face immobile, trying not to give anything away. Telling him about Cane would endanger all of them.

A full minute ticked by while she stayed silent. His ruddy complexion grew redder with each passing second. She took one step away from him. His hands shot out of his pockets to grab her by the forearms.

"He's not the same as he was when he took over the gang." Chubs lowered his voice to a hissing whisper. "Tell me what happened."

She would have preferred him to yell or try to shake it out of her, anything other than this dark look of evil intent. She thrust her knee toward his groin, but he straightened his arms to keep her from hitting the mark. He held her tight, away from him.

"Now." The word was a growl.

She shook her head while struggling to free her arms. She could shock him, but the smell of Violet's sizzling flesh hadn't faded from her memory and probably never would. Still, if he went too far, she'd give him a little jolt. If she could control it.

He ground his teeth, his eyes flashing rage. Then, like

a waterfall rushing over a cliff, the anger drained from his face. Hopefully, the temper tantrum was over. Kaleo would be here soon. He could handle Chubs, could force him to keep their secret.

He lifted one shoulder in a half-shrug and said in a passive voice, "Well, you're supposed to be dead anyway."

He drew his arm back and punched her in the face. Her head screamed in pain for a split second before the edges of her vision began to darken. The shadows collapsed in on her, and she faded away.

CHAPTER TWENTY-ONE

BRIGHT LIGHT FILTERED through her lids, burning her eyes and making her head pound. She opened them to tiny slits, then pressed them shut again. Too bright. She tried to put her hands up to shield her eyes, but her limbs were frozen in place. She yanked at her arms. They were stuck behind her back.

Where was she? She bent her head, letting her hair fall in front of her face like a dark curtain. Somewhere she must have lost her ponytail holder. She lifted her eyelids again.

After a few minutes, her eyes adjusted to the glare; however, the striking hammer blows continued to pummel her skull. She eased her head up. Amber wood timbers, angled ceiling, and sloping walls in a spacious room. This was the tree house where she and Cane had spent the night. But she was on the floor leaning against the wall, not on one of the cots.

She yanked at her arms again and felt rope digging into her wrists. Why was she tied up? How did she get here? In a rush, the events of the morning came back to her. The trek to the compound. Running into Chubs. He'd hit her. And must have put her here. Why?

The trap door in the floor jerked open and slapped onto the wooden planks. Chubs's brown hair poked through.

He gave her a relieved look. "Glad to see you didn't go anywhere."

As if she could. She glared at him as he climbed in. "Untie me, right now."

He ignored her and focused on the opening as another head popped through the trap door. This one blond. Her stomach twisted into tight knots. Chubs had brought Daric.

No place to hide or escape. If Daric didn't kill her right away, he would use her to take Kaleo down, and then he would kill her. She wrestled with her numb arms, trying to find a way out of the bindings.

He climbed all the way in and loomed over her. "If it isn't Snow White in the flesh. Chubs, I've gotta give you credit. You weren't lying."

"You said you needed proof before you'd take on Kaleo. Here she is."

Daric crouched down to her level. "Now, I can stare at you without watching my back for your boyfriend."

His eyes roamed over her entire body, lingering on where her T-shirt had come up in the front, exposing a swath of her stomach. She tried to scoot away from him, but her back was pressed against an old wooden trunk and her left side was hemmed in by a cot.

When he'd finished gawking, he ran his hand down the side-seam of her jeans from her belt loop to her ankle. At some point, Chubs must have taken off her boots. "Small, but well-proportioned."

She scowled at him. Hopefully, more anger than fear shone from her eyes.

"Don't worry, Snow. You'll live longer than most of the women I've met, simply because of a lack of other options. Though, I can't say the same for your boyfriend." He placed his hand back on his knee. "By the way, have you seen Violet recently? She went looking for you."

Oakley turned her eyes to the cedar plank flooring. Admitting what happened would probably make things worse. She could lie, but an experienced manipulator like Daric would see right through it.

"Not in the mood for conversation? I'll give you some time to think about it. When I get back, you're going to want to make yourself useful." He fingered a lock of her hair.

Her blood burned through her veins like acid. If she could get even a finger on Daric, she'd make him sorry he'd ever laid eyes on her.

"What about me?" Chubs threw his hands down to his sides where they smacked his legs.

"Relax. Unlike Kaleo, I'm willing to share."

"You didn't share Violet."

Daric looked offended. "You didn't ask." He waved a hand in the air. "Besides, that was different. Violet came here to be with me."

Chubs nodded like ownership of a woman made perfect sense. If only she could shock them both until they begged her to stop.

Daric pulled a handkerchief from his back pocket. He folded it and whipped it around her head, covering her eyes. Her hair pulled painfully as he twisted some in with the knot.

"Why the blindfold?" Chubs's voice sounded as if he'd moved away from her.

Daric answered from right by her ear. "Probably not necessary, but in my experience, prisoners are less likely to escape if they can't see."

Feet shuffled to the trap door. The creaking of the rope on the ladder rungs indicated that one of them had descended.

"You rest." Daric's saccharine voice came from above her. "We'll be back as soon as it's all over with Kal." He ran a finger underneath her chin, tilting her head up. His next comment was a hot whisper against her cheek. "I can't wait to kiss your whole body, like licking whipped cream off a ripe peach."

Grateful she couldn't see his expression, she summoned the anger hovering just below the surface of her skin and pushed it with all her might. His thumb traveled over her lower lip, then quickly jerked away.

"More intense than I expected." He laughed. "I'm going to enjoy the sparks between us, Snow."

Not if she could help it.

More shuffling noises as he made his way to the door. The creaking of the ladder. The door snapping shut.

She had to find a way out of here before they came back. For a long time, she struggled with her bonds. The rope cut into her flesh, and she managed to gain only an inch of slack. It wasn't enough.

She let out a frustrated breath. Her major adrenaline spike had waned and fear stole her bravery. Fear of what Daric might do to Kaleo. Fear of what he would do to her. Fear of what she might do to him and Chubs to get away. Any violence could be considered self-defense, but her fragile psyche might not be able to handle adding two more to her body count.

Godlike power with no spiritual compass. Cane's words floated through her head, resonating in her heart. When she killed Violet, she wielded her power like Daric —to get the results she desired. Sure, she'd done it to protect Cane and Kaleo, but it was all for nothing. Here she sat, in the same situation that she'd killed Violet to avoid.

We are programmed to kill. Adler might be right, but she wasn't a robot. She could choose not to kill. Ever again. There had to be another way out of this.

CHAPTER TWENTY-TWO

"CHUBS, SPEAK UP." Kaleo had bumped into Chubs and Daric while searching for Oakley. When they had insisted Kaleo come back to the compound, he'd warily complied and followed them to the courtyard. After all, he couldn't admit to searching for her. Thankfully, neither of them had seen Raptor, who'd ducked into the bushes to avoid them.

"This time *you* have to listen to *me*. It's better to do this in private." Chubs finally met his gaze.

The petulant child Kaleo recognized in those eyes made his shoulders tense. What was he up to? Kaleo led them inside and to his room. There were plenty of weapons stashed around in case things went bad. He allowed the two men to enter before he rounded on Chubs. "What's your problem?"

He closed the bedroom door as he answered. "You."

Kaleo blinked at the venom in his voice.

As if emboldened by the reaction, Chubs took a step closer. "I've had enough of your mood swings—"

He laughed. That was certainly the pot calling the kettle black.

"I don't know why you've changed, and I don't care anymore." Chubs straightened to his full height, just a couple of inches shorter than Kaleo. "You need to leave quietly and never come back."

Over Chubs's shoulder, Daric smiled with smug assurance, his arms folded across his chest. Uncharacteristically quiet, but menacing all the same.

Kaleo raised his eyebrows. "Really?" He took a fast step toward Chubs, bumping into his chest.

Chubs jumped back, shooting a panicked glance at Daric.

"You know I can beat both of you," Kaleo said.

Recovering, Chubs mimicked Daric's stance by crossing his arms. "I know." He paused for several seconds. "I also know you'll leave to save *her*."

He shook his head in disbelief. Chubs had to mean Oakley since he was the only one who suspected she might be alive. But she was safe with Cane. He was bluffing. Had to be. "She's dead."

"Luscious pale skin, just a little sun burnt. Flashing blue eyes. Tiny, with curves in all the right places. She seemed very much alive to me." A corner of Chubs's mouth lifted. "Captive, but alive."

Kaleo grabbed his chest and fisted his shirt. "Did you touch her?"

Chubs pinwheeled his arms, trying to get away. Kaleo held fast. When Daric didn't immediately jump to the rescue, he stopped struggling. "I wanted to, but she was unconscious. I'm not into sex with girls who just lay there." The wicked glint returned to his eye. "I may have lifted her shirt a little though, traced along her lavender bra. Purple brings out the slight honey tone to her skin, don't you think?"

Every muscle in Kaleo's body ached to shove Chubs's nose into the back of his brain. He controlled himself for Oakley's sake. It sounded like she hadn't been hurt. He would know if Chubs was lying.

Daric cleared his throat. "I wouldn't have had the same restraint, but Chubs insisted we give you a chance to leave peacefully. In fact, you should be proud of your little protege, Kal. I never would have guessed he had the guts to challenge you, much less kidnap your woman."

Peacefully. If only he could simply take the deal and walk away with Oakley. He released his grip on Chubs. "You're throwing your fate in with Daric?"

He nodded. All compassion for him—for the abuse he suffered from an older woman, for being dumped here at seventeen, and for the taunting and teasing from the other inmates—it all fled in the face of this betrayal.

Clarity of purpose hit Kaleo like a massive swipe from a sauropod's tail. Why was he fighting? His time here as a leader had come to an end. Protecting Oakley was the only thing that mattered. "How do I know you have her?"

Chubs rolled his eyes. "Would I be stupid enough to try to force you out if I didn't?"

Kaleo gave him his most disparaging look. Oakley would have been proud.

"In addition to knowing the color of her bra, she had these on her." He held out a pair of silver fleur-de-lis earrings—the only jewelry she had brought to the island.

Pretending to think it over, Kaleo ran his hands through his hair. "If I agree to leave, you'll release her and let us walk away?"

Chubs nodded, extending his hand to shake on it.

He ignored the gesture. "Not good enough." He pointed at Daric. "I want to hear him say it."

Daric placed his hand against his chest in a mock gesture of surprise. "Of course. You and Oakley can leave. Just don't come back."

Insincere, but what else could he do? They had backed him into a corner.

Chubs walked to the bedroom door and opened it. "She's in the safe house."

The tree house. He had taken Chubs there a year ago and told him to use it in case of dinosaur attack or problems at the compound. The treachery of holding her captive there burned acid through his chest. Chubs had better hope they never ran into each other again.

Chubs turned his attention to Daric. "Follow him and make sure they both leave."

Daric ran his tongue over his teeth. It obviously grated on him to take orders from a kid, though he merely nodded. For a criminal, Chubs was extremely naive. He had no idea what Daric would do when given complete power.

Daric swept a hand toward the hallway. "After you."

As Kaleo walked into the hall, the lights flickered once, then went out completely. He hesitated, almost expecting Daric to stab him in the back.

Chubs waved them on. "Go. I'll fix it, just like I fix everything around here."

Strange how he wanted more power, yet was willing to still do the mundane maintenance. Perhaps he was making himself indispensable to Daric. Well, they deserved each other. It was time for Kaleo to get away from them. Unlike Chubs, he wasn't naive enough to believe Daric would let him walk away.

With every muscle taut, he led the way out of the compound and through the chirping and rustling forest. His agitated nerves made him painfully aware of a nearby predator, and not the dinosaur variety. Though he could kill Daric in a head-on fight, Daric had the advantage simply due to his ruthless nature.

Kaleo side-stepped around a large pile of dinosaur dung, his mind occupied with options for the best defense of Oakley and himself. As he shifted positions, he glanced back at Daric. He was reaching around to his back for something, causing the front of his T-shirt to pull tight along his chest.

What was he hiding? More importantly, when would

he use it? Perhaps he would wait until they had reached Oakley in order to kill them both at the same time.

No, too risky to try to fight off a pair. He would do it sooner.

Warning tingles raced down Kaleo's spine. His ears had been attuned to Daric's every movement behind him and the noise, though barely a blip on his ear drums, sounded like a knife sliding out of a sheath. Of course, it could also be Daric scuffing those ridiculous black tennis shoes, but better to be paranoid.

A casual glance behind to check. Daric's hand still lay hidden along his back. His raised brows and set jaw spoke to his intentions.

Ahead, two ostrich-looking dinosaurs scraped their mouths along the ground, searching for freshly fallen leaves. They would have to circle around the pair without disturbing them. Even these relatively small dinosaurs could do damage if startled.

He twisted into the trees on the left, his attention momentarily focused on the animals. Daric shifted to stand in his blind spot. Not good.

Twisting his neck, he caught a glimpse of Daric poised with a knife in midair. He held the weapon for a split second as if relishing the tension of the kill before he swung the blade down hard.

The blow aimed for Kaleo's back. He darted to the side, shifting his torso away from the blade. Not all of him escaped the knife's deadly arc. The blade sliced through his upper thigh. Blood welled up from the cut and spilled onto his jeans.

Daric pulled the knife up for another strike while simultaneously punching Kaleo in the jaw. He groaned as the impact knocked him back.

Taking advantage of the successful hit, Daric swung again with the knife, this time aiming directly at Kaleo's left eye. Kaleo reached for the whip at his back, bringing it up in time to deflect the knife with the hilt.

Daric barely controlled the weapon, narrowly keeping it from gouging his own leg.

The whip cracked against the ground as Kaleo unfurled it, sending the ostrich-dinosaurs scurrying into the jungle.

Kaleo brought the whip back, ready to aim at his head.

Daric kicked him hard in the thigh, directly in the knife wound.

He crumpled halfway to the ground. The flick of his wrist was weak. Even so, the whip cracked through the air, missing Daric's head by an inch.

They stared at each other for a moment. Kaleo doubled over in pain. Daric with shock evident on his face.

Then, Daric did the worst thing possible—he took off into the jungle, sprinting toward the tree house.

CHAPTER TWENTY-THREE

A SCRAPING SOUND CAME from below Oakley's perch in the tree house. Her heart skipped a beat, then raced at full speed. They'd come back already? She shifted her position on the floor toward the noise as if she'd be able to see someone through the heavy blindfold.

Squeak. Slam. The trap door.

She held her breath. Scuffling sounds. Someone was scrambling into the room.

"Is this a bad time? You seem tied up." Adler's deep voice surprised her.

She blew out a trapped breath. "How did *you* get here? Never mind, come untie me."

A low chuckle. "I followed those guys from the compound. Good thing I'm the curious sort."

She bit back a sarcastic comment, something about leering instead of helping, and tried the nice approach. "How about you untie me? Please?"

His footsteps shuffled closer. "You really can't see through that?"

What a stupid question. "Does it matter?"

"Actually, yeah. If you can't see me, then I can do whatever I want."

He had to be toying with her. "Um ... Are you getting naked out there or something? If so, I'll keep the blindfold on, just untie me."

He laughed again, this time a deep, unamused sound. "I'm supposed to free you."

Wherever that directive came from, she should be grateful, but something in his tone gave her pause.

A zipping noise. Perhaps a backpack opening. "Unfortunately for you, I've got other plans."

Fear tightened her throat. "You're going to leave me this way?"

"No." The single word slithered with menace.

The metallic click of a gun cocking sent adrenaline sparking through her body. Why would Adler point a gun at her? He could have taken any one of several opportunities to kill her in the last week.

"Why now?" she whispered.

Quieter shuffling. Was that him spreading his feet? Or did the sound come from outside the tree house? It was hard to tell spatial relationships with just her ears.

"Because no one's watching. I can convince my boss something went wrong. With all the killers running around, a stray bullet managed to find you. It was always one of the risks of sending you here."

His boss? Did he mean someone at Asperten? This person must have been watching them until now. But how? "I don't get it. Why send me here just to kill me?"

He heaved out a sigh. "I told you, you're here to find the creator. And you're doing a poor job of it."

"Because your boss wants to find him?"

"*Her.* And yes. But I couldn't care less where she is, which means I couldn't care less about you. Goodbye, Oakley."

The finality in his voice hollowed out her stomach. She held her breath and braced for the impact of the bullet. Would it hurt or would her system block it out until she slipped away? Another, more important question surfaced. Would Adler make the rounds of the island, killing everyone who knew he'd been here? Kaleo, Cane, Raptor—they could all be in danger.

A thundering thump shook the floorboards. Something large had hit the wooden floor next to her. Rolling and grappling sounds met her ears. She released her trapped breath. Someone else had interrupted her execution.

Low grunting, then a growl. Wait, the growl sounded familiar. She'd heard it many times while wrestling gators. *Raptor!*

She wriggled, trying to get out of her bonds or at least to dislodge her blindfold. It was torture, not knowing what was happening.

A deafening shot echoed through the small room. She felt no impact, heard no cry of pain from the others.

Heavy weight crashed into her right side, knocking her over and partially under the cot. The blindfold caught on a splinter sticking out from a board. When she tried to sit up, the splinter dragged the right corner of the blindfold down her nose a few inches.

She gasped at the sight before her. Raptor lay on the ground with his hands clutching his abdomen. Adler stood over him, pointing a gun at his head.

She opened her mouth to scream, but fear made her mute. No blood darkened Raptor's orange T-shirt, but he groaned in pain.

She scrambled to a sitting position. The blindfold pulled all the way down, ending up around her neck.

"You can't save her." Adler kept his eyes fixed on Raptor as he moved the gun in slow motion. His arm inched along a flat arc until the barrel pointed directly at her, but he still didn't look at her.

Her right eye twitched, suddenly burning and itching. It was the least of her concerns. Adler took a step back and shifted his gaze to her. When their eyes met, his expression morphed from determined desperation to outright shock.

Perhaps it wasn't so easy to kill someone who was staring directly at him, though he'd been ready to do it one second before. His determination had been a tangible force surging off of him in waves. Then abruptly, when their eyes had connected, fear had taken over.

He lowered the gun. With barely a glance at Raptor,

he circled to the trap door, jumped onto the ladder, and descended through the opening.

His retreat didn't make sense. Why lower the gun and run away just because she could see him?

Raptor crawled to her and pressed a pocketknife into her hand before bolting out the trap door. Using her fingertips, she flipped open the blade and went to work sawing through the rope.

She had freed one arm when another booming shot rang out. Dread tingled through her nerve endings. The shot was close, very close.

CHAPTER TWENTY-FOUR

OAKLEY STRIPPED the bindings from her wrists, ditched the blindfold, then cut the rope off her ankles. She flipped the knife closed and shoved it into her back pocket. Maybe it wasn't too late to help stop Adler. She grabbed the edges of the ladder and slid down. The gunshot had come from the west.

She hadn't gone far when she spied a dark orange stripe peeking through the tree branches. *Raptor's T-shirt.*

She ran to him and dropped to her knees. He lay on one side facing away from her. A small circle of blood darkened the orange into rust just below his rib cage.

"Raptor?"

He rolled over to his back. "Oak, get out of here."

"He shot you."

"Exactly why you need to go." With one hand, he pushed at her knees. "He might double back to see if I'm dead."

She listened to the surrounding jungle. A distant rustling in the trees heightened her fear. It came from the south, right where Adler would emerge if he doubled back. Before she got a chance to reach for the pocketknife, Raptor placed something in her palm—a large, serrated hunting knife. Better than the pocketknife at least. She squeezed her fist around the hilt and nodded.

The sounds came closer, joined by a faint high-pitched noise. She jumped behind a tree, holding the knife across her body.

The high-pitched sound turned into a chirp. *Cody!*

A green head poked out from under a bush. She whistled for him to come to her. He closed the distance in two fast hops and nuzzled her thigh. She rubbed the downy fuzz on his head.

Behind Cody, Cane stepped into view, carrying a bow and quiver. He gave her a sideways smile. "Took him out for a hunting trip, and he ran away. I figured he would find you."

She grabbed his hand and pulled him down as she dove next to Raptor again. "He's hurt."

Raptor pushed Cane away as well. "Go after Adler. He tried to kill Oakley." He pointed to the northwest. "That way."

Cane scooped up his bow and quiver, then turned to look at her. His green eyes had darkened with murderous intent. Surely, he wouldn't go against his peaceful ways just to protect her. Without a word, he ran into the jungle.

She almost called him back. Not only did she need to

get Raptor some help, but the rare show of hostility in Cane had unraveled her nerves. The pastor had a dark side—a side he pretended didn't exist.

The blood spot on Raptor's shirt grew with each passing second. She had to control the bleeding. She secured the bottom of her tank top while pulling off her T-shirt, then rolled the fabric into a ball and pressed it to the wound. Neve was the only person on the island who qualified as a healer. Oakley couldn't drag Raptor through a mile of jungle to Neve at the cave. Maybe if she could get the bleeding stopped, she could bring Neve here.

Raptor's eyes fluttered closed.

"No! Keep fighting!" The absurdity of her rant echoed with her screams. Her eyes misted with tears as she continued to push on his wound.

Nearby leaves rustled. Someone tall stepped out from the trees. She almost didn't have the strength for one more startle reflex. Almost.

Her eyes locked on to the pitch-black tennis shoes first, splayed at a cocky angle. Her stomach plummeted like a ship plunging down a rogue wave. *Daric.*

She snatched up the knife that she'd laid next to Raptor. Her fingers, slick with his blood, bobbled the grip. She held the knife out while still trying to keep pressure on his chest.

Daric came closer, his eyes shifting from her to Raptor. She let go of the T-shirt and scrambled backward. Maybe she could lead him away from Raptor.

At first, it worked. Daric moved in her direction,

looming over her. Since he was unarmed, it might be a fair fight. He glowered at her for a moment before he lowered to one knee beside Raptor's unconscious form. The hilt of a knife stuck out of the back of his jeans. So much for him being unarmed.

He unsheathed the knife and drew it back. "Might as well take care of you right now."

The blade hovered over Raptor's chest. He didn't open his eyes. The muscles in Daric's biceps flexed as he prepared to thrust the knife downward.

Oakley jumped to her feet, flipped her knife around, and grabbed the blade, ready to throw it. "Stop!"

Daric didn't turn, merely watched her from the corner of his eye.

She pulled her arm back, taking aim at his spine. Hopefully, he couldn't see her fingers trembling. "I said stop."

This time, her commanding tone halted him midstrike. He stared up at her for a brief second. Slowly, he got to his feet. "Okay, Snow. I get it. You'd like to have your fun before I get too bloody. It's not like he's going anywhere." He advanced on her. "By the way, I like how you're getting all fired up. It's hot."

Her trembling hand bounced the knife around until it looked like it might jump from her fingers on its own accord. "I will throw this."

"I believe you. Go ahead."

He'd called her bluff. But she wouldn't be so stupid as to let go of her only weapon.

He lunged at her, knife pointed down. Apparently, he wasn't trying to hurt her yet. His hand grabbed for her wrist.

She wrenched it away, then flipped the knife around and jabbed the blade toward his chest.

He twisted his shoulders sideways to dodge the blow. In the same instant, he swiped his knife at her hand. Their blades met with a clang. His knife sliced into the flesh on her palm, causing her to drop the blade to the ground.

Before he raised his knife again, she turned and ran. She evaded tree trunks and swatted her way through vine curtains. Hopefully, she wouldn't run blind into something just as deadly.

A quick glance over her shoulder. He was right behind her, reaching out with long arms.

She sidestepped away from him and jumped over a dry stream bed. One foot slipped on a patch of rotting leaves. She swung her arms to keep balance.

A sharp tug yanked her backward. Daric had caught the lower edge of her tank top. He hung on, using her momentum to spin her around and slam her into a tree.

The impact took her breath away. Rough bark scraped against her shoulders.

He pressed his body onto hers, pinning her, and cutting off more of her air. Her knee came up. He was ready for it and easily blocked her. Wedging both legs between hers, he made sure she wouldn't get another chance.

Her flimsy white tank top had pulled tight and the

press of his body pushed her breasts up and out. Primal fear reared up inside.

His breath was fire against her ear. "How many times did Kaleo take advantage of this lovely view?" He put a finger to her lips. "No, don't tell me. I'll only be jealous."

The panic threatened to drown her senses. With it, came the deep, restless pulse of energy. The spark grew until her cells begged for release.

This would be justified. Self-defense.

But the pungent smell of charred flesh was still too fresh in her memory. Her stomach roiled with nausea. Maybe she could use her power to wound him instead?

With two fingers on his arm, she let a sliver of panic flow out.

"Whoa!" He pulled back, eyes wide. "You really are juiced." With a smile on his face, he slid a rough hand down her neck. Of course the shock would only spur him on. A man like him would never fear a woman.

He lowered his head to her neck. Her skin crawled as he trailed wet kisses from her ear lobe to her clavicle. A husky moan. She needed to stop this.

Wait. The moaning wasn't coming from him. Soft breaths puffed behind her left shoulder, like something sniffing. The smell of rotting meat gagged her as she glanced behind. The exhalations came from a source she couldn't see—until her gaze caught on three spots next to a long, dark scar.

CHAPTER TWENTY-FIVE

OAKLEY SCREAMED AS CAMOCROC ROARED. Its teeth gleamed pearly white against the camouflaged green and tan of its head. The creature lunged, bulldozing between them, and knocking them apart.

Its teeth grazed her arm near her elbow. She pressed her hand to the wound while ducking around to the back side of the tree. For once, her small size worked in her favor. Camocroc went after the bigger target.

Daric staggered backward. Not fast enough. One of Camocroc's teeth carved out a chunk of flesh near his collarbone. Blood quickly seeped through his shirt.

He yanked the knife from his pants and swiped at the creature's mouth, slicing into its gums. Its blood spurted and dripped down his arm.

She crouched lower. Camocroc had followed her around almost as faithfully as Cody. It could probably smell her somehow, perhaps detect her pheromones? Hopefully, it wouldn't hunt for her behind the tree.

Scanning the area, she searched for weapons. Raptor's knife lay twenty yards to her left, out of reach. It wouldn't help anyway. Daric's knife was having the same effect as a mosquito on Camocroc.

Daric circled behind into the trees on her right. His shift in position exposed her to its sniffing snout.

Camocroc switched directions. Digging both feet into the soft soil, its muscles went rock hard and the camouflage slipped a bit. It was getting ready to charge at her.

She dashed into the jungle. As the leaves whipped by, she worked on a plan. She only had a few options. She couldn't hope to outrun it downhill like before. This area was flat ground.

Daric ran parallel to her, his arms pumping, his breath coming in desperate pants. The thunderous crash of branches behind them signaled Camocroc's pursuit.

She angled away from Daric while pushing her legs furiously forward. Ahead, she saw an open stream. Bad idea. The water would slow her down, making her an easy target.

She swerved in the other direction. Just as she caught up to Daric, the flash of a carved image drew her attention. Splayed out lines indicated a trap. Except she didn't recognize the symbol coupled with the trap.

She veered toward the tree anyway. The nature of the trap might be a mystery, but it was her only hope.

In the scant seconds before she hit the trap, she tried to decipher the sideways arrow sitting on top of an upside down three-sided box. Kaleo had told her the arrows meant razor blades or spears. Blades on top of a platform maybe?

With no more time to guess, she flew past the tree, then pivoted to her left, and lunged for the backside of the same tree. As her hands connected with the rough bark, she shot a glance over her shoulder. Both Daric and Camocroc adjusted to her new course.

But neither one of them could turn on a dime like she could.

Daric jumped to a stop and looked as if he might pursue her. With Camocroc barreling behind him, he instead leaped in the other direction, narrowly avoiding a collision with the beast.

Camocroc shifted its body to come after her, but its momentum carried its massive bulk sideways several feet. It slipped on the carpet of fallen leaves, then its belly shuddered and compressed as it slid over something large.

Vines and leaves fell to the ground exposing a short metal platform.

Clunk! Whoosh!

The metal plate on top unhinged and flipped straight up. It wasn't a platform so much as a launching pad. The mechanism flung Camocroc's body into another curtain of vines.

Shtick!

The sickening sound of knives cutting into flesh.

An agonized roar tore through the air. The pinpoint

tips of spears poked through the opposite side of its tough skin. Blood dripped like crimson snakes down its still-heaving rib cage.

She turned away from the repulsive image as its breathing began to slow. Then, her head snapped back to it when she heard a loud crack.

The creature hadn't moved. In fact, its lungs barely wheezed.

"Finally, we're alone." Daric walked around Camocroc's flank, holding a spear with a broken handle, ripped from the trap. "I lost my knife in the struggle, so ..."

Her heartbeat crashed inside her chest, drowning her ears in the strong *thump, thump, thump.* She'd eliminated one threat, only to be left with her original nightmare. He glared at her, his blue eyes as dark as midnight. The tip of the spear glinted in the scant rays of sunlight.

Kill or be killed. On the boat, Officer Lewis had pushed her to survive, but Violet's death taught her that killing was too easy. It was a steep incline of horror paved with icy intentions. She wouldn't give in to the desire for control. She wouldn't be like Daric.

A whisper crawled through her mind. *He deserves to die.*

Yes, but who on this island was innocent? Not even her. Taking Violet's life wasn't completely self-defense, just the easiest path at the moment.

Daric stalked closer, his feet silent on the littered jungle floor. Was this how he'd hunted his prey on the mainland? A breeze blew the hair off his forehead, giving him a feral look. His face broke out in a twisted grin.

He will never stop.

The spear angled toward her, bridging the short distance between them. It pricked the hollow of her neck. "As much as I'd love to hear your high soprano scream, you'd better stay quiet. I'd hate for us to be interrupted."

A torrent of anger welled up from the unending supply inside her. Her fingers tingled, the tips burning like matches ready to light. But he was too far away. Even if she wanted to, she couldn't electrocute him through the wood of the spear.

In a quick horizontal swipe, he sliced a cut along her jaw. She yelped and covered the wound with her hand. It was nowhere near deep enough to truly injure her. It was meant as a reminder of what he could do. He'd had a lot of practice.

He used the spear to gesture behind him. "I'd rather not have roadkill in the background for our first time."

She moved around the side of the tree. The spear tracked her position, not straying from her throat. Drops of warm blood dripped from her jaw to her neck.

When they reached the opposite side, he lowered the weapon and stepped closer. She could almost reach him.

In a quick motion, he grabbed both of her wrists in one hand and pinned them over her head. Before she could release her rage, he slammed the back of her head into the tree. Stars swam before her eyes.

"Don't worry. I'm not going to kill you. You're the

hottest commodity on this island." He pressed a knee between her legs and lifted her slightly. "I've got to know something, though. Violet's not coming back, is she?"

She opened her mouth. No words came.

He inferred the truth. "Did you kill her? Or was it one of the men who follow you around?"

It didn't matter if he knew now. Still, she dropped her gaze, refusing to give him what he sought.

"That's all the answer I need." He ran the tip of the spear along the side of her body.

The sound of an alarmed chirp drew her gaze over his shoulder. Cody had found her. Hope flared up inside. Maybe Cane was following Cody again.

But no one else came into the clearing.

With barely a glance, Daric reared back and kicked Cody hard. The animal whimpered and took off into the trees.

The distraction had given her a split second of valuable leverage and a whole lot of anger to work with. She sent a pulse of heat through her hands.

Daric grunted and loosened his hold on her wrists. Not the reaction of a man being electrocuted, but she'd take what she could get. Yanking her arms down hard, she slid underneath his right arm. He fell against the tree trunk as she darted away.

At the edge of the creek, he tackled her from behind. Her palms hit the ground first, and she rolled away.

He grabbed for her, tugging her toward him by her

thighs. Her shirt came up and her back scraped along rough pebbles.

Water splashed over them as she thrashed against his hold. Her loose hair flipped into her face. She couldn't see, but reached out anyway, trying to find him. She hadn't been able to shock him enough through her wrists. She needed to get her hands on him.

He smashed her head backward onto a rock. The world spun and nausea swirled in her gut.

He straddled her waist, holding her tight with his knees, and grabbed her wrists again.

She bucked against him.

His hand circled tightly around her throat, cutting off her heaving breaths.

Her power released, and current shot through her body. Her wrists burned as if they were on fire. The tips of her fingers sparked, heating up the water around them.

Daric relaxed his grip for a second and smiled as if he enjoyed absorbing the heat. The terror inside her grew as she realized she couldn't make him stop.

"I have to tell you a secret, Snow. It's something they never talked about in the newspapers." He leaned down to brush his scruff across her cheek. "I have a fetish."

CHAPTER TWENTY-SIX

OAKLEY'S BLOOD turned from boiling hot to ice cold in an instant. Daric had a fetish. He enjoyed cutting women, but what else was he into?

He rose up to peer at her face, then laughed. His voice came out in a hoarse whisper. "I want to watch you struggle to breathe."

The hand around her throat constricted. A tiny whimper escaped her lips.

His palm pressed against her windpipe. She couldn't make any other sounds, couldn't draw air in or push it out. His fingers crushed the tendons in the sides of her neck.

He focused intently on her face. Unmistakable joy built behind his eyes, lighting the blue on fire, making them almost iridescent with spiraling delight. He wanted to watch the life drain out of her, to see when her lungs collapsed, to feel her body go limp.

Her lungs clenched in anguish. Her head throbbed

with the misery of a thousand stabbing needles. She tugged on her arms, trying to free her wrists. She had to find a way to get her hands on him.

Except she was having trouble focusing.

Just as the need to breathe eclipsed everything else, he released the pressure with a satisfied grunt.

She gasped and coughed, drawing in every air molecule she could fit into her starving lungs.

Mere seconds later, the hand around her throat tightened again.

She sucked in a large breath before the misery became too great. He increased the pressure swiftly, his eyes searching for her desperation, for her breaking point.

Her vision dimmed. Her head throbbed and pulsed. She desperately needed air. Still, she closed her eyes and lay anchored to the ground, refusing to give him the satisfaction of begging for her life.

He grunted, then gave a low growl.

Her eyes still shut, she could only imagine the frustration on his face. She would have smiled at bursting his fetish bubble, but was afraid her lips would part on a guppy-like gasp.

He whipped her neck back and forth.

Her eyes flew open. Trees jumped in the same rhythm as her head bouncing off the wet rocks. When he stopped shaking her, she settled her gaze on him.

Instead of becoming clear, his features wavered and oscillated, fading in and out. The short blond hair morphed into long, stringy brown locks. His face shifted into the softer features of a woman. The ice blue eyes deepened and elongated, changing into the aqua eyes of her mother. She ignored the burning in her lungs as the image of her childhood bathroom took over her senses.

The cream-colored porcelain of the bathtub closely matched Mama's pale skin while she leaned against it. Mama's eyes stared at a spot high on the bathroom wall nowhere near Oakley. Not unusual for Mama, but this time Oakley couldn't just leave her alone. The bathroom door was locked.

"What are you doing, Mama?" Oakley knelt next to her.

Mama sighed before answering. "I'm deciding."

"Deciding what?"

She tapped her head against the tub. "Whether to give you a bath."

"I want a bath!"

"I know you love baths, sweetheart. This one would be different." A few seconds later, Mama nodded as if she'd made up her mind. "This bath will wash you completely clean, inside and out, but only if you stay under a long time. Can you do that?"

"I can hold my breath good." She wanted to be clean more than anything. She felt dirty ever since she scalded Brandon Wilson's arm two days ago. At least that was what Mama had called it, a scalding. She burned him, but the bully deserved it for stealing her roller skates and pushing her down on the sidewalk when she came to get them.

Mama ran a hand down her face. "Okay. Climb in."

She took off her nightgown and got in. The huge tub

was already half full of cold water. She shivered as it closed over her body. "Can I turn on the hot water?"

"Yes." Mama's head appeared over the side of the tub, her silver fleur-de-lis earrings winking in the light. Oakley loved those earrings, sweet like a flower and also tough like the head of a spear.

She turned on the hot water and sank down against the bottom of the tub with her ears underwater. She let her hair flow freely and pressed her feet together, pretending to be a beautiful mermaid.

Mama stepped into the tub, her feet on either side of Oakley's. "Mama, you have to take your nightgown off first."

She frowned. "It's okay this one time. I'll wash it later."

Oakley shrugged and went back to sweeping the ends of her hair through the water. She was small, even for a seven-year-old, and the tub was big, so there was room for both of them. She shifted to move over for Mama, but Mama shifted her back to the center of the tub.

She dropped to her knees, sitting on Oakley's legs. It didn't hurt, and Oakley enjoyed the touch. Mama didn't touch her much. She preferred to read her work papers at home and didn't care for hugs or cuddling.

Tears leaked from her eyes as she touched Oakley's wet cheek. Why was she sad? When she spoke, Oakley had to stop moving to hear the words under the water. "You won't understand this. I'm doing this to save you."

Oakley raised her head just above the water and squinted at her. Her words didn't make sense. "Will it make me clean?"

"I hope so. Hold your breath."

She nodded and took a huge breath. Mama slid her under the water and pinned her shoulders to the bottom of the tub.

Closing her eyes, she imagined the air running through her lungs like on the treadmill Daddy used for exercise. At first, a roadrunner ran on the treadmill, then a cute puppy, and finally a lazy coyote. When the coyote could barely walk anymore, she needed air. Hopefully she was all clean by now.

She tried to sit up.

Mama held her down.

Her eyes flew open. She thrashed and splashed, leaking the tiny bit of air she had left out of the corners of her mouth.

Mama shifted farther up her body, holding her tight. Mama's words were slurred as they met her ears through the wavy water. "I'm sorry. You shouldn't be here."

The words cut to the core of her heart. Mama didn't want her here, had never wanted her? Why would she hate her this much?

Deep down, she knew the answer. Whatever had caused her to burn Brandon had come from inside of her. There wasn't any soap or water that could clean the burning part of her away. It was lodged too far down.

Needle-like pains shot through her chest. She opened her mouth, but sucked in only water. More pain sliced into her lungs, carving them up like Dad carved their Christmas turkey.

She pushed against Mama's legs. It didn't help. She was too tiny.

A strange and desperate heat flowed through her face and spread to her head and neck. This was bigger and sharper than the anger she'd directed toward Brandon. The feeling grew until her head ached and it felt like she was exploding.

Mama's hands trembled, shaking Oakley up and down. No, wait, she had grabbed Mama, and Mama was trying to hold on.

Her lungs ached for air. The raw liquid fear kept coming. Water sloshed in the tub as she and Mama vibrated as one.

A slow, blistering fire spread across her skin, like the water was boiling. She cried out, or was that Mama?

The next instant, the pressure released.

Oakley was free.

She bolted straight up while sucking in the longest, sweetest breath of air she'd ever tasted. The fire on her flesh cooled, leaving reddened skin over her whole body.

Mama fell backward and slumped against the back of the tub.

Oakley drew her knees up, wrapped her arms around them, and cowered against the other side. But Mama didn't move. Only the small rise and fall of her chest showed that Mama was still alive.

CHAPTER TWENTY-SEVEN

THE PRESSURE on Oakley's neck eased. She sucked in air in raspy gasps. As her vision began to clear, her soul ached as much as her lungs. Her mother's death had been no accident. The revelation blasted a gaping hole through her carefully constructed walls of denial. Her mother had known what she would become.

You shouldn't be here. Her mother had tried to kill her. And Dad kept it a secret because she had put her own mother in a coma.

No wonder she'd repressed her power for so long afterward. She'd inherited the heart of a killer. Like mother, like daughter.

Her neck throbbed from the compression of Daric's fingers. Her body was desperate to live, though a small part of her questioned if this way might be better. No matter what Cane said about God allowing their creation, she could no longer escape the truth. She wasn't meant to exist. Why should she fight for a life that was an abomination?

She could allow Daric to end it all for her. Then, she'd be free of this awful place. She'd never have to wake up afraid that today was the day her insides would be gouged out by a raptor. Or if this were the day an inmate would shoot her in the face for looking at him the wrong way. If she submitted to death here and now, she'd take back control from Daric and win over the fear.

But she'd also miss out. No longer would she blush because of Kaleo's passionate protectiveness or bask in Cane's quiet peace. Between the two of them, her biggest regret would be Cane. He wouldn't understand why she hadn't valued her life enough to fight to live.

A twisting motion at her waist sent her into another panic. With his free hand, Daric had unbuttoned her jeans. The desperate impulse to survive resurfaced and careened through her body.

The choice to live or die had to be hers.

She swallowed through her swollen throat. Abomination or not, she wanted to live.

While working to pull off her jeans, Daric let go of her wrists, leaving his one hand on her neck. This was her opportunity.

Grabbing his nearest forearm, she pressed her fingers deep into the muscle. She drew her anger and fear out, pushing and intensifying, willing the pulse to move through her fingertips.

He screamed as his muscle fibers seized. His hand

clamped tighter on her neck. He couldn't let go if he wanted to, but it meant he was strangling her again.

She peeled her fingers off his arm. Immediately, he jumped back and glared at her, his expression a blend of malice and fascination. "That was intense."

On all fours, she scrambled backward until she hit deeper water, where she stood. His eyebrows rose and his eyes narrowed as the malice morphed into predatory desire. Clearly, he'd come to the conclusion she was dangerous, and it continued to turn him on.

She backed farther away. The cool water hit her knees.

"Why run? You can't deny the spark between us." He whipped off his T-shirt and held it out in front as if to insulate himself from her power. He stepped toward her, then must have decided it wasn't enough protection because he ran to the edge of the creek and picked up the spear again, this time wrapping it in his shirt.

Her stomach lurched at the lust on his face. The shock had only increased his need to possess her. She'd given him a new fetish.

He deserves to die. The voice wasn't her mother's—it came from her own thoughts—but it might as well have been Mama's. She had known what Oakley hadn't. Killing was a part of her biological makeup. As natural as a snake squeezing a mouse or more accurately, an electric eel shocking its prey.

Daric took a step toward her, wielding the spear like a club. She had to do something before he hit her with it. Searching around, she saw only water and a few rocks.

But water was a good conductor.

She dipped the fingers of her right hand into the creek. With a psychic push, she sent unrestrained anger and pain flowing from her head, through her arm, and to her fingers. Cool water swirled over her fingertips for a few seconds before it began to heat up. As a circle of heat surrounded her legs, she swept a rush of it toward him, imagining the flow of water as a string connecting them.

He took a step back, but couldn't get out of the water fast enough. The muscles in his legs spasmed first. Next, his torso seized up, and finally his neck. His eyes rolled back into his head. The spear waved about wildly as his body convulsed.

The warmth on her legs intensified, along with the pounding in her head. Within a minute, her flesh beneath the water screamed in pain. Although her muscles didn't react to the current, she was burning her skin like she had in her childhood bathtub.

She pulled her hand out of the water. Hopefully, she'd given him enough of a jolt to stop him for the moment.

He slumped to the ground, half in and half out of the water. The spear had crashed into the shallows beside him. He moaned and rolled his head.

A strange mixture of relief and regret swamped her. She hadn't killed him. Yet.

But now that he knew what she could do, he'd never

stop trying to dominate her, use her, and abuse her. For her to live, he had to die.

She stepped through the water to stand beside him. With his eyes closed, he looked young, like he could pass for a random college guy on any campus. Never would she guess at the evil lurking inside.

Perhaps he felt the same way about her. Could he have seen a hint of the evil programmed into her genes?

She'd been created for this. Being sent here may have been a mistake, but there wasn't any better place for her to be than where everyone had been sentenced to die. Here, the judge and the jury had already served their purpose. That only left ...

Daric opened his eyes, his hand grasping for the spear, not finding it. When his gaze met hers, he appeared only curious. "What are you?"

"I'm your executioner."

She shifted her feet out of the water, squatted, and grabbed his elbow while pressing her eyes closed. This time, the push felt different. More forceful. Sharply directed. Jagged, like her energy encased him in lightning. She could almost experience the pain along with him, and that anguish, above all else, kept her pushing and pushing.

He groaned and tried to roll over, but his taut muscles obeyed only the current pouring out of her. She yanked him flat on his back again. A dense cloud of burning agony swirled between them, churning and thrashing, until it crashed in a thunderstorm of charged air.

Daric let out a tormented whimper.

Ignoring his cry, she squeezed every potential ounce of electricity from her muscles and propelled it through her hands. As her energy waned, most of the pain faded away, except for a knife-sharp ache centered on her left thigh. She opened her eyes. The spear stuck awkwardly out of her leg. He must have found it right after she'd closed her eyes.

She turned away from her injury, immediately regretting it. Her gaze fell on Daric's face. His eyes bulged unfocused, yet staring into the jungle.

The smell of burning hair and flesh suffocated her. She pulled her hand off his arm and gasped at the residual outline left from the contact burn. She examined her throbbing palm. The surface was as red as the head of a matchstick.

She scooted backward to get away from him and slammed her leg onto the ground, dislodging the spear. A trickle of blood dripped down her thigh onto the rocks under her feet. She was injured, but alive.

No relief came. Only the regret. Not for Daric's life, exactly. But for the little piece of her spirit that had died while his flesh burned under her fingers.

CHAPTER TWENTY-EIGHT

MORE BLOOD from Oakley's leg splashed onto the rocky edge of the stream. Leaving a trail of blood in the jungle was an awful idea. At least the wound on her jaw and the scrape on her elbow from Camocroc's tooth had both stopped bleeding.

She pushed herself to a standing position and backed away from Daric's body as if she still needed to keep an eye on it. At the edge of the woods, she smacked her back into a tree trunk, startling her out of her shock. She should have grabbed Daric's shirt to wrap around her thigh and staunch the blood, but she wouldn't go back. She wouldn't revisit the carnage.

Forcing a breath through her tight throat, she heaved out a sigh. It was over. He would never hurt anyone again. She'd done this little corner of the world a favor, so why didn't she feel good about it?

Another heavy breath. She needed to ease off the adrenaline high. Wrapping her arms around her midsection, she focused on breathing in through her nose and out through her mouth.

Movement on the other side of the creek brought her back to alertness. She quickly relaxed as she recognized Cane stepping through the bushes. She pressed a hand to her tense stomach, coaxing the muscles to slacken. Would he cross the creek and carry her away from this scene of death?

A ridiculous thought.

He caught her eye and gave her a relieved smile. Before she could return it, he glanced to her left and his expression froze. His smile fell little by little, and then his lips began to move with no sound. He was praying.

Using her hands as guides behind her, she shifted around the tree and tilted her head to catch a glimpse of whatever had frightened him. Standing six feet tall and only ten feet away, the *Utahraptor* had a raised red crest between the eyes. It had to be Red Grizzly.

Her clenched stomach did a painful barrel roll. The creature snorted and took an extended, deep breath, moving its head up and down. It was smelling her. A shiver raced down her spine as its nose approached her injured leg. No way would Red Grizzly pass on fresh blood.

She couldn't run with her wounded leg, and trying to would probably just incite its prey drive. Even worse, she didn't have the strength left to shock it. Her best bet would be slow movements away.

Perhaps, RG would take an interest in Daric instead of her. She suppressed a scoff. More than likely, it would kill both her and Cane, then feast on Daric for dessert. Still, she wouldn't just stand here and wait to be disemboweled.

Slowly, she crept around the side of the tree. Red Grizzly moved closer, tilting its head to keep an eye on her, alternating between sniffing her upper body and her thigh.

At the same time, Cane moved to the edge of the water. She shook her head at him, not wanting him to sacrifice himself for her. But he refused to meet her gaze or acknowledge her.

As Red Grizzly came even closer, it danced side to side as if it couldn't decide what to do with her. She held her breath to block the putrid scent coming from its mouth. Maybe if she punched it in the snout, it would go away. Animal noses were usually sensitive.

The next time it dipped its head toward her thigh, she slammed her fist into its nose. It reared back with a stunned honk, followed by a low rumble. She'd only made it angry.

Yellow saliva strung out in a line as it flexed strong jaw muscles. It splayed a set of dagger-encrusted fingers in a terrifying illustration of its deadly capabilities. She searched for options. She could jump up to catch a branch above her head, but the creature would probably grab her or leap at her before she got far.

In the distance, her ears picked out the squeaks of Cody's distress. Maybe he would leap from the bushes to save her like a valiant guard dog. Even if he did create a distraction, it wouldn't help much. She'd only be able to run slowly through the jungle, leaving a tasty blood trail to follow.

RG shifted its stance to sniff the air. When its head came down, it pointed directly at Daric. A fresh wave of saliva slipped through its jaws. It took a small step closer to Daric, then her, apparently unsure who to eat—live prey or barbecued.

Cody broke through the trees several yards to her right, followed by Kaleo. Her heart flipped over at seeing him for the first time since they'd faked her death and at the hope his presence brought. Three of them against the large *Utahraptor*. The odds were improving.

Red Grizzly scratched its fearsome back claws into the soft gravel of the river bank. Too much prey had agitated it.

Cody darted to her and nuzzled at her knees. RG ignored him, instead continuing to alternate between smelling Cane, Oakley, Kaleo, and Daric. But how long would this standoff last before the fearsome creature picked one of them?

Kaleo gave a cursory glance to Daric's body. He directed his words to her. "I've got an idea." Louder, he shouted at Cane, "Slowly back away. I'll give Red Grizzly a reason to choose the easy meal."

Cane glanced at her, a pained expression on his face that said he wanted to be there for her, wanted to argue. But he didn't. He retreated to the trees. As he disappeared, she shifted her gaze to Kaleo. What was he planning?

With Cane gone, Red Grizzly focused its black eyes on her. Its upper lip curled over its teeth. Was it remembering how she'd punched it in the nose?

"Hook ..." The nickname sparked a live wire somewhere inside her. "When I give you the signal, circle behind the tree and duck down."

RG snarled, its attention flipping to Kaleo.

"What signal?"

From the corner of her eye, she saw him reach behind his back. The jumbled flop of the unfurling whip sounded sweet to her ears.

He flicked his wrist to make the whip crack in the air above her head. That must be the signal. She grabbed Cody by the neck, circled behind the rough trunk, and crouched down.

A whip strike hit where she'd been standing.

Although Red Grizzly wasn't struck, it seemed confused by the rush of air coupled with her disappearance. But it probably wasn't stupid enough to believe she'd evaporated into thin air.

"Come to me behind the cover of the trees," Kaleo yelled.

Easing Cody behind her, she backed up until several thick trees were between her and Red Grizzly. Through the leaves, she caught glimpses of Kaleo's standoff with the dinosaur. RG sensed her escape and tried to follow.

He cracked the whip again.

The dinosaur jumped back with a screech. A tiny spot of blood appeared on its snout, almost exactly where she'd punched it. It directed a savage glare to him and tightened its leg muscles, a prelude to a charge.

He snapped the whip at its feet. RG jumped to avoid the strike without losing ground. It was getting bolder and angrier.

She approached Kaleo quietly from behind. Maybe they could back away and melt into the forest. Instead, he remained in place. Only then, did she see his wound, almost identical to the one in her thigh, except deeper. Neither of them would be able to travel fast.

A few more snaps with the whip. A few more superficial cuts.

Red Grizzly took the next blow on the snout undaunted.

Kaleo growled, "Stubborn creature. This one's going to hurt."

He twisted his wrist and flicked the whip sideways. A bright red stripe stretched across the creature's chest. RG roared and tried to get a look at the wound, but couldn't dip its head far enough.

With one last fierce glare, it went in search of the corpse waiting by the edge of the water. As the creature tore into Daric's stomach, she averted her gaze. The feast was too gruesome to watch.

Kaleo pushed her silently in to the trees. She hushed Cody while dragging him along. They didn't speak as they walked, though the questions were evident in his curious glances. He wanted to know what had happened to Daric. Even though he could probably guess at the events, she wasn't ready for a confession just yet.

CHAPTER TWENTY-NINE

KALEO FOCUSED on the wooden rafters of the tree house, wincing as Neve stitched up his leg. The clove gel she mixed as a topical pain reliever worked well, to a point. Cleaning the wound had hurt much worse than the stitches, though it was all at once. The process of sewing the stitches went agonizingly slow.

Neve slipped the tiny needle into his flesh for the final time. "Fifteen total, same as Raptor." She gave him a teasing grin, knowing he would be competitive even in the number of stitches.

Oakley's wound was the least severe, only five stitches, but those covered half of her small leg. She leaned against the wall, waiting for him to get done.

Raptor lay on one of the cots in the corner of the tree house, holding the bandage covering his side. Fortunately, the bullet had gone straight through. Neve planned to stay here with him for several days to keep an eye on his recovery.

Kaleo breathed easier as she tied off the last stitch. "Thanks." He allowed her to place a bandage over the area, then sat up and directed a question at Raptor. "Where do you think Adler might be hiding?"

Raptor folded an arm behind his head. "There are plenty of abandoned shelters across the island. But I think he'll stay close. He's not done with Oakley yet."

Kaleo glanced at her. She stared out the open window of the tree house, giving no indication that she'd heard them.

"The man is dangerous," Cane said. "We have to be careful about how we look for him."

Oakley turned her head and nodded along with Cane. So she had been listening. Her expression was one of respect, if not affection. A sharp dagger of jealousy shot through Kaleo's heart. He could never match the connection she shared with Cane because of their abilities, and yet he loved her—loved that she had trouble biting back her sarcasm, loved that she could be the smallest person in the room and not cower, loved that she tried to protect that crazy mongrel dinosaur—he loved the whole imperfect beautiful mess that was her.

A shadow darkened the bright bloom of emotion inside him. Despite his feelings, he couldn't stay with her. He'd have to leave her with Cane.

Cane met his gaze with those knowing eyes of his.

"Are you coming back to the cave or will you stay at the compound?"

There was no other reasonable conclusion. He could still do the most good by staying at the compound. It would keep Oakley and all those at the cave safe, even if she was with Cane. "I'm going back to the gang."

She bristled and put her back to the window, her hands gripping the lower sill. Her expression crinkled as questions filled her eyes. The answers wouldn't give her peace. This decision weighed on his heart. Leaving her again would be awful.

At least he could help in her search from the compound. His crew could cover more ground looking for Adler than Cane's people. She desperately wanted to know her origins, and Kaleo would help for her sake. In fact, he'd have no problem beating the answers out of Adler. But when it came down to it, it didn't matter where her ability had come from or who'd made her. She wasn't the sum total of what the geneticists had tinkered with. When he tried telling her so, she always shut him out.

He rose and tested his leg. Not too bad. Neve was a gifted healer. He'd be able to limp back to the compound and have Taye help him until he recovered.

"What are you going to do about Chubs?" Oakley asked.

He matched her pose, leaning against the opposite window. "He'd better not have said anything to anyone about you."

"What if he did?"

"If the guys in the compound believe you're alive, they'll hunt us both down." He ran a hand through his hair. "If Chubs told anyone, I'll have to kill him to prove it's not true."

She absorbed this without comment like swallowing a bitter pill. With a sideways nod of his head, he motioned for her to follow him down the ladder of the tree house. He hobbled down each rung, and then helped steady her bad leg as she came down.

When she made it to level ground, he stayed close and waited for her questions. It wouldn't be long.

A moment later, she stared at his chest, refusing to look him in the eye. "Why do you have to go?"

He shuffled his feet. This was hard. Too hard. "Nothing has changed. You're still better off at the cave. I still need to be at the compound." If only he could explain it in a way she'd understand. He had to make up for his past, to show he'd changed. More than that, Cane and Oakley both made him want to be a better person, to put others first.

Besides, she had her own issues to process. She hadn't made a true decision about who she was, who she wanted to be, and especially who she wanted to be with. He owed her the space to figure things out.

Also, the cave wasn't his home. Even though Cane was like a brother to him, Kaleo simply felt more comfortable with the guys at the compound. He still resembled the people in his gang more than he did Cane.

The frustration in her eyes spoke of the war going on

inside her. It seemed that she wanted him to stake a claim on her. But if he did, it was a claim he couldn't defend.

Her fingers brushed the bandage on her jaw line. Then, her left thumb rubbed along the stub of her missing fingers. She didn't need to be self-conscious around him. He grabbed her damaged left hand and wrapped it completely in his. "You're beautiful. Every scar on your skin is a reminder of what you've survived. You never give up. Be proud of that."

She pushed her shoulders back and gave a slow nod.

He lowered his head until their lips were a breath apart.

Her gaze flicked from his lips to his eyes. Tension rippled from her. She narrowed her eyes, though her voice was soft. "I'll probably forget about you immediately."

The halfhearted words were meant to push him away. He wouldn't let her go so easily. He traced the curve of her uninjured cheek, savoring the silkiness of her skin. "Then let me give you something to miss."

With one finger, he tilted her chin up, bringing her lips to meet his. The soft sweetness he found there melted his heart.

When she responded, her passion set the rest of his body ablaze. He swept his hands through her flowing hair before cradling the back of her head in one of his palms. He pulled her closer, melding her body to his, bringing the kiss deeper. This was torture, but so worth it.

He heard her breath catch as he feathered kisses down her neck. When he found her lips again, she speared her hands through his hair and leaned in. The burning ache of not touching every inch of her body was eclipsed only by the bitter realization that he wouldn't see her gorgeous face every day.

Finally, when he could barely control his erotic thoughts, the spark jolted through him, propelling him backward. He gasped as he absorbed her electricity, a sharp tingling sensation like trying to tame a lightning bolt.

She opened her mouth to apologize, but he placed a finger on her lips. Then, he brushed stray dark hairs from her face, tucked them behind her ears, and looked deep into her ocean eyes. "I'll come to see you, Hook." He rubbed a thumb along her lower lip and winked. "A lot."

THE CAMOUFLAGED concrete bunker beckoned Raptor like home. He paused behind a tree to catch his breath. His body needed sleep and healing. Neve had done a competent job sewing him up, but he'd refused her offer to babysit him for a few days. He could take care of himself.

Just as he was about to step out from the trees, something on the other side of the clearing caught his eye. A figure crept toward the steel door. The guy moved like an expert tracker, a predator, and an alpha male all rolled into one. *Adler Calais.*

Adler would surely have spotted him had he not

stopped to rest in the cover of the jungle. He stood motionless as Adler strode up to the door and punched in a code. The door swung open instantly.

To have the code confirmed that Adler worked for Asperten. Even though Asperten paid half of Raptor's salary to come down here and check on the dinosaurs—the other half being paid by the government—the inner workings of the secretive company remained a mystery. After what Oakley had just told him about her power and the possible connection to Asperten, he now trusted the company even less.

He waited several minutes to give Adler time to move away from the door, then he punched in the same code. The door opened silently and gave a small click when it closed. Hopefully, Adler had gone deep enough into the building to miss the noise.

On light feet, Raptor crept down the hall. His tiny room appeared undisturbed with his large pack on the cot and his rain jacket slung across the solitary chair.

A telltale click sounded farther down the hall. He soundlessly moved in that direction. As he rounded a corner, another door was just swishing shut—the door to the secure area of the bunker. He stared at it, unable to follow because he didn't have access.

The questions piled up in his mind like a Baton Rouge traffic jam. How was this guy connected to Asperten? What did he really want with Oakley? First, he said he wanted to talk to her, then he tried to kill her, and in the end, he ran when he got the chance. None of the puzzle pieces fit.

Returning to his room, he grabbed the satellite phone from his pack and went back outside. No way did he want Adler overhearing this conversation.

When he was a good distance from the bunker, he dialed FBI Agent Noah Brooks. Though Raptor didn't trust the government much more than Asperten, he needed answers.

Agent Brooks's pinched voice greeted him. "Mr. Greene, I've been waiting for your call."

He shook his head. Government types had no patience. Rather than give the agent the apology he sought, Raptor launched into his questions. "What do you know about Asperten?"

A short pause during which static filled the connection. "Why do you ask?"

"There's a guy here who appears to work for them. Name is Adler Calais." Raptor hesitated, then hedged a bit. "He's threatening some of the inmates."

"I've never heard of him." Agent Brooks cleared his throat. "As far as the company goes, they're into Biotech and Bioresearch. They've never been in any trouble, other than the dinosaur fiasco."

He meant the unauthorized biological regeneration and release of the dinosaurs many years ago. Perhaps the company had done other illegal things they hadn't been caught doing. "Did you approach them to sponsor me?"

"No, it was their idea. All they asked for was access to

the data you collected." Agent Brooks huffed out a breath. "Now, for your report. What about Oakley Laveau?"

"I found her. She's alive."

"Really? That's surprising." His tone, like he'd just discovered a toy prize in the first layer of a cereal box, ticked Raptor off.

No matter how many death confirmations he did, he never lost sight of the humanity of the prisoners. Many of them had people who still cared about them. Maybe Agent Brooks should do his own dirty work next time.

"What happened to her tracker?"

Raptor steadied his breathing and neutralized his voice. "She doesn't know." Technically, it was a lie because he had detected the truth in her eyes. She had an idea of what happened, but Agent Brooks didn't need to know of his suspicions.

"Okay. We'll make arrangements to get her tracker re-installed."

Re-installed. Like replacing a defective fuel pump in a government vehicle. Oakley was no longer a person to Agent Brooks. Her life had become property of the U.S. government.

But the agent wasn't heartless and callous. He simply had to keep a certain amount of emotional distance, some-thing Raptor couldn't do with Oakley.

"In the meantime, initiate Protocol Two," Agent Brooks said.

He gulped. Protocol Two required him to find Oakley

again, handcuff her, and hold her at the bunker until surgeons could arrive.

"I trust it won't be a problem. I'd hate to think your prior relationship with her would compromise your responsibilities."

It was a not-so-veiled threat. Raptor had signed a document stating that if he aided any criminal in an escape attempt, it would be considered an act of treason. Not obeying Agent Brooks's order would cause him to end up here permanently as well.

"I understand." He ended the call with a knot of tension balling between his shoulders. Perhaps he should have lied and told him Oakley was dead. But if the agent discovered the truth, he would face the same treason charges. He'd never considered helping an inmate escape before. Never thought it would be an option. But with Oakley's tracker disabled, the possibility was tempting.

CHAPTER THIRTY

OAKLEY TURNED from her mother's determined face. A heavy weight pressed on her chest and legs. Pain lanced her lungs. She gasped for air; sucking in only water. The burning ache in her hands would come next, followed by Mama's cry.

Instead, Mama stood and climbed from the tub, her nightgown dripping water on the tile. Oakley sat up, drawing air deep into her lungs.

Mama crossed the bathroom floor with one arm sweeping back and forth, beckoning her to follow. She climbed out to trail behind her. By the time Oakley reached the other side of the bathroom, the pale blue walls faded away, replaced by the dull gray of another room entirely.

A tight corridor curved in front of them. Mama faced her, while continuing to walk backward. Her mouth was moving as she gestured with her hands, but the words were muted. She opened a thick, gray metal door and stepped through.

When Oakley followed, a warm, humid breeze blew through her hair. She stood on a catwalk across from Mama. The metal grate hovered over the ocean, far enough out to sea that no land was visible on the horizon.

Mama's voice broke through the silence like the sudden tuning of a radio. "We made you here. Come home."

Before she could ask how, Mama shoved her with both hands, sending her tumbling over the low railing. With a silent scream, she twisted and flipped as she fell. The ocean rushed closer and closer, its foaming waves ready to suck her under.

OAKLEY CRIED out and sat bolt upright as the dream broke its hold on her. The smooth walls of the cave echoed her scream back to her. She was here, with the others, with Cane. Despite her racing heart, she was safe.

Dreams about her mother weren't unusual. This one, though, was more vivid than most. Before she'd remembered the truth about her mother, the dreams were fuzzy and indistinct, leaving her with an aching longing. But she'd take one of those dreams over the stark reality of this last one.

The floating fortress in the middle of the sea had seemed familiar and empty. No one else was around, but like any fortress, it had to be guarded. Were there secrets in that building? Her mother's secrets?

A stirring of cave dust brought her attention to the nearby wall. Cane stood there, looking completely at ease and somehow intensely interested in her. "Are you okay?"

"Just a nightmare." She licked her dry lips.

He merely stared at her. She had more to say and he knew it, like always.

She pushed loose hair off her forehead. "I have to find out who manipulated our DNA. It might have been my mother, but I don't think she was the only one."

"Why not?"

"Adler said I was supposed to find the creator. If it was simply my mother, then Asperten would have known what happened to her. She died in the hospital after being in a coma for a year."

"Okay." He drew the word out until her declaration sounded ridiculous. "Adler's not trustworthy. And if Asperten wants you to find the creator, maybe you shouldn't do what they want."

He made a good point. But this wasn't for Asperten. *She* needed to know her origins. Unfortunately, finding Adler hadn't made anything clearer. "I have to do this. A few days ago, you asked me what I was chasing. Well, this is it. I need to find these answers."

A corner of his mouth lifted into a smirk. "And if you fall off a cliff while trying to get there?"

The certainty of her decision continued to grow inside her. "I still have to try."

He dropped his shoulders as if conceding. "How exactly are you going to find this person?"

We made you here. Her mother's words echoed from the dream. Here had meant the building. Who was the we?

"I have to find this floating—" Then it hit her. The building in the middle of the ocean had to be the world headquarters of Asperten International. Her father had described it several times. "My dream pointed me to the place where my mother worked and my father still does."

Cane crossed his arms. "Suddenly, the nightmare was a dream?"

"Don't act so skeptical. What if this dream came from God?" A guilty flush welled up. Hopefully, it didn't show on her face. Even if God spoke in dreams, this one didn't have any type of spiritual stamp on it. She'd only thrown it out there to persuade him.

He paced for a minute. When he turned back to her, he shook his head. "If you leave, they'll hunt you down."

She shook hers vigorously right back. "Not if they don't know I'm gone. Temporarily gone." Her tracker had been fried. She had a limited window to discover the truth about who she was. Eventually she might try to clear her name of Monica's murder, but only if she wasn't a danger to others.

She raked her hands through her hair, tugging it back from her face. Getting off the island presented its own set of challenges. "You came here somehow, right?"

He didn't answer.

"Help me find a way to get a boat. Please?" she added for good measure.

He took two steps and planted his feet in front of her. "Only if I can come with you."

His offer firmed up her resolve. She probably couldn't get off the island without his help. They could do this together. Finding the truth would benefit them both.

If only she didn't have to leave Kaleo behind. Her chest ached at the thought. What if he forgot about her? Perhaps he would move on to the next woman he protected.

Anything could happen once they started this journey.

She stood and grabbed the backpack from under her cot, trying to push the doubts away. It was a risk she'd have to take.

If she didn't go immediately, she'd miss her chance.

LUMAS VERRET, the Director of Asperten, patted his assistant on the back. "Good work, Glen. It looks like she's coming home."

Although the mission on the island hadn't made much progress, at least their back-up plan had been executed perfectly. While Oakley was sleeping, Glen inserted the image of their headquarters into her consciousness using the camera lens attached to her right eye. The device had been implanted with her tracker before she'd left for the island and had proved invaluable for surveillance.

Ever since her arrival, they recorded her actions,

without any sound, as she used her power to electrocute a dinosaur, a woman, and then Daric Perkins. Her skills grew with every kill.

As much as Lumas would prefer to leave her on the island to discover more of her capabilities, the risk wasn't worth it. If he left her there much longer, her high levels of pheromones could cause her death. Her genetic manipulation was attracting the very animals used to manipulate her genes. Not surprising, but concerning, since the creatures had consistently tracked her.

Taking in a slow cleansing breath, he savored the small victory. They hadn't found Dr. Penna Gallardo, but if Oakley came to him, perhaps he wouldn't need Penna after all. Her disappearance fifteen years ago had left him incapable of continuing their genetic experiments, but with Oakley, he might be able to breed his own.

The computer screen held a freeze frame image of her gesturing toward the man from the cave. Of course, Lumas couldn't hear what she'd said to the man, but she was passionate when she awoke, most likely passionate about coming to headquarters. If fortune favored him, the man from the cave would come with her. That man had a mutation Lumas had never seen. Penna had kept many secrets from him.

"What do you want to do about Adler?" Glen asked.

"Good question. He tried to kill Oakley when he thought I wasn't looking." Lumas brushed a hand down his goatee. "He needs to know his place. Send him a message to return here."

Auburn grabbed his hand, startling him. She managed to sneak around often without being detected. "Don't hurt Adler. He didn't follow through. Plus, he told you about Oakley's disabled tracker."

She batted her pleading dark-lashed eyes at him. Her chocolate hair and bright blue eyes were similar to Oakley's; however the features of her face, just a bit sharper in the cheekbones, more slope to her nose, gave her away as a fraternal twin. As it turned out, her abilities were much different from Oakley's, although just as terrifying.

How genetics shuffled the deck, one could never be sure. Two similar eggs from the same parents, implanted into the mother's womb could create two vastly different people. Or maybe that was how Penna had planned it.

"Dad?" Auburn still waited for him to answer.

He folded his arms over his chest. He had a hard time disappointing her—such a strange mixture of fatherly affection and the desire to protect his investment—but Adler had crossed the line.

"He's still valuable to you," she pleaded.

She was right. The perfect cross between a sociopath, a charming extrovert, and a ruthless assassin, except he didn't have any special abilities, other than the pheromones ensuring his attractiveness to others. His greatest talent seemed to be manipulating Auburn. Lumas again blamed the pheromones. Auburn's love for Adler compromised her vision and her ambition.

"We can talk about this later. Let's go celebrate the possibility of your sister coming home."

She nodded without enthusiasm, her indifference to her twin understandable. She'd watched all of it, absent of sound, as Oakley killed people. The carnage spoke for itself. Perhaps competition with Oakley would force Auburn to take her power to the next level.

Lumas wrapped an arm around her shoulder and indulged in a self-satisfied smile. It was about time the twins were reunited. He had great plans for these two.

More bloody Red Grizzly, Adler the assassin, and electrifying Oakley to come in book 2 ...

Dear Reader,

I hope you enjoyed this tooth-and-claw-filled adventure with Oakley. It was so much fun to write! My passion is to explore the limits of science and human endurance.

Along those lines, I modeled all of the special abilities in this book after the superpowers of real animals. To explore this, as well as dossiers on characters, a special author interview, exclusive bookmark/postcard files, and more, visit the secret Jurassic Judgment Junkie page (link: https://janiceboekhoff.com/jurassic-judgment-junkie). Note: you cannot access this page from the menu on my website, only from the back of this book or by typing the above link into your browser.

If you enjoyed *Extinction Island*, I would appreciate it if you would consider leaving a review on Amazon or Goodreads. Your opinion counts! Even just a few sentences can help more people to enjoy the same adventure and it is the kindest thing you can do for an author.

If you're interested in learning about my new releases and book recommendations, sign up for the quarterly newsletter on my website. I'd love to connect with you.

Blessings,
Janice

ACKNOWLEDGMENTS

Over the years, I've been blessed to have such encouraging and talented people on my writing journey. This series exists because of all of you.

Todd—Thank you for listening as I struggled with one more version of the beginning (how many did I have?). You keep me grounded when my head is always up in the clouds.

Zach, Jenna, and Riley—Your support means more than I can ever say. Not to mention your willingness to answer every time Mom asks, "What's the most gruesome way to kill a dinosaur?" I love the brainstorming help and how proud you are of the work I do. And I'm so proud of all of you!

Crystal Joy and Amelia Judd—Every writer should have such talented critique partners. You made this book what it is (the good parts at least). I'm grateful for the brainstorming, the critiques, and the help with the emotional arcs.

Jennifer Beckstrand, Carol Brandon, Donna Feld, Lisa Lee, Mary Johnson, Martha Robinson and Charlotte Sanchez—You brought different perspectives to this novel and your comments have enriched it greatly. Thank you for spending your precious time reading the first draft.

Kim Mesman (Mesman Designs)—You created much more than I expected for the cover. I'm blown away by your talent.

Linda Yezak—This was our first project together and I'm sure it won't be our last. You are a gifted editor and have a way of bringing out the best in a manuscript. I'm grateful for your insights and corrections (all further mistakes are mine).

Dear reader—You are my reason for writing. Thank you for each adventure that we take together. I am blessed to have you here and hope to see you again at the end of Book 2.

Happy Reading!
Janice

ABOUT THE AUTHOR

Blessed with an insatiable curiosity and a low tolerance for boredom, award-winning author Janice Boekhoff (pronounced Beau-cough) has worked more than twenty jobs ranging from Loan Consultant (important, but mortgage paperwork makes her sleepy) to Landfill Environmentalist (literally her smelliest job) to Research Geologist (the job that gave her the best suntan and the most adventures). She began writing as a way to express all the unique ideas colliding in her head. A Midwest native, she writes from Eastern Iowa where she lives with her hubby, three basketball-loving kids, and one adorable Vizsla.